Safe Haven: Hope Street

Christopher Artinian

CHRISTOPHER ARTINIAN

SAFE HAVEN: HOPE STREET

CHRISTOPHER ARTINIAN

DEDICATION

To Lorraine.

CHRISTOPHER ARTINIAN

ACKNOWLEDGEMENTS

Thanks to my incredible wife, Tina. I could never ask for anyone more patient and understanding. She is just as responsible for each of these books as I am, and I'm boundlessly grateful for everything she does.

Thank you to Arita and the wonderful Glasvegan staff. Glasgow will not be the same without you.

Thanks to my mate, Dee, for the technical advice.

Thank you to the gang across in the fan club. I'd struggle to find a friendlier group of people to chill with.

Thanks to my dear friend, Christian Bentulan, for another brilliant cover. Also, many thanks to my editor, Ken – a fantastic editor and a lovely chap too.

And finally, a huge thank you to you for buying this book.

CHRISTOPHER ARTINIAN

PROLOGUE

Billy, Galli, Decko and Gummy had not stopped since leaving the van and entering the forest. It seemed everything was working against them despite Billy's affirmation that this was their best and only way out.

They had stumbled upon numerous infected during their journey. Decko and Billy had brought them down quickly and quietly, but it had highlighted a problem that they had not thought about before entering the woodland.

Night had fallen, and it was far too dangerous to carry on, so they had scaled a giant sycamore tree in the hope they could eke out a few hours' rest before daylight. Even though the foliage was just budding at this time of year, there was enough cover from the branches for them not to be seen from below should a few stray infected pass by.

"They're following the smoke," Billy whispered.

"Do you think?" Decko replied. Sleep had come quickly for Galli and Gummy, but the other two men knew they would not get a wink. They were in the dragon's lair and could literally feel fire breathing down their necks. "You do realise the wind's changed direction, don't you?"

"Yeah. Thanks for pointing that out, Decko; I wouldn't have figured it out for myself."

"I'm just saying. We don't know how far this forest stretches. We don't know how many of those things could have seen the smoke and be heading in this direction. Continuing is a risk. Going back is a risk."

"What were we meant to do?"

Decko let out a long sigh and began to splutter as he breathed in once more. The masks they wore could only filter so much and large intakes of breath often made their lungs burn. He shook his head. "There was nothing else to do. I'm sorry. I'm just…."

"I get it. It's grim." There was enough moonlight bleeding through the smoke and clouds for them to see basic outlines and Decko watched as his friend shook his head despairingly.

"If we do get out of this, what's the plan?"

"Ha. Man, you're optimistic tonight. You mean how do we survive with just the clothes on our backs, the bullets in our guns and the boots on our feet?"

"Pretty much."

"I'm struggling to focus on that at the moment."

"I thought you could multitask."

Billy laughed. "I'm sorry, Decko. I'm sorry I got you into this."

"You've got nothing to apologise for. I was a dickhead for following you." They both laughed this time.

"There is one possibility that I've been giving some thought to."

"Oh?"

"I think we could do worse than head down to Skye."

"Skye? The Isle of Skye?"

"Well, I don't know of any other."

"But why?"

"Our people went down there looking for Beck. There were loads of infected around Portree. If we can get to the north, the chances are we'll be safe from Olsen."

"So, let me get this straight. You want to go to Skye because there are a load of infected? That sounds like a fucking brilliant plan. Maybe we could find a portable PA system and carry it around with us so they wouldn't have any trouble finding us."

"Clever arse, aren't you? What I'm saying is if we bypass Portree, we could find somewhere to hole up for a while. Olsen would have no reason to look for us down there and we know Beck's no longer there. We'd pretty much have the place to ourselves."

"Sure enough. But how do we survive? What do we do for food and supplies?"

"Scavenge. Maybe get ourselves a couple of fishing rods. Maybe hit some of the houses around Portree. I don't know exactly what our people scavenged down there, but they couldn't have got everything, could they?"

"Jesus, Decko. You make it sound like we'd be nipping out for a fucking kebab."

"Remember Ellon?"

Billy's mind drifted back to the town north of Aberdeen. It had been one of the first places they'd liberated in the name of Chancellor Olsen. It had also been something like a nightmare. The information they'd had on the place was all wrong. In addition, thousands had fled Aberdeen and the surrounding area in the hope of finding safety. They didn't.

The place was overrun with infected, and after an initial massacre, Billy, Decko and a few others, through planning and subterfuge, were able to get the upper hand. Fires, sirens and other decoys were all employed to lure the creatures, splitting them up, trapping them, and killing them. With planning, anything was possible.

"I'm not likely to forget it, am I?"

"That was on a huge scale. You and me were bang in the middle of it. We wouldn't be facing anything like that on Skye and we wouldn't have to worry about a load of panicky newbies."

Billy thought for a moment. "Well … I suppose it's as good as anywhere to catch a breath."

"That's what I mean."

"Okay. Assuming—"

"Shush!"

They both held their breath as a familiar and eerie sound drifted towards them. Gradually, it got louder, and the unmistakable song of multiple infected rose into the night air.

"Shit," Billy hissed.

"Billy! BILLY!" Gummy suddenly cried out, waking from his dreams like a frightened child.

"Be quiet," Decko hissed.

"Billy. Infected."

"Keep quiet, Gummy," Billy urged this time.

He saw Galli's hand shoot out and grab Gummy's arm. The sound of the creatures drew nearer and the tension mounted further with each second that passed.

There was a thud as a single beast smashed against the tree. A second thud followed. "Shit. They know we're here," Billy whispered.

"Yeah. I wonder how."

"Can you see how many?" Billy asked as a third and fourth smash against the trunk sent vibrations upwards.

Decko squinted down through the branches. "I don't know. Five, maybe."

"What should we do, Billy?" Gummy asked way too loudly, causing the growls of the creatures to rise higher with excitement.

"We can't just sit here," Decko whispered. "There could be a hundred of the bloody things by morning."

"Don't do anything stupid, Billy." Galli's hushed words lingered in the air just above the sound of the creatures' growls. He closed his eyes for a moment and breathed in, realising he could smell something other than smoke. He could smell the foulness of death and decay. As much as he'd wanted the stench of something other than the fire to coat his nostrils, this was not it.

Thud. Thud. Thud.

Billy turned to Decko. "Get them somewhere safe."

"What do you mean?"

Without replying, he eased himself from the comfortable nook he had thought he was settled in for the night and began to shimmy along a strong, wide bough.

"Billy, no!" Galli hissed as she saw his outline begin to move.

For the time being, the creatures remained around the thick trunk, clawing and hammering. Billy continued pulling himself along. Nodules poked and prodded at his ribs and he had to stop a couple of times to straighten the shoulder strap of his rifle. Eventually, the bough began to bend, letting out a loud wooden groan, and the growls and hammering stopped momentarily.

Shit! It's now or never.

He swung his left leg over to meet his right and felt the wind rushing around him as he dropped to the ground. *Bend knees and roll.*

He was back on his feet again in a second and cast a look towards the trunk, where the five creatures now launched into a run towards him.

"Billy!" Galli's desperate scream gave the beasts a momentary pause, reminding them of the prey in the tree.

"Get them to safety, Decko!" Billy's shout was all it took to gain the monsters' full attention and they started towards him with fresh verve.

A pain stabbed his heart as he heard Galli's pleading cry echo, but he did everything he could to block it out. He could hear the pounding feet behind him. *These things can see perfectly in the dark.* He didn't need to remind himself of the fact. It had always been a hard and fast rule to avoid confrontation with the infected at night time unless it was completely necessary. This was completely necessary, and he felt responsible for everything that had happened and was happening, so if someone was going to pay the ultimate price, it was only right that it should be him.

He cast a glance over his shoulder, and even though all he could see were shadows and outlines, he could make out Decko on the ground next to the tree, helping Galli down too. The pain in his heart eased a little as the knowledge that his actions would not be in vain warmed him.

His head turned back to his direction of travel and the darkness that extended in front of him. They had been walking in this forest for hours and managed to avoid dozens, possibly even hundreds of infected, but now, every silhouette, every shadow could spell death.

This is shit. Billy could feel his run was awkward. He was lifting his feet far higher than normal as fear of stumbling over a root or partially buried stone gripped him. The result was that he was running nowhere near as fast as he needed to get any kind of distance between himself and the pack of blood-crazed beasts in pursuit.

Death had stalked him many times in the past, but he had never faced it alone, and a shiver trembled through him as he sprinted. He threw another glance over his shoulder. *Fuuuck!*

They were only six metres behind him. One stumble, one pause, and it would all be over. Their eager, hate-filled sounds raced to catch up with him, sending greater waves of panic surging through his system.

Ahead, darkness. Behind, darkness. His lungs burned as he ran. He'd begun with no plan other than getting as far away from the tree as quickly as possible in order to give Galli and the others a chance to escape, but now the full weight of what he had done began to bear down on his shoulders.

Billy spluttered through his makeshift mask as the night air, thicker than ever with the smell of smoke since the breeze changed direction, punished him.

It's no good. I can't keep this up for—"Waahhgg!"

The thing he had feared finally happened. Despite all his precautions and silent prayers, the toe of his boot caught on an exposed tree root. The scorched air left his lungs and his chest smashed against the forest floor.

Shit!

He ignored the pain that jolted through him. He pushed the fear down deep inside. He resisted the temptation to cry or scream out in fear. He pushed hard against the ground, launching into a run.

The growls were louder than ever and Billy could almost feel the outstretched fingers brushing against his jacket as he ran. *This is useless. They've got me. But if I can get just another few metres, it's a few metres closer to safety for the others.*

The black outline of a giant fallen tree stretched out in front of him. He hurdled it, his boot scuffing on the rough bark in the process, causing another adrenaline surge. He landed heavily wondering whether he would remain upright. A loud thud followed by several more made him glimpse over his shoulder and a small wave of relief flowed through him as he saw all five of his pursuers stumble.

A sound of a different kind echoed into the air, but he carried on running for a moment, desperate not to waste the advantage. CRACK! It came again, but this time, he slowed and looked back.

In the shadowy darkness, he could just make out three more figures. They were not running or scrambling to their feet. They were upright. Two wielded their rifles like giant truncheons, smashing them down on the heads of the fallen creatures. A third swung a tyre iron like a baseball bat. WHACK!

The sounds reverberated around the woodland. POP! Billy ran back to his friends, slipping the rifle from his shoulder and joining in the life-or-death whack-a-zombie game.

His SA80 felt like it was going to spring apart in his hands as the butt made contact with one of the struggling creature's heads. The vibrations ran through his arms and up to his shoulders, but it was a pain he was more than willing to trade for the dire fortunes that had awaited him just moments before.

CRACK! CRACK! CRACK! Then silence but for the heavy breathing of the four of them as they looked down at the still figures.

"What the bloody hell are you playing at? What if they'd got you?" Billy asked.

"Don't mention it. Ungrateful twat," Decko replied.

Billy let out a deep breath. "I got you into this shit. It was up to me to get you out of it. You should have run in the other direction ... saved yourselves."

"You'd love that, wouldn't you?" Decko said.

"What?"

"You'd love to die a martyr, a hero, and leave me stuck here with your grieving bird and this dopey fucker, wouldn't you?"

There was a short pause before they all laughed, even Gummy.

"Funny bastard."

"He's right, Billy," Galli said. "We're all in this together and we need to stick together. If we're going to survive, there's no room for heroics, no going it alone. There's one way we come out of the other end of this, and that's together."

Billy shook his head. "We've got no food, no water. Hell, we don't even know where we are. This forest—"

"This forest saved us. It might not feel like it at the moment, but if we hadn't headed in here, we'd probably be dead now. There are still a few more hours until dawn. Let's find somewhere new to get a little rest and then start out again at first light. Who knows how many more of these things are still wandering around in here?"

"Listen to your girlfriend," Decko said. Even though Billy couldn't see the smile on his friend's face, he could hear it in his voice.

"Screw you."

They wiped off their weapons without really knowing how clean they had gotten them and started their search for a new camp for the remainder of the night.

It took them just over ten minutes to find a tree big enough to shield them from any potential hunters, and it was another half hour before Galli and Gummy drifted to sleep. No matter how hard they tried, Billy and Decko could not relax long enough to fall into slumber.

"Thanks, Decko," Billy whispered, seemingly out of the blue.

"For what?"

"For coming back."

"Don't thank me. It was Gummy who set off after you. Fucking knob started running like one of those wind-up toys as soon as he hit the ground. I'd have left you to get on with it."

"Uh-huh. Thanks anyway."

"Just remember what Galli said. We're in this together."

"Yeah. I suppose we are."

1

Mike and Mya sat side by side on a wide flat rock that jutted out over the narrow, pebbly shore. Muppet lay at their feet, his head resting on an errant growth of heather. They had watched Les's boat disappear into the darkness some time before, but now they just sat there in quiet contemplation.

It had been a day like no other. They had lost their people, their homes, and their future. The smell of smoke was still in the air, although on this small island it was not as acute as it had been on the mainland.

"Y'know," Mike began, "there's a good argument to make for us heading over there too."

"The weapons. The ammo. The supplies," Mya replied as proof the same thing had been going through her mind.

"Exactly."

"We won't be able to take all of it."

"What we can't take we can destroy." He paused for a moment. "There are going to be a lot of infected milling about."

"You led a hell of a lot of them out of the village with you."

"Yeah. But there were a lot that we didn't take. It would be a massive risk."

"Oh, come on, Mike. Since when haven't you enjoyed taking a risk?"

He let out a long breath. "Since I made a promise to Em."

"So, you're telling me that you're scared of your sister?"

"You've met her. What do you think?"

Mya shrugged. "You make a fair point."

"A fair point about what?"

"Jesus!" Mike and Mya hissed in unison as they turned around to see Emma standing there.

"I woke up and I saw you weren't there," Emma said, looking at her brother. "What are you doing?" She cast her eyes over the water in the direction both of them had been looking.

"Les set sail for the village a little while back," Mya replied sadly.

"Oh."

"He wanted to do something. He wanted to try to get some payback however he could."

"Do you think he will?"

"No. I think he'll die over there."

"What were you two talking about before I got here?"

"Heading across there," Mike admitted.

There was a long pause before Emma spoke again. "For the supplies and weapons?"

"What we can get of them. Yeah."

"I think it's a good idea. I mean the supplies that Raj brought across will probably last a little while, but it wouldn't harm to bolster what we've got while we get settled on Skye."

"Err … yeah. That's what we were thinking."

Emma walked around and plonked herself down next to her brother. "So, how do we do this?"

"The headland about two miles out of the village," Mya replied, pointing.

In the dark, it was merely a black patch of rock set against many others, but the two siblings knew where she was talking about. "What about it?"

"We start a beacon fire there."

"Who's starting a fire?" The three of them jumped and turned to see Wren, Robyn and Mila standing there, weapons and all. "Who's starting a fire?" Wren asked again as Wolf sat down beside her.

"You couldn't sleep either?" Emma asked.

"There's something about being forced out of my home that gives me insomnia."

"Yeah. I get that. We're thinking about heading across to get some of the remaining supplies. Mya was talking about setting up a beacon fire on the headland to draw any infected in the village away from where we need to be."

"Makes sense. We could do that."

"Surprise, surprise," Robyn muttered.

"What do you mean?" Mya asked.

"Stick around my sister long enough and you'll find out. Fires are her thing."

"Said the girl who tried to burn down Inverness," Mila replied.

"Trying to save my sister and some old German tart."

"So, now I am old as well as fat. What else—"

"I think we've gone a little bit off point," Mya interrupted.

"My sister does that," Wren replied. "The three of us can light the beacon. I mean we'll probably need to take some of the dried wood. It wasn't raining that heavily earlier, but it probably dampened stuff and I don't fancy messing around trying to get a blaze going."

"Makes sense."

"Listen," Mike began. "You set up the beacon fire and you get out of there straight away. There are hundreds of those things up and down—"

A blinding flash followed by a seemingly apocalyptic eruption made them all gasp and they turned to their former home to see fire shooting into the sky. More explosions boomed and fear-filled cries and shouts rose from the other side of the island.

"Oh shit!" Mya shouted above the noise.

Further booms, cracks and rumbles made the air around them tremble as the giant firework display laid waste to what had been their supply warehouse and much of the campground.

"What the hell's happening? Is it Olsen?" Shaw screamed as he appeared in the arc of light provided by the continuing pyrotechnics.

"It's Les," Mike replied.

"What?"

More people were emerging from the darkness as Mike repeated himself. Some were carrying branches ripped from the campfires in order to illuminate their paths. "It's Les ... was Les. He went over there. He wanted to do something to put a spoke in Olsen's wheel. I suppose he stopped her getting our supplies and ammunition at least."

The cacophony and light show continued for several more minutes. Despairing cries flittered around the semicircle of gawkers. This was the finale to a terrifying and devastating twenty-four hours.

"Oh, God!" Jenny sobbed. "There'll be nothing left when that fire takes hold.

Shaw placed his arm around her. "Don't worry, Jen. The main weapons store was positioned well away from the rest of the caravans just in case an accident of some kind happened."

"And how do you think that plan's working out right now?" she asked, leaning into him and placing her head on his shoulder.

The crowd maintained their vigil long after the final explosions sounded. A bright orange glow beyond the trees told them all that the flames were licking high and their hopes of ever returning to Safe Haven diminished a little more with each moment that passed.

"Well," a familiar voice said and everyone turned to see George standing there with his walking stick for support. In the flickering light from the torches, his face appeared long and drawn, but his eyes were fixed on the opposite shore with a steely gaze. Jules and her brothers were by his side. Forlorn expressions painted their faces too. "Looks like everyone's up. I dare say we're best making a move now rather than just standing and gawking, don't you think?"

"It's the middle of the night," one woman cried out as she clutched the hand of the child by her side.

"That it is, but I doubt if any of us are going to get any more sleep, and watching our home go up in smoke isn't going to do a single one of us any good, is it?"

"George is right," Shaw said. "It'll take us a while to get the boats loaded and the journey down to Skye's not going to be a picnic." He turned to his friend. "Jen. Do you think you can start getting people organised?"

The small handful of children who had survived had not stopped crying since being woken up by the explosions, but now, as they were led away, things on the east of the island began to quieten.

"Somebody should row out to the yacht and tell Raj what's going on," Mike said.

"I'll radio across to him in a minute. Assuming his battery's still got a bloody charge. One of the handsets is already dead," Shaw replied.

"Are you okay?"

"Peachy. Why do you ask?"

"Look, when we get down there, it'll give us a little bit of breathing space. We'll be able to figure out our next move."

Shaw let out a huff of a laugh and shook his head. "You always make me smile, Mike," he said, walking away.

Mike watched him go and sadness crept over him. He had never seen Shaw give up. He'd never seen him down or weak despite everything they'd been through before, but maybe this was one disaster too many. Maybe losing Barnes and being left with a ragtag mob of survivors like this was the one thing that could push him into the jaws of depression and hopelessness. He felt a cold hand close around his and he looked down to see Sammy's silhouette.

"Hey, Sammy Bear," Mike said, doing his best to hide his sadness.

"We're never coming back here, are we?"

"We don't know that, Sammy. We don't know anything right now. All this has only just happened. We're going to head down to Skye, take a breath and figure out what to do next."

"Mike's right," Emma said, taking her little sister's other hand. "The important thing is that the three of us are together, and whatever else happens, nobody's going to change that. Now, go find Jenny and we'll be there to pack up in a minute."

Mya watched as Sammy's silhouette disappeared after the last of the torch lights and then turned to Mike and Emma. "It's not going to be easy, y'know."

"What isn't?" Emma asked.

"Getting everyone to the centre in Skye."

"It was your idea."

"Yeah. And out of all our options I think it's the best one. But there are people on the yacht who are frail, there are young kids, and there isn't going to be anything like enough fuel in the Land Rover to ferry them all."

"So, what are you saying?"

"I'm saying we're going to have to march a few miles through hostile terrain and there's every chance we could run into trouble." Muppet lay down by his mistress's side despite her dire warning.

"Well, this day's off to a great start."

"What's your plan?" Wren asked as she, Wolf, Robyn and Mila joined them.

"It's not ideal."

"There's a switch," Mike muttered under his breath.

"But we use the Land Rover to carry the old and infirm to the centre and keep going until the fuel runs dry. Everyone else is just going to have to go on foot and we'll just have to hope we make it without incurring any losses."

"What happens once we're all there and the food starts running out? We're miles away from Portree." He turned to Mya. "My guess is you and your people scavenged everything that was useful from the surrounding area."

"Pretty much," Mya conceded.

"Exactly. If we use all the fuel up, we'll be trapped there. Any scavenger teams would have to go out on foot with no means of bringing back any supplies that they couldn't carry on their backs, and that's if they made it."

Even though it was too dark to see anyone's facial expressions, a sombre mood fell over them all. "I think this is something we need to talk to Shaw about," Wren said. "If we run into trouble on our way to the centre, then it's all over for a lot of people before it's even begun."

"My brother's right," said Emma. "It was a million to one that we escaped Safe Haven alive. What was the point if we're going to wither away and die down there?"

"What's the point if a lot of us don't make it to the centre?"

"What's the point if we don't make it when we reach the centre?"

"Like I said, I think this is something we need to speak to Shaw about."

"Shaw's been through a lot."

"We all have."

"You got all those people from Stroon and the other villages to safety by yourselves, covering a much greater distance."

"Yeah," Robyn replied. "But it was going over rough ground and sticking to the coast. From what I've seen, there are a lot more roads and a lot more hiding places down there. We could be walking along and a horde could come at us from nowhere."

"It might," Mike said. "But then again, it might not. I say that we take as many of the least mobile people in the Land Rover as we can in one journey. Whoever drives them secures the grounds of the centre and prepares for the rest of us to arrive. We save the remainder of the fuel for when we need to go scavenging."

"And I still say this is Shaw's call," Wren replied.

"Fuck it," Mike hissed. "We're just going round and around in circles here. Speak to whoever you want. I'm going to go and get our stuff together." He turned and walked away.

Wren and the others were taken aback. He had never flared up at her like that before and it made all of them feel uneasy.

"I...." She didn't know how to continue and Wolf rubbed his head against her, sensing his mistress's shock.

"Everybody is stressed. Everybody is on edge, yes?" Mila began. "It is important that we do not start finding reasons to fight amongst ourselves. All of this comes from wanting what is best for everyone. Maybe there is a middle ground that we can find."

"You're right," Emma conceded finally. "But first things first. Let's get all our stuff together and get down there."

*

Beck was still struggling to get to sleep when the sounds of the blasts thundered. He had been lying next to Trish in quiet contemplation as Regan and Juno slept quietly in the other bed. He had rushed out onto the deck to find Raj already standing there with Humphrey by his side. For once, the Labrador Retriever did not have his trademark happy-go-lucky expression painting his face.

The two men stood in silence as they heard the sound of others joining them. They could not pull their eyes away from the village, however, and even when he heard his daughters crying, Beck did not turn.

"Oh, dear God," came the cry from one of the older women as she stumbled out onto the deck.

After a moment, Beck felt a familiar hand clutch his own and he instantly knew it belonged to Trish. He looked to his right to see Talikha had joined her husband and beyond them stood Darren. A knowing glance passed between the two men in the subdued glow of the solar-powered LED lights Raj had positioned around the deck before they returned their gaze to shore.

The frightened cries of Regan and Juno finally abated as they realised their world was not coming to an end and Trish took them back downstairs to the warmth and safety of their beds.

The minutes dragged on, but they continued their vigil of the orange glow. Eventually, the radio hissed, jerking them all from their contemplation. "Raj, this is Shaw. Is everybody okay across there? Over."

"We're all fine. What happened? Over."

"From what I can tell, it was Les's attempt to make sure Olsen didn't get her hands on the weapons and ammo. Look, we're packing up. I don't think we're going to get any more sleep tonight, so we may as well just head down to Skye. Over."

"Okay. What do you want me to do? Over."

"We're packing up the gear now. We'll ferry what's practical across to you for the journey down and spread the rest between the other boats. Over."

"Okay, Shaw. We'll be waiting. Over and out."

"Are you okay, Darren?" Beck asked.

There was a single tear running down Darren's face as he continued to look out over the sound towards Safe Haven. "I worked with Les for a long time, sir. He was a good friend, a good man."

Beck nodded. "They don't come much better than him."

"It wasn't right that he went out like this."

"No."

Darren shook his head and walked away.

"This day has not started any better than the last finished," Talikha said.

"You noticed that did you?" Beck replied.

One by one, the other spectators returned below deck. Trish eventually re-emerged while Raj and Talikha prepared for the arrival of the supplies from the small island.

"They drifted back to sleep holding each other tight," Trish said.

"Won't they panic if they wake up and don't see you there?"

"I'm heading back down in a minute. I just wanted to make sure you were okay."

"What possible reason could you have for thinking that I might not be okay?"

"Funny man," she replied, clutching his hand. "You know, people are going to need you more than ever now."

"Me? What the hell will they need me for? They need a miracle; that's what they need."

"And you're the man to provide that miracle."

"Ha! I love your faith in me, Trish. But I'm all out."

"All those files. All the things you've been planning and working on over the past months. Are you telling me it was all for nothing?"

Beck gestured towards the glow. "I don't know if you've noticed, darling, but they've just all gone up in smoke."

"You've still got that one file and I've never met anyone in my life with a more photographic memory when it comes to facts, figures and locations."

Beck turned towards her. "They're all meaningless now."

"No. They mean more than ever."

Beck shook his head. "A lot of that information would have been pertinent if we had an army. We've got nothing, Trish."

"No. We've got people who are relying on us, people who are looking to you."

"Nobody is looking to me. Shaw's the one in charge here."

"No. He was in charge of Safe Haven."

"I'm not about to get into a leadership contest with anyone. Those days are gone."

"I'm not talking about a contest. I'm talking about bringing these people on board. You don't have the army you hoped for, but there are people here who are going to fight until their last breath. Mya, Darren, Shaw, Vicky, Emma, Mike, Wren, Robyn, Mila, Jules and her brothers. None of them are ever going to give up."

Beck let out a long breath. "Let's get down to Skye first, shall we? We'll figure everything out from there."

Trish squeezed his hand once more and the pair stood in silence, watching the hypnotic, orange glow across the water continue to spread.

2

The journey down to Skye had taken much longer than anticipated, but otherwise, it had gone without a hitch. Mya, Shaw, Mike, Emma, Jules and her brothers were the first to set foot on the narrow shingle beach. Muppet stood by Mya's side with his tail wagging, but even he couldn't put a smile on any of their faces for the moment.

The fleet had moored a little way off the coast and a discussion as to the next step had taken place on the yacht before the nine of them had headed to shore.

"Okay," Mya said. "Everybody knows what they're doing. Let's not waste any time." True to her word, she and Muppet headed towards the trees and up the steep incline that would take them to the road.

Shaw and Andy remained by the dinghy watching the others as, one by one, they disappeared into the woodland. "I don't like any of this," Andy said in a hushed tone.

"You and me both, mate."

*

Mya and Muppet continued their climb, scouring the area for any sign of movement. Mike, Emma and the others followed. It only took them a few minutes to reach the road, and as soon as they did, they longed for the seclusion of the trees.

They continued along the narrow lane until Mya veered into another section of woodland and proceeded to uncover the old army Land Rover. She climbed inside, grabbed the keys and, after a few attempts, coaxed the engine to life. She looked towards the others with a relieved expression painting her face. They stayed put for a moment, carefully surveying their surroundings. When nothing appeared, Mya grabbed the radio on her belt. "Shaw, this is Mya. Over."

"This is Shaw. Go ahead. Over."

"We're with the vehicle. No hostiles in sight. Heading back to the rendezvous point now. Over and out."

*

Shaw clipped the radio to his belt, looked across towards the yacht and waved. His and Mya's were the only radios that were switched on. All the charging stations were back in Safe Haven and it wouldn't be long before radio communication was a thing of the past for them, so it was deemed prudent to save the batteries on the others.

Within ten minutes, he and Andy were dragging boats onto the shingle. Robyn, Wren and Wolf were the first to disembark. Mila helped George out, who struggled a little on the pebbly beach. With them were the most vulnerable of the people who had been brought up from Malbaig and the surrounding villages. Liz accompanied them and she shared their disconcerted looks as Wren and Robyn aimed their respective bows into the woodland.

"There was no better place to land than this?" Wren asked Shaw.

"I'm just a passenger on this trip. Mya's the one who knows this island."

Wren turned to see the yacht moored out in the bay while the smaller boats continued their journey towards the shore. "If there are infected in the woods, this could be the shortest escape in history."

"That's a cheerful thought," Robyn replied, looking down at Wolf. "He seems happy enough, so that's got to be a good sign, right?"

"I suppose."

"Okay," Shaw said as the final passenger was helped out of the first boat. "This is everyone who's going in the Land Rover."

Wren looked at her grandad then the other seven old folks who had been at the hospital when Olsen had attacked. "It's going to be more than a bit of a tight squeeze, isn't it?"

Shaw shrugged. "It is what it is."

"Are you okay?"

"I wish people would stop asking me that. I just want to get today out of the way."

There was an untold story in his words and Wren didn't press him further. "Okay. I get that."

A dinghy was dragged onto the shore next by Vicky, Ephraim and Kat. Ruth, Richard and a small handful of others climbed out. Ephraim and Kat were armed and they walked across to join Wren and Robyn. "Well, isn't this nice? We got the band back together for one final gig," Ephraim said, smiling.

"Seriously," Robyn replied. "Don't start with that weird stuff today."

"Sounds like somebody got out of bed on the wrong side."

"Right then," George called out, leaning on his stick and doing his best to disguise the discomfort he was feeling in his ankle. "Time's wasting. The sooner we get to where we're going the sooner we can warm ourselves around a nice fire."

The people who had travelled with Vicky and the others each paired with a former hospital patient and began the slow climb up to the road beyond the trees.

"Come," Mila said to George. "You will take my arm."

27

"Best chat-up line ever," Robyn said. "It sounds like an offer and a threat at the same time. How can anyone resist?"

Andy and a few of the others chuckled, lightening the mood for just a moment. Wren turned to Vicky, Ephraim and Kat. "I suppose this goes without saying, but the guns are a last resort. Bobbi and me will lead the way; you take the flanks and the rear."

"Yes, sir," Ephraim replied, saluting.

Wren and Robyn ignored him, turned around and entered the woods with Wolf following closely by their side. It was an overcast day and it had rained several times during their journey south, so the forest was a little darker than usual for this time of the morning.

It made little difference to the two sisters, however. They had honed their skills ever since leaving Edinburgh and now there were few better people to have in a situation like this. Indeed, it was why Mya had specifically asked for them to lead the second group up to the road.

Robyn cast a glance back over her shoulder to see the progress of the others was slow. "Hold up a minute." Wren needed no explanation as to why and the pair of them stayed put, panning their weapons slowly from side to side, waiting, listening, sensing anything out of the ordinary. Wolf sat between the two of them, his nose twitching, his ears pricked up, ready to sound a warning if one was needed.

"Not tired already, are you, girls?" George said with a smile on his face as he and Mila finally reached them.

"Are you okay, Grandad?" Robyn asked.

"Don't you worry about me."

She cast a weak smile towards him before she, Wren and Wolf continued. "I don't get why he's so chirpy."

"It's the old British spirit. Stiff upper lip and all that. Somebody needs to remain positive around here. I don't think I've ever seen Shaw so down before. Even when we lost Lucy, he was the one who stayed strong, kept us all going," Wren said.

"Maybe he thinks this is it for us."

"Yeah, well. He needs to snap out of it."

"That's caring of you. It's usually me who comes out with something as arsey as that."

"I'm serious. Everybody looks to Shaw. Everybody depends on him. Without him bulling people up, telling them that we can get through this, things are going to get worse and worse. If enough people start believing there's no hope then guess what; suddenly, there's no hope."

"I still say we should give him a breather. There are other people who can take up the slack here for a while."

"I suppose you're right."

They both fell silent as they scoured the treescape.

*

Mike and Emma had proceeded to the next bend while Jules, Jon and Rob had headed down the road in the other direction. "It looks quiet enough," Emma said, gripping her hatchet tighter than ever.

"Yeah. For the time being."

"I hope Sammy's okay. She wasn't too happy about us both leaving her again."

"She's with Talikha. She'll be fine."

They both stood looking down the road for a few seconds before Emma spoke again. "We're going to have to keep a close eye on Shaw."

"What do you mean?"

"I was speaking to Jenny earlier and she says that she's never seen him so low."

"We've just lost over four-fifths of our people. We lost Barney, Saanvi, Prisha, and that doesn't even scrape the surface. It'll take time for us all to come to terms with what's happened, but before that, we need to get to safety."

"I get what you're saying, but Jenny said this is different. She said that a part of him died too yesterday. She said he was changed."

Mike shrugged. "She's just being dramatic. Shaw's like the rest of us. We have good times and bad times.

29

Yesterday was disastrous, and he probably feels it more than anyone, but that's not to say he's not going to bounce back like we all do."

"I hope you're right. I really do."

"I'll have a word with him when we've got today out of the way."

"Oh Jesus, no."

Mike laughed. "Don't worry. I can be caring and stuff when I need to be." The pair of them remained there for another few moments. "Come on then. Let's head back to the car."

*

Raj had been the last to leave the yacht, and now, as he stood with Shaw looking at all the supplies, he placed his hands on his hips. "We're going to have to divide all this up and hope we can transport it in one journey," he said. The other man didn't respond. He didn't even give Raj any indication that he'd heard him. "Hello. Shaw?"

"Sorry, Raj, I was miles away. What did you say?"

"I said we'll have to divide all this up and hope we can transport it in one journey."

Shaw looked at the other man, but there was little recognition or understanding on his face. "Hmm."

"Are you alright?"

Again, it took a moment for Shaw to respond. "I'm just tired."

Raj nodded slowly. "Yes. Yes, of course. It will be good to get where we're going. Maybe then we can all rest and process what has happened."

Half a smile appeared on Shaw's face, but he did not answer.

*

Robyn and Wren came to a halt. They'd seen movement up ahead, and just because Wolf wasn't growling, it didn't mean there was no danger. Robyn pulled her bowstring taut and Wren raised her scope, carefully placing her finger over the trigger.

They held their breath despite those behind them being completely unaware of the potential danger. It was only when Mike and Emma appeared in the clearing that they breathed out a sigh of relief and lowered their weapons.

"Nice to see you're both on the ball," Emma said.

"If you're here, I'm guessing that means the road is clear," Wren replied.

"For the time being anyway." They all looked down the hill as the others slowly made their way up. "It's going to be a tight squeeze in the Land Rover."

"It beats walking."

"True," Robyn replied. "Have we decided who's heading to the centre first?"

"I think we're going to draw straws," Mike replied.

"What? Really?" A smile cracked on his face. "Knob."

"I think it's going to be Mya. If anyone can look after herself and a bunch of old invalids, it's her."

"I know you were waiting until I was in earshot to say that, but don't think for a second I won't crown you with my walking stick," George said, smiling as he and Mila joined them.

"How're you doing, old man?"

"Old man me again and you'll find out."

Mike nodded to Mila. "I'll walk with George the rest of the way."

"What the bloody hell have I done to deserve that?"

"Funny."

Mila, Wren, Robyn, Emma and Wolf carried on while George took Mike's arm and continued up the ever-steepening incline. "So, what's happening?"

"What do you mean? Can't I just help a friend out?"

"Oh, is that what this is?"

"How are you doing? I mean really?"

"My ankle's bloody killing me, I've got sweat pouring down my back, and I'm scared to death that not all of us are going to make the journey to the centre."

Mike nodded. "I get that."

"Okay. So, I've been honest with you. It's time for you to be honest with me. Why are you back here?"

"Genuinely, I wanted to see how you were doing."

George didn't speak for a moment. Instead, he looked at the younger man trying to see if there was a hint of facetiousness on his face. "Okay, I'll bite. Why?"

Mike looked back down the hill. The beach was well out of sight, but he knew it wouldn't be long before the remaining population of what had once been Safe Haven were trudging up with the rest of the supplies. "Honestly, without you, I don't see us making it."

"If you're trying to make an old man feel needed, you don't have to. I'll do what—"

"I'm not trying to make you feel anything. I'm being serious, George. We've got fewer resources than we've ever had. You can make something out of nothing and we're going to need your skills and your knowledge more than ever if we're going to survive."

"We'll need more than that," he said with a chuckle.

"True enough. But you're the one who gives us a fighting chance."

"That's kind of you to say, Mike, but no one's irreplaceable. We've got Jack and James. They're both very handy. They can—"

"Yeah, but they're not you. Something that seems impossible to others isn't for you. I'm telling you, George, back in Safe Haven, I'd have said our weapons and the militia were our greatest resources. Here, it's you. You're the one who is going to give us a fighting chance."

"Well, I don't know about that, but I'll do my bit. I've got no intention of going anywhere in the foreseeable future."

Mike smiled. "That's good to know."

"But I'm not the only one who's going to have to step up, y'know."

"What do you mean?"

"You've got a good head on your shoulders, Mike. It's about time you started using it." Mike laughed. "I mean it. There isn't a person here who doubts your courage or your loyalty, or your devotion to your family. But it was you who saved Beth. You knew exactly what needed to be done and you did it. You've saved plenty of people, and not just through fighting harder than anyone else. Shaw doesn't have Barnes anymore. He's going to need someone he can rely on."

"He's got Vicky, Em, Darren. He's got plenty of people."

"But he's going to need you too."

Mike paused again. "I'll do my best, George."

"I know you will."

*

There were more than a dozen boats that had made the journey down from Safe Haven. In them were the last of the supplies and the last of what had once been a happy population. Shaw, Raj and Jenny had organised the distribution of the food, tools and some of the weapons among the survivors.

Everyone carried more than they were comfortable with, and if an attack came, there was no possible way they could make a quick escape. As everything was divided up, they began their journey up the wooded incline in groups. Jack and James, carrying rifles as well as bags of tools that George had ferried across, led one group. Raj, Talikha and Humphrey headed another group. Jenny and Meg spurred on a third group. Tommy had not spoken since the previous day, but he did nonetheless follow every instruction his sister had given him.

During the journey down, everyone had been in a kind of limbo, still unable to believe or process all that had happened. One by one, as their feet hit the pebbled shore, the startling reality of what was happening struck them. More than a few gasps and cries left the lips of the survivors, but knowing that their journey was still far from over they did their best to pull themselves together and prepare for the reality that now faced them.

Meg brushed up against Jenny's leg as they climbed the wooded hillside. "It's alright, darling," she said to her beloved companion. "We're all going to be alright." She said the words in the hope that vocalising them would help her believe them, but it didn't.

"Do you need any help with that, Jen?" Ruby asked as the older woman struggled to get a better grip on the crate she was carrying.

She looked across at her and smiled. Ruby had a rucksack on either shoulder and a large bindle resting between the two. Many people carried hastily assembled bindles made from blankets, branches and whatever they could find to make the transfer of the supplies more convenient. "And where are you going to carry this exactly? On your head?" Jenny asked, smiling.

"Maybe we can take some of the stuff out of there and make it a bit lighter for you."

"You're a sweetheart, but I'll manage." She looked across to Tommy, who also shouldered two heavy rucksacks. His wide, staring eyes were fixed on the ground. "How is he?"

The smile was suddenly gone from Ruby's face. "I'll be glad when we've reached wherever it is we're heading. I think he will too."

Jenny nodded sympathetically. "I'm sure he'll be back to his old self in no time." *Another lie.* None of them would ever be the same again. So many friends and loved ones had died it overwhelmed the senses. They had been torn from their homes in the most horrific circumstances, and even though they were on the Isle of Skye, it did not fully compute. There was a part of all of them that struggled to believe or comprehend this was their life now. There was a part of all of them that thought this was just a day trip and they'd be heading home before dark. Their minds had yet to catch up to current events.

She looked down at Meg again and a sad smile curled the corners of her lips as her doting dog, seemingly sensing Jenny's eyes upon her, returned her gaze. Jenny swallowed hard. *She knows. She knows this isn't just an adventure. She knows this is the next chapter ... the final chapter.*

*

Jesus. This is like a scene from some weird Cocoon *reboot.* Mya dragged her eyes from the rearview mirror and returned her gaze to the road ahead. The debate about who would be the one to head to the Skye Outward Bounds Centre had been a short one. It had been decided that she was the obvious choice. No one was more capable of defending the passengers she carried and securing the centre before the arrival of the others.

George was in the passenger seat, and although he was still nowhere near back to full strength, he carried one of the M16s and knew how to use it. Muppet was in the footwell, and if nothing else, those were two individuals Mya could rely on if they got into a scrape.

Gasps and cries went up each time she went around a bend at speed and Mya's shoulders sagged a little more. "It's like being the driver on an old folks' home outing," she muttered under her breath.

George laughed. "This will be you one day."

"Somehow, I doubt that."

"Yes. Actually, so do I."

She took another bend and to their left was a sprawling meadow. "Screw it," she hissed as she immediately focused on a dozen creatures who turned and started running in the direction of the engine sounds. They would be gone long before the beasts reached the road, but it wasn't herself and her passengers she was concerned about. "I hope to God Mike's had the good sense to switch his radio on now we're on the road." She pulled the handset from her belt and hit the talk button. "Mike, this is Mya. Over."

"Go ahead, Mya. Over."

A moment of relief swept over her until she looked at the fuel gauge. The dial was hovering just over red. *Dammit.* "Just spotted a pack of creatures about two miles in. They're probably going to be on the road before the time you get to them. Over."

"How many? Over."

"About a dozen. I'll let you know if I see more. Over and out."

*

Mike clipped the radio to his belt and looked back at the line of refugees, some of whom were still emerging from the woods. A sad smile crept onto his face as he glanced towards his little sister. She was the only one Daisy ever followed now Jake was gone, and although there was a loop of rope placed loosely over her head, it was there as an emergency measure only.

His eyes drifted from her to Jules, to Emma, to Rob, to Talikha and to the rest, some of whom he still didn't know the names of even after all this time. Seventy-three people had escaped Safe Haven and about half that number could put up some kind of meaningful defence if they were attacked.

"Looks like we've got our work cut out," Darren said, shouldering his rifle.

Behind him were Beck and his small entourage. "I thought they'd have been going in the Land Rover."

"The PM insisted he wanted to be with everyone else. Plus, it wasn't great optics taking up space in the car and forcing some old people to struggle."

Mike smiled. "He's not running for re-election, y'know."

"Exactly what I said to him."

"I never got a chance to tell you how sorry I am about Les."

"Let's just make sure his death wasn't in vain."

Mike nodded and Darren headed over to the small group he was responsible for. Mike pulled the radio from his belt and hit the talk button. "Shaw. I'm guessing you heard Mya's transmission. How close are we to being ready? Over." Raj and a small handful of other men and women suddenly emerged from the woods onto the road.

"Speak of the devil," Jules said, walking up to join Mike. They watched for a moment and both shared the same confused look when Shaw didn't appear.

"Raj," Mike called across as Humphrey happily greeted his owner. "Is Shaw with you?"

"He said he'd be right behind us."

Mike raised the radio to his mouth once more and hit the talk button. "Shaw, this is Mike. Are you on your way? Over." He stared at the radio as his heart began to pound a little faster in his chest. Most of the people readying themselves for the journey were lost in their own worlds, their own fears, but those around him knew only too well how unlike Shaw this was.

"Maybe his battery's died," Emma said, joining her brother.

"Shaw. Come in. Over." Silence. "Shaw, this is Mike. Come in. Over."

"I'll go find him," Robyn said.

"I'll come with you," Mike replied, turning to Emma. "Get everybody moving."

She stared at her brother for a moment then nodded.

3

In the bunker, Beck had been shown how to use a weapon. Back then, he could never have envisaged a day when he would need to, but as he walked with his wife and family out in the open, he realised that day may well have come.

Doug walked a little behind with Liz and Mel. All of them were well out of their comfort zones. In fact, most of the people in this sad procession were out of their comfort zones. There were a few, though, who had walked similar roads a thousand times before.

"I'm scared," Regan said, clutching Juno's hand tighter than ever.

"I know you are, precious. But we'll be back at the Outward Bounds Centre soon. You liked it there, remember?" Trish said.

"It was better than running."

Trish's heart broke a little at that moment. Her girls had already been through so much and she felt sure there was worse to come.

*

"You okay, Jen?" Jules asked as she dropped back to walk with her friend.

Meg had been practically glued to her side ever since leaving the boat.

"You know me. Battling on. How are you doing?"

"I'd be a lot fuckin' happier if we weren't traipsing around in the middle of fuckin' nowhere."

A weak smile appeared on Jenny's face for a moment. "And other than that?"

"I still can't believe we're here. I can't believe what's happened. I can't believe we lost our homes." Jules carried a large, heavy sack over her shoulder. She could handle herself, but she was never the fiercest of fighters so she was not part of the response team if there was an attack.

"We'll be back there soon enough."

"You don't really believe that, do you?"

Jenny looked further up the line. Emma led the way with Andy, Rob and Jon by her side. She let out a long sigh. "No. No, I don't. But there are others who do."

"Yeah. And I love them like my own blood, but I think when things calm down and they start to understand what's happened, they're going to realise that they're fucking dreaming."

They walked a little further before Jenny replied. "That's the problem with dreams and nightmares, darling. You never know how they're going to turn out until it's too late."

*

Wren, Mila and Wolf brought up the rear of the long line. "They will be okay," Mila said, reaching out and placing a comforting hand on her friend's arm.

Wren shook her head. "I'm not worried about Bobbi and Mike. I'm worried about Shaw."

"He will be okay too. Shaw is a...." She clicked her fingers irritably as her mind searched for the term. "How you say, a war horse?"

Wren smiled weakly. "Yeah, a war horse."

"He has got us through so many disasters, so many scrapes. He is not someone you ever need to worry about. It will be just the radio. His radio is used more than any others. It makes sense his battery will die before the rest."

"Okay, I get that. But where is he?"

"Knowing Shaw, he was probably checking all the hawsers were secured, making sure every last grain of food, every last bullet had been collected from each boat."

"I hope you're right."

Mila nodded. "I am German. Of course I am right."

Wren laughed. "Y'know, the two don't necessarily go hand in hand."

Her friend smiled and shrugged. "In which case, I am Mila. Of course I am right."

*

Robyn and Mike broke from the tree line simultaneously, fully expecting to see Shaw. Instead, they saw nothing. The small fleet of vessels were all beached on the shingle, their hawsers secured to trees or suitable rocks.

"Shaw!" Mike called out.

Silence.

"Shaw!" Robyn yelled this time.

Nothing.

"Shaw!" Mike cried out again, louder this time.

"Err … maybe it's not a great idea for us to be making this amount of noise, y'know, considering."

"You make a good point."

The pair turned slowly. "We probably passed him and didn't even know it. He might have veered off a little bit or something."

"Possible, but not likely."

"That's us arriving at the centre. I'm going to do a sweep and then get everyone inside. Over."

Mya's voice hung in the morning air as Mike and Robyn stared at each other with shocked expressions. The radio on Mike's belt wasn't the only source of the

41

transmission. Mike grabbed the handset and hit the talk button but didn't speak. The pair just listened for the crackle and moved a little nearer to its source. He released the button and hit it. Again, they heard the hissing crackle, a little nearer this time. "Oh shit!" Robyn cried, looking down into one of the boats.

"Fuuuck!" Mike's eyes fixed on what she'd seen. A folded piece of paper was lying in the middle of the boat. On top of it was a walkie-talkie.

"Are you reading me? Over." Mya's voice echoed, but still Mike did not respond. He slid the radio out of the way and grabbed the piece of paper. His face was inscrutable as he read it.

"What? What does it say?" Robyn asked, taking it from him.

I'm sorry.

"This is Mya. Is anybody reading me? Over."

"Mya. This is Mike. Are you still in the car? Over."

"Negative. I'm just about to start my sweep. I thought something had happened when I couldn't get through. Over."

"Is anyone with you? Over."

"Does Muppet count? Over."

"Mya, we've got a problem. Shaw's gone. Over."

"Gone where? Over."

"I don't know. He left a note saying he was sorry. There's no sign of him. Over."

"He can't have got far. Can't you go look for him? Over."

Mike glanced at Robyn before returning his gaze to the radio. "Where would you suggest we start exactly?" This time he dispensed with the sign-off.

"Shit, Mike. This is the last thing anybody needs after yesterday. Shaw's like a rock. We need to find him. We need to get him back. Over."

"I'm open to suggestions, Mya. Right now, there are sixty-odd people heading in your direction. There are maybe ten of them I trust to put up a proper fight if something happens. You've already told me there are infected along the trail and now you want me to go looking for a needle in a haystack. If you've got some magic eye in the sky you've not told me about, please point me in the right direction. Over."

There was a long pause before Mya spoke again. "This is bad, Mike. This is really, really bad."

"Yeah. I kind of figured that out. Maybe when we've got everyone settled, we can get in the Land Rover and try to track him down."

"That's a negative, Mike. There's probably enough fuel left to get to Portree if we're lucky, but not back again. The next time we take the Land Rover out, we'd better find more diesel; otherwise, we're walking. I'm going to finish my sweep. We'll talk when you get here. Over and out."

Mike let out a long, deep breath. "Shit."

"Nicely put. We're pretty much in it up to our necks, aren't we?" Robyn said.

"I've known Shaw a long time. This isn't like him."

"I suppose everybody has their breaking point."

"Not Shaw. He's always been the one to drag people back from their breaking point."

"Looks like it's going to be up to you now."

"Ha! Yeah, right. I couldn't replace Shaw if all our lives depended on it."

"That's a shame. 'Cause right now, everybody's lives do depend on it."

*

Mya had circled the main building at least half a dozen times in the Land Rover but seen nothing. The last time she, Mike and Jules had left this place, they'd closed the gate behind them, and unless there was a break in the fence or the infected had somehow learnt to fly, there was no way she was going to find any, but all the same, she had to make certain.

The news about Shaw was a devastating blow. Yes, they had Beck, but Shaw had the trust and faith of the people of Safe Haven. Beck was still seen as a little aloof by most, not the kind of man who would get his hands dirty. His taking over could be one adjustment too many.

Mya felt something against her leg and looked down to see Muppet's wafting tail. For the first time in a while, a smile crept onto her face. The dog was clearly at ease, which was another sure-fire way of knowing there were no infected about to spring out. She searched the offices then headed to the accommodation area. One by one, she checked the rooms, making plenty of noise along the way. She finished her sweep in the cellar and when she was a hundred percent sure there were no dangers lurking inside, she headed back to the car.

George had already climbed out by the time she and Muppet reached it. "How is everyone?" she asked.

"Looking forward to getting out of there."

"Yeah. I don't blame them. Listen, don't say anything to the others, but Shaw's gone."

George looked at Mya as if she had spoken to him in another language. "Gone? What do you mean gone?"

"I mean he left a note. Mike went to look for him and he was nowhere to be seen."

George reached out, taking a grip of the Land Rover to steady himself. "Dear God."

"Like I say, keep it to yourself for the time being."

"Yes. Yes, of course. It's just ... he's the last person I would ever believe would do something like that."

"Yeah. I suppose it was too much for the poor guy."

"Are we going to go look for him? I mean, when the others arrive, are we going to try to find him?"

"There's nothing I'd like more, George, but I know for a fact that you saw the fuel gauge on our drive here. The food we've brought with us might last ten days, maybe a couple of weeks at best. The next time we go out, we need to find diesel and supplies; otherwise, people will go hungry. As much as I want to find Shaw, we need to think about the bigger picture."

"But...."

"Trust me. I get it. There isn't anything I like about this, but you and the rest of the council are going to have to show a united front more than ever now. You're going to have to be there in Shaw's absence. Do what needs doing. Give people the strength to carry on."

George put more of his weight against the Land Rover. "And if we don't have the strength?"

"Then you do what every politician since the dawn of time has done. You fake it."

*

It had not been possible to conceal the news of Shaw's disappearance, and the morale of the Safe Haven refugees sank to a new low as they continued their journey towards the Skye Outward Bounds Centre.

Mike had joined his sisters, Jules and Jenny at the front of the long procession. Jenny was crying and, despite Meg's best efforts, there was no sign of her stopping. She held on to Jules' arm tightly, and in the space of the few minutes she had learnt of her friend's disappearance she seemed to have aged ten years.

"We're going to need a council meeting as soon as we get to the centre," Mike said.

Emma let out a huff of a laugh. "Oh yeah, sure. That'll solve all our problems." She was in shock as much as everyone else. She stared down at the road, gripping her little sister's hand as she walked along.

"If people know you guys are still discussing things, still trying to figure out how best to proceed, it will make a difference. They don't expect you to have all the answers, but the fact that you're looking for answers will make them feel better."

"Answers? Jesus, Mike. I can guarantee that every member of the council will feel as lost and bewildered as I do right now."

"Look, somebody's going to have to make decisions, plan what happens next, keep people informed, organise food distribution, defences, all the stuff that Shaw and the council did before."

"Shaw and Barnes were the ones who coordinated all the security aspects of Safe Haven. The rest of the council never got involved in that."

"Okay, well, maybe you draft Mya or Darren in. Maybe you—"

"Maybe we just don't talk about this right now. I mean Jesus, Mike. Shaw was your friend. Aren't you at least a little bit concerned about him? Does everything have to be about what we do next? Can't we just have a little time to process it all?"

"Please don't fight," Sammy said, looking down at Daisy as she happily trotted along by her side.

"We're not fighting, Sammy. We're just having a discussion."

"In answer to your question, yes, of course I'm concerned about him, but he made a choice, the same way you made a choice when you got up and left. The thing is, when someone leaves, life goes on. Stuff still needs doing or everything grinds to a halt. Do I wish Shaw was still here? Of course I do. But I also know that if we don't step up and do what needs doing, we're signing our own death warrants."

Mike looked back towards Jules and Jenny then cast his eyes further to the line of people behind before returning to his direction of travel.

"Okay," Emma said eventually.

"Okay what?"

"Okay, we'll have a council meeting the second we get to the Outward Bounds Centre."

"Thank you. That's all I'm asking."

"Jesus Christ. We know we're in fuckin' trouble when Mike's the voice of reason," Jules said, causing Emma and Sammy to laugh. Even Jenny laughed a little through her tears.

"Thanks, Jules. Always nice to have you weighing in."

"For what it's worth, I think you're right. I'm as sick to my stomach as everyone else is about Shaw disappearing on us, but unless we're proactive, everything's going to turn to shite in a heartbeat."

"There we go," Mike said. "You heard her. "Everything's going to turn to shite in a heartbeat," he said in his best Irish accent.

"Why couldn't it be you who fucked off?"

"I couldn't deal with the guilt."

"What guilt?"

"The guilt of knowing that you'd be left so broken-hearted. Let's face it, Jules, all this hostility towards me is just your way of masking your true feelings."

"In your fuckin' dreams."

"In my nightmares, more like."

Jules quickened her step for a few paces to catch up with Mike and give him a shove. He turned and they locked eyes with each other. They both smiled. She winked at him. It was just a simple gesture but one that let Mike know that she was backing him and she wasn't giving up either. He nodded and turned to the front once more.

*

"That's the thing about the zombie apocalypse. Sure, it's all fun and games for a while, but no one ever thinks about the mental toll it takes on some people," Ephraim said with a barely noticeable smile.

"Don't make jokes like that around here, Ephraim. If Mike hears you, he'll snap you in half," Wren replied.

"Oh, come on. Where's your sense of humour?"

"I think I left it with the hundreds of my friends who died yesterday." She looked down at Wolf at the same moment he looked up at her. No matter how bad things were, he was always there to reassure her, always devoutly loyal.

"Wren is right. What is wrong with you?" Mila asked. "These people took you in. They have lost everything and now you make fun of them?"

"Technically, I was making fun of the situation rather than them."

"Well, that is fine then. I feel better knowing this. Carry on. Let us all join in. Let us laugh at the people who died, at the ones they left behind, at those who lost their family homes, their hopes, their—"

"Minds?"

"Screw Mike," Robyn hissed. "I'm going to gob you if you say one more word."

"Okay, okay!" Ephraim said, putting his hands up.

"Don't be a dick, Ephraim," Kat added.

"All I was saying was—"

"Don't."

Ephraim took a breath and thought for a moment before deciding to continue. "All I was saying was that nobody has ever really stopped to think about the toll this takes."

There was another pause before Wren spoke again. "What do you mean?"

"I mean think about this. After President Doom over there gave his address to the nation, our lives were turned on their heads. Yes, we did the whole stiff upper lip thing for a while, and give Beck his due, he actually did a remarkable job, for a politician, keeping us fed, safe and organised and busy, but at the same time, our entire world had changed forever. From that moment on, it was like we were on a war footing."

"A war footing?" Robyn repeated.

"Yes. I mean don't get me wrong. Some of us had it a lot easier than others. We were very lucky in Malbaig until Collingwood and his thugs showed up, but for most, things progressively got worse and worse until the eventual outbreak."

"Oh yeah. Things got so much better then."

Ephraim smiled. "That's my point. Things got a whole lot worse and continued to get worse and the pressures on the few who were left grew and grew. There is only so much the human mind can take until something gives. Trust me; I know whereof I speak."

"It sounds like you're saying you're surprised more of us haven't cracked," Wren said.

Ephraim thought for a moment. "Well, to an extent, I am. I think your council have done an incredible job, but at the same time, I think all of this will have taken a toll on them, and here we are today with Shaw as the proof of the pudding. No one has had more pressure on him and everyone was prepared to let him take it because that was the way it's always been."

"You're saying Shaw leaving is our fault?"

"I'm saying it's my fault, your fault, Olsen's fault, everybody's fault and nobody's fault. I'm saying that Shaw is probably the thin end of the wedge. I'm saying that even though we were living in that artificial haven that we all believed was worth fighting and dying for, nothing was ever okay. It was just a … a religion almost. We threw ourselves into it without ever questioning the truth behind it, always believing that it would give us salvation if we gave it long enough."

"You don't believe in God?" asked one of the villagers from Polness who had been earwigging on the conversation.

Ephraim looked irritable for a moment before replying. "You're asking me if I believe two kangaroos hopped and swam thousands of miles to get on a boat built by a six-hundred-year-old man, stayed on it for forty days and forty nights while the world flooded, then hopped and swam all the way back? No. No, I don't. That being said, I don't rule out the concept of a deity. I merely reject all the deist concepts that have been created by mankind, but that is completely by the by. What I'm saying is that everyone held on to Safe Haven as if it was this unwavering, unquestionable constant, that the very idea of it was something that we had to hold true in our hearts and our heads be damned."

"You're saying it was that belief that pushed Shaw over the edge?" Mila asked.

"Yes and no. He was the one who ordered the evacuation, so there was part of him that believed it, but the fact that he was prepared to leave suggests there was a part of him that didn't. The fact that Barnes and a whole lot more people died and he got out is probably what pushed Shaw over the edge."

"If you brought any of this up to try to make us feel better about things, it really isn't working," Robyn said.

"Well, once again, you've missed the point completely, but thank you for taking part. No, what I'm saying is that in Safe Haven we were in a protective bubble of sorts. But the bubble's burst."

"Are you saying that you think we're going to have an epidemic of nervous breakdowns?" Wren asked.

Ephraim laughed a little. "And you're meant to be the clever one. No, I'm saying that we need to be more watchful, more understanding and more supportive of everyone than we ever were in Safe Haven. I'm saying we need to provide more than just free meals and a place to sleep. People will be feeling more pressure than ever, more pain than ever."

"And do you honestly give a damn?"

A thin smile decorated Ephraim's face for a moment. "Despite what you might think, yes, I do."

They carried on walking for a little while before Wren continued. "You had a breakdown, didn't you?"

Ephraim laughed again. "Oh, my dear girl, I had the mother of all breakdowns. But I'm fine now. Just ask Mother," he said, gesturing to the empty space by his side.

"Very funny. We're talking about a serious subject here."

Ephraim took a deep breath. "Yes, Wren, I had a nervous breakdown. The thing is, even when you can see the signs in others, you can't always see them in yourself, and it's never the same for everyone."

"What was it like?" Robyn asked.

Ephraim looked at her for a moment. "It was the most frightening experience of my life."

"Why?"

"Looking back, I see how it all unfolded, and talking to friends afterwards, they spoke of the change in my personality too. A lot took place and I was completely oblivious to it. But then things started happening that I couldn't help but notice."

"What kind of things?"

"I started hearing things, seeing things. I started feeling presences."

"Okay. Now you're starting to freak me out," Robyn said and Ephraim chuckled again.

"Yeah. Imagine how I felt."

"What kind of things?" Wren asked.

"The kind of things that you don't want to see and don't want to hear. The kind of things that make the hair on the back of your neck stand to attention and goose pimples run up and down your arms. I remember one evening, I was in my office sitting at my desk marking papers when I suddenly looked up. There was a black hooded figure standing in the corner with its face to the wall."

"Honest to God, I would have pooped myself there and then," Robyn said.

Wren shook her head irritably. "Go on, Ephraim."

"Well, if it wasn't for a knock on my door at that very moment, I don't know what would have happened. One of my colleagues walked in. Well, actually, they were more than a colleague. I looked from the doorway back to the corner of the room and the thing I'd seen was gone. For a moment, I just stared and then I burst out crying. If it wasn't for Embeth walking in, I honestly don't know what I'd have done, but I can guarantee it wouldn't have been good. Within twenty-four hours, I had voluntarily committed myself, and the rest is history."

"Holy cow."

"Indeed, young lady. Holy cow."

"But you're, like, okay now," Robyn said.

"Yes. That's not to say it couldn't happen again, but I think the whole experience helped me understand a lot more about my mind and how it works."

"That's good then."

"Oh yes. It was totally worth it."

This time it was Wren and Mila who laughed. "Get lost," Robyn said.

"Thank you for sharing that, Ephraim. It can't have been easy," Wren said.

"It was actually easier than you think."

"Well, hopefully, I'll never find out."

4

The sun broke through the clouds and with it came the warmth that had been an uncharacteristic partner to the early spring months. Mike looked back to see the procession all keeping good time behind him.

"At this pace, we should be there within the hour," he said, turning back to the road ahead. To either side of them were fields, once full of crops, now merely brown patches with stubborn growths of scrub grass breaking through the surface.

"I can't stop thinking about Shaw," Jenny said as Meg brushed up against her once more. Humphrey nudged Jenny's other leg and a smile flickered on her face for just a moment.

"Shaw is strong," Talikha replied. "Maybe a little time alone will help him see things more clearly."

"Time alone is all well and good, darling, but when armies of those things could jump out from anywhere, it's quite difficult to find time alone, isn't it?" Talikha reached out and took her friend's arm.

Suddenly, growls rose from the back of Meg's and Humphrey's throats. "Shite!" Jules said, preparing to slip the rucksacks from her shoulders. The leading group all came to a stop and Sammy took a tight grip of Daisy as if she was some kind of comfort toy.

"Anybody see anything?" Mike asked. It would normally be Shaw standing where he was. It would normally be Shaw asking the same question, but in an ever-changing world, this was just one more change that Mike had to get used to.

"I don't see a thing," Emma replied, flicking her rucksack off and unslinging her rifle.

The rest of the procession had come to a stop, too, and the escalating tension was palpable as they all surveyed the fields and the trees up ahead, searching for infected.

Pounding feet drummed along the road and Mike turned to see Robyn, Mila and Wren joining them. Mike brought Shaw's radio up to his lips and hit the talk button. "You see anything, Andy? Over."

Andy, Rob and Jon were bringing up the rear. It was too important a position for it to be someone Mike didn't trust. "Nothing. Over."

"Keep your eyes peeled. Over and out."

Mike returned the radio to his belt and looked down at the three dogs as the growls continued and their heads turned in multiple directions.

"What's happening?" Darren asked as he approached with his Glock drawn and Beck and his entourage following closely behind.

"We don't know yet, but the dogs aren't happy," Emma replied.

"Remember," Mike called out, "guns are an absolute last resort." Despite the warning, several more people dumped the bindles and rucksacks they were carrying in order to raise their rifles.

"This could turn bad quickly," Robyn said, her bow raised and an arrow already nocked.

"Ah, yes. Because things have been going so well up to now," Mila replied, withdrawing both her swords.

Then it happened. Almost as if it was a coordinated assault. At least ten creatures emerged from the trees beyond the field to their left. Double that number began to charge from the woodland, running parallel to the road up ahead while another dozen or so started sprinting down the road itself.

"Oh Jesus," Emma whispered.

Everyone froze for a moment as the beasts advanced.

"We're not losing anyone else," Mike said; then he shouted, "We're not losing anyone else." He ran into the field, attracting the attention of the two largest groups, and most of the creatures began to converge on him.

He felt a presence by his side and turned to see Mila matching him pace for pace. "Here," she said, slowing down to a stop twenty metres or so from the road. "When this is over, you and I will have a long chat about communication."

An arrow then a bolt blurred by the pair of them and they watched as the two lead creatures from the pack to the south collapsed, making more stumble. "Bloody hell, those two have got some serious skills with their bows."

"We should be grateful, yes?"

"Definitely."

"FIRE!" It was Emma who shouted the order, conscious of the fact that Mike had said using guns was a last resort but understanding that the sheer number of infected descending upon them meant there was no other option.

Booms and cracks began to echo around the clearing, making it sound like the scene of a military re-enactment. All of those with rifles had undergone training, and although not all possessed perfect aim, at least a quarter of the beasts fell within the first few seconds.

Mike withdrew the shotgun from his rucksack and pumped the fore-end. BOOM! Pump. BOOM! Pump. BOOM! Pump. BOOM!

Four creatures fell, causing more to trip and collapse. He threw the weapon to the ground and withdrew his machetes, kicking out hard as the first of the beasts reached him.

Mila's blades blurred as she split to the south. Only four of the creatures from this direction remained standing. Swipe! Three. Slash! Two. Wumph! One. A lightning-fast upward thrust through the palate took care of the final beast. She withdrew the blade straight away and turned as an arrow disappeared into the head of the monster nearest to her. A bolt took down the next and Mike finished off another creature with a single, powerful downward smash. At least half a dozen more fell around her as the bullets continued to fly.

She ran forward to join Mike as the second wave of infected approached. More arrows, bolts and bullets flew, decimating the ranks of the undead army before they even got close to either of them. They looked to the road to see the beasts that had been closing in on the convoy were all down too.

Within a few more seconds, silence hung over the clearing once more. "Holy shit!" Mike said, regarding the fallen creatures as he slowly turned.

"Ja," Mila replied.

They had both expected a drawn-out attack. They had both expected to come close to death as they had so many times before. They had not expected this.

Mike stared across at his sister and they shared a smile. He looked down the line. Jules, Raj, Talikha, and even Jenny all had their weapons still raised. Vicky, Ephraim, and Kat also had their rifles braced against their shoulders. Darren was the first to return his Glock to its holster and Mike's eyes locked on Beck, who also carried a gun. He shielded his family behind him, and whether he had taken any of the creatures down or not Mike didn't know, but the fact that he was prepared to fight edged him up a little further in Mike's estimation.

"I suppose we better get back on the road before we come across any more," Mike said.

"Ja. Something tells me we will see plenty more before our day is over."

*

Shaw had left the woodland behind some minutes before. He stared into the distance as the faint sound of gunfire still echoed in his ears. He almost collapsed onto a wide flat rock and let out a shuddering breath as sadness overwhelmed him.

I left them. He'd left them not for selfish reasons but in the firm belief that they would be better off without him. Now doubt engulfed him. *If I'd stayed, I could have at least been an extra gun.*

He'd had more experience than most and he knew that whatever fight had ensued, it was well and truly over. It had not lasted long, and there were no draws, no ceasefires in the war against the infected, so it had gone one of two ways, and there was a big part of him that feared the worst.

It was only a matter of time. If I'd been there or not, it probably wouldn't have made a blind bit of difference. If some of them lived through today then there's nothing to say they won't face the same fate tomorrow or the next day or the one after that.

A single tear ran down his face, but he quickly wiped it away. He had never felt so confused or conflicted in his life, and the only thing he did know was that it was not a state of mind conducive to marshalling a group of survivors through a time when they would need strong leadership the most.

He did not want to die, but he didn't want to go on as he was either. Barnes was dead. Hundreds of people were dead, all while he was at the helm. He'd lost Safe Haven. He'd lost the place he and all the rest had depended on. It was all down to him.

Even now, as he sat on the rock with just the sun and the breeze to keep him company, he didn't understand what had happened. He didn't know how Olsen had carried out her plan. *Couldn't have been choppers. Couldn't have been planes. Those things couldn't have been fired from a trebuchet. How the hell did you do it? How did you do it?*

This time, more than a single tear fell from his eyes. His head drooped and he watched as the drops fell onto his jeans one by one, spreading. A vast emptiness grew inside him. In the space of a day, he had lost everything. He'd lost one of his best friends. He'd lost his home. He'd lost many of the people he loved, and now he was losing himself. He could feel it. He could feel that, inch by inch, he was being devoured from within. *Soon there'll be nothing left. There'll be nothing left of me. I've already lost so much.* "What's a little more?"

Suddenly, he saw Lucy's face in his mind's eye. He had shared more secrets with her than he had with anyone. *That's when it all started going wrong.*

It was an epiphany of sorts, but it didn't make him feel any better. If anything, it made him feel even more hopeless, more pathetic. Lucy dying had affected everyone, but as he sat on the rock staring down at his jeans, he understood that was when he'd started disappearing too.

He'd had to stay strong for the others, for the community. He'd had to stay strong for Mike and Emma and Sammy and all the rest. He'd had to be compassionate and understanding but unwavering in his pursuit of defending the idea of Safe Haven too. He'd had to be a rock. He'd had to be the one that everyone turned to, but who could he turn to? He had Jenny, but she wasn't Lucy. No one was Lucy.

And all the stuff that he used to talk to her about, it just built and built and he had to push it down further and further inside until there was no more room and now … now … this.

He climbed to his feet, this time not bothering to wipe the tears from his eyes. It would be like washing a car in the rain, completely pointless.

He took one final look towards where he'd heard the sound of the gunfire and then he was on his way once more.

He didn't know how long he would walk or where he would end up, but he knew that this would be the last journey he would ever take.

*

"I'm really hungry, Billy," Gummy said as they continued their seemingly endless march.

They had finally left the forest and were walking over croft land. The breeze had shifted and the smell of smoke, although not completely gone, no longer demanded that they wear their makeshift masks to breathe.

"I know, Gummy. We're all hungry, mate. Hopefully, we're going to find a house or something soon, and with a bit of luck, there might be food there."

"Oh, you fucking belter," Decko said.

"What?" Billy asked as he, Galli and Gummy all turned towards him to see his eyes cast towards a white cottage in the distance. "Oh, thank Christ."

They all changed direction. Out there in the open, they could identify threats much sooner than when they were in the forest, and with the sun shining down on their tired bodies, something close to a smile lit on all their faces.

"Do you think we can rest up for a while?" Galli asked, almost apologetically.

"I think that'd be a good idea."

"Too right it would," Decko replied. "My feet are killing me."

The quartet continued towards the house like four people in a desert heading towards an oasis. With each stride their hearts lifted a little more. By the time they reached the yard encircling the property, they were almost running.

The heavy-panelled oak door was locked when Decko tried the handle. He took a step back and booted out hard. Rather than the door moving, he catapulted backwards and fell to the ground. The others all burst out laughing as he lay there flat on his back.

"Nice work, Decko. You showed that door," Galli said between giggling breaths.

"Don't worry about me, will you?" he said, rubbing his coccyx as he climbed to his feet. "That bloody hurt."

"Aww. Poor Decko."

"I can go off people, y'know," he said, this time taking a run at the entrance. There was a loud crack and the door juddered inwards slowly as the fragments of the jamb fell to the ground.

A wave of warm, stale air struck them all. "Okay. Let's see what we can find." They all filed into the kitchen and immediately walked to the cupboards, eagerly swinging the doors open like kids searching for Christmas presents while their parents were out.

With each cupboard they searched the hope that had built in each of them diminished a little further. "They're all empty, Billy," Gummy said, almost in tears.

Decko walked over to the sink. He turned the tap only to hear air escaping. "Son of a bitch."

"Whoever lived here is long gone, and they took everything worthwhile with them."

"But I'm starving," Gummy said.

Billy exhaled a long frustrated breath. "I know you are, mate. We're just going to have to be a little more patient though."

"Hey. Wait a minute," Galli said excitedly. She rushed back out of the house and around to the front where she disappeared from sight for a few moments. There was a look of unbridled joy on her face as she reappeared in the kitchen. She held the hem of her T-shirt out in front of her, using the material as a kind of bag as around twenty freshly harvested potatoes jostled around, flaking off soil as she walked over to the kitchen counter. "Whoever lived here must have planted them before they left. Not the best crop I've ever seen, and they've probably been in the ground a bit longer than they should, but they're something at least."

"Can we eat them?" Gummy asked.

"Not a good idea to try eating them raw. They can cause stomach upsets," Galli replied.

"I'm guessing you haven't just dug them up for the fun of it," Billy said.

She walked over to the cupboards and crouched down, grabbing an old pan missing its handle. "When they went, they obviously didn't see the point of taking up any extra room with this.

"Okay. So, we've got potatoes and a pan. There's old furniture all over this place. Break some of it up and we'll get a fire going in the range." The range sat in the fireplace. It was a giant cream-coloured thing from another time.

"Will it still work?" Decko asked.

"There's not an awful lot that can go wrong with them, but there's one sure-fire way to find out, isn't there?"

"Err … Toni dearest, what are we going to do for water?" Billy asked. "Take it in turns spitting?" Galli walked outside again and came back a minute later carrying an old pickaxe. "What the hell are you going to do with that?"

Galli disappeared further into the house without bothering to explain what she was doing. The three men looked at one another with confused expressions. When a thunderous banging began to ring out from one of the other rooms, they all rushed out of the kitchen in search of its source. They found Galli in the bedroom with the carpet peeled back. There was already a sizeable hole in the wooden floor, but each time she brought the heavy axe down, the gap got bigger and bigger. She finally stopped what she was doing, walked by the three men and headed down the hall.

She passed them once more as she re-entered the bedroom with the pan and placed it in the hole where the floorboards had once been. It was next to the skirting board and underneath the radiator. The gap between the floor and the foundation of the house was only about eighteen inches, and a small shudder ran down Galli's spine as she saw signs of rodent droppings.

She grabbed the pickaxe, took a stride back, then swung it down and to the side with all the strength she had.

There was a metallic ring as it struck the copper piping below the radiator, which dented noticeably. She brought the axe back up and swung again. This time, it cut all the way through and a steady stream of water began to flow.

"Err … your girlfriend's pretty bright, Billy," Decko said.

"In fairness, compared to you three, the potatoes I just picked are pretty bright. Now, can one of you go put the plug in the sink while another keeps an eye on the flow? I'm guessing I don't need to explain that you'll need to put your thumb over the pipe when the pan's not underneath."

Billy laughed. "Err … I don't think we should be using that."

"Why not?" Galli asked.

"They add chemicals to stop corrosion. It was a nice thought, but I think we're better off cupping water out of the cistern."

"I'm not using toilet water."

"It's not toilet water. It hasn't actually been in the toilet. And, y'know, we're going to be boiling it too."

Frustration flashed on Galli's face. "Whatever. I trust I can leave you to do that then?"

"Why? What are you doing?"

"I'm going to check all the wardrobes to see if there are any clothes we can wear. I don't know if you've noticed, but we all smell like foundry workers' armpits. Oh, and when you're done, get the range going, will you?" Galli smiled and headed back out of the bedroom.

"You heard the woman," Billy said as they all smiled now. "Let's get to work."

*

"There's going to be a council meeting as soon as we get to the centre," Emma said as she dropped back to walk with Beck, Trish, Doug and the others.

"That's probably wise," the former prime minister replied.

"I'd really appreciate it if you'd come along."

"We're all in this together. I'd be happy to help in any way I can, although I don't know how much that will be."

"Well, we've just used up a hell of a lot of ammo. We've got less than two weeks' worth of food if we ration it, and from what I understand, we've got hardly any fuel left in the one vehicle that's at our disposal, so any help will be useful at the moment."

Beck turned to look at Juno and Regan. They were walking along, clutching Mel's hands. Tears had been streaming down their faces during the attack, but for the time being, at least, they weren't crying.

"Like I said, I'll be there."

"Thanks," Emma replied and sped up, heading to the front of the line.

"You do realise that we're going to have to break the glass, don't you?" Doug said.

Beck looked across at his long-time friend and confidant.

"What does that mean?" Trish asked.

Beck ignored her. "Do you really think we've got to that stage?"

Doug thought for a moment. "Well ... speaking as your special advisor, I'd tell you to let them show their hand first, but I'm pretty certain I know what they're holding."

"Hello," Trish said. "What are you two talking about?"

Beck sighed. "Break glass in case of emergency. Doug's saying we've reached that point."

"Okay, I still don't understand."

"Let me put it like this," Doug said. "We're on the canvas, the count is nine, and the bell is about to ring."

"Jesus Christ, can someone just give me a straight answer, please?"

"We're going to have to go into survival mode, Trish. We're going to have to offer up the one thing we can."

Trish carried on walking for a few paces. "You're saying that as if it's going to help."

"It might."

"Yeah. If Mike and the others have been hiding a couple of thousand soldiers somewhere that they've not told us about."

"Look, I don't think we need to think like this for the time being. A group's heading out to Portree tomorrow or the next day. If that's remained untouched, as Mya believes, it could keep us going for months … more than that even."

"So that's the plan?" Doug asked. "We just squirrel away down here, living on scraps. We turn native."

"I hate to break it to you, Doug, but we've been native for some time now."

"Honestly, Doug," Trish said. "You talk about it as if it's something indecent. These are good people."

"Exactly," Beck chimed in. "We escaped with our lives when so many more didn't. But for a quirk of fate we wouldn't be here now."

"Quirk of fate, my arse, Andy," Trish replied, making even Darren break his zen-like state of concentration and look towards her. "Shaw and Mya and Raj and Talikha and Mike and Wren and the rest of them made sure that as many people got out of there as they could. Fate had nothing to do with it. It was sheer bloody grit. And right now, we all need to show a bit more of it."

5

Although not uneventful, the remainder of the journey to the centre was not as treacherous as it could have been. The first encounter with the infected was, by far and away, the worst. There were two more, with smaller packs, both of which were dispatched quickly and efficiently by Mike, Wren, Robyn and Mila, with little fuss and even less noise.

When they finally reached the gates of the Skye Outward Bounds Centre, some of the refugees began to cry with relief and others with sadness. Safe Haven had been more than a home. It had been an idea. It had been something that promised a future. This place would give them safety and respite for a short time, but with the greatest imagination in the world, it would not be somewhere they could call home.

"I haven't been able to check the fencing," Mya said to Mike and Emma before they'd even got through the gate. "I thought it was too much of a risk for me to leave everybody and do a circuit of the place."

Mike had ended up carrying the crate that Jenny had struggled with in addition to one of Jules' rucksacks. "I'll drop this stuff off up at the house and then I'll go round."

"I'll come with you," Wren said as she and Wolf walked up behind them.

"Ja," Mila added. "Robyn and I will head in the other direction. This way, we will get the job done in half the time."

"Why do I have to go?" Robyn asked.

"To keep me company."

"As long as it's for a good reason then."

It took several more minutes for the procession to reach the house. Wren, Robyn and Mila all squeezed the life out of George before they reassembled in the foyer of the former asylum and waited for Mike.

"The expanded council meeting's about to start," he said, appearing at the top of the staircase as pots and pans began to clatter in the kitchen. The smell of smoke drifted down the hallway and a wave of heat wafted into the foyer as they walked towards the front door.

"Expanded council meeting?" Mila asked.

"Yeah. They've got Beck, Mya, Darren and Doug in there too."

"I understand Beck and Mya. I don't understand the other two."

Mike shrugged. "Nobody seemed to object, and without Shaw around here, it probably won't harm to get a bit of extra input."

"We shall follow the fence to the right, yes?"

Mike nodded and looked towards Wren and Wolf. "I guess that means we're taking the left."

They headed through the entrance in silence. So much had happened in such a short time that none of this quite seemed real. They gave one another little more than nods as they finally reached the gates at the end of the long drive and split up. They continued walking for a few more minutes before Wren broke the silence.

"I'd like to go with you to Portree."

Mike smiled. "I'm not in charge here, Wren. I'm guessing that's what's going to be decided in the meeting." Wolf brushed up against Mike's leg and he bent over to give his mane a friendly tussle.

"It's obvious, isn't it? You, Shaw, Barnes and Hughes were always the ones to head out on scavenging expeditions. In the absence of the other three, there's no one with more experience. I survived in Inverness for a long time by myself and I'd like to go. I think Bobbi and Mila should too. If we're heading into a small town that's going to be brimming with infected, doing it by stealth is the only way people are going to get out alive."

"I don't disagree."

"So, you'll put in a word for us?"

"Like I said, I'm not in charge. But if anyone asks my opinion, I'll tell them. Why are you so eager to head there anyway? Have you suddenly developed a death wish?"

Wren reached out and let her fingers run along the chain-link fence for a while. "This is our last chance, Mike. I'm not saying that for effect. I mean this is really our last chance. I'm not blind and I'm not deaf. I'd say we've got a couple of weeks' food at the absolute most and after the bloody gunfight at the O.K. Corral that we had on the way here, I'm guessing our ammunition reserves are pretty dreadful too."

"Actually, I reckon it's closer to a week."

"Ha! At least it won't be a long, drawn-out death then. But that's my point. When we go to Portree, we need results. I'm not being arrogant, but me, Bobbi and Mila lived out there longer than anyone for a reason. We know how to survive."

Mike put his hands up. "You're preaching to the choir."

"So, you'd want us out there with you?"

"Given the options, I don't really think there's anyone else."

"Given the options? Wow! Has anyone ever told you that you can be a complete dick sometimes?"

"I didn't actually mean it like that."

"Really? How did you mean it then, Mike?"

"I mean that I don't like the thought of you guys out there any more than I like the thought of Em or Sammy or Jules out there."

"So, you're telling me that you're a sexist pig. Is that what you're saying?" Wren's face had turned a little red. There was no playfulness in the words, only anger.

"No. I'm saying that you're my family. You're my family and the last thing I want is for you to be in harm's way."

Some of the bluster left Wren. "And did you ever feel that way when you went out with Shaw or Barnes or Hughes?"

"No."

"And you say it's nothing to do with being sexist."

"Shaw, Barnes and Hughes were all soldiers. Yes, they were like brothers to me, but I always felt like they'd be okay." Mike shook his head. "I can't explain it. It's just a feeling, a state of mind. They've all gone now, and it hurts, but we're here and we're carrying on. I've lost Luce and Jake, and if it wasn't for Em and Sammy and you, I don't think I'd have come out of the other end of that. If I lose any other people I really care about, really love, I don't know how I'm going to carry on."

"But if we don't come back with food when we head out there, you're going to lose everybody. That will be it. There'll be no future, no anything. You, me, Bobbi, Em, Sammy, we're going to slowly starve to death. Everyone here will. It will be like a death of a thousand cuts. It'll happen slowly and you'll get to see every slice, every drop of blood."

"I'm guessing you did pretty well when it came to creative writing back at school, didn't you?"

Wren let out a little laugh. "I'm serious."

"I know. And you're right. If I'm involved, I'll tell them I want the three of you to come along."

"Four of us," she said, nodding down towards Wolf.

"Sorry. The four of you."

"And if they say no?"

"Then we take the Land Rover before anyone gets up and we head there ourselves."

*

The desk that Beck had resided behind during their first stay at the Skye Outward Bounds Centre had been pushed to one side and a circle of chairs had been assembled in the spacious office.

"This doesn't feel like a council meeting without Shaw here," Jenny said.

"Well, let's call it an extraordinary meeting of the council until we get back on our feet, shall we?" Beck replied. "So, Shaw was the one who always chaired these meetings as I understand it, and in his absence, I suggest we elect a new chair." He looked around at all the faces. Most were still in shock.

Ruth and Jenny looked bewildered by what was going on. Vicky and Jules stared down at the floor. Their eyes were heavy and full of sadness. Mya sat with Muppet directly across from Beck. She had her arms folded and would clearly rather have been anywhere than there. George sat between Emma and Raj, doing his best to stay positive despite having as little reason as everyone else.

To Beck's left was Doug. To his right was Trish, and beyond her, Darren. Everyone had been through so much in the past day. All they wanted was a little respite so they could come to terms with what had happened, but when they had joined the council, they had assumed a responsibility, and now it was time to pick up that mantle.

"I propose Emma," Trish blurted.

"Seconded," said Beck.

"Wait. What?" Emma replied, shaking her head. "Propose what?"

"You should be the new chair," Trish said. This had been something Beck had suggested before the meeting started. Doug had wanted him to take control, but he and Trish had believed this was a smarter play. Emma would be full of insecurity and the fact that Beck and Trish had nominated her would immediately make her trust them a little more. It would be far simpler for Beck to steer things through Emma than overtly lay out his own agenda.

"Show of hands, please. All those in favour of Emma being the new chair," Beck said. He looked around the room. "It's unanimous then."

She straightened up in her chair and suddenly felt very self-conscious. She ran her fingers through her hair and cleared her throat. "Err … well, I suppose we'll be doing this quite a bit to start off with. The first thing we need to look at is food." She turned towards Raj. "You think we've got about two weeks' worth?"

"That was a guesstimation," Raj replied. "We bundled what we could onto the yacht and got it across to the island just in case the flames hit. There was no science behind it."

Emma turned to Jenny. "After the meeting, do you think you and Ruby could do an inventory?"

Jenny's eyes were red and tired, but she shuffled up in her chair too and nodded. "Yes. Yes, of course. But I know they've already started cooking downstairs."

"People need to eat. They need to feel warm. They need to feel as comfortable as possible today. They've just been torn from their homes, and hope isn't exactly plentiful at the moment, so today, we won't be food fascists." The term prompted a small ripple of laughter from the others. Emma turned to Mya. "The fuel situation for the Land Rover isn't good?"

Mya crossed her legs over Muppet as he sprawled out in front of her chair. "The dial's well into the red. I'd say we've got enough to get to Portree, but we'd struggle to get back again. We'd need to find fuel when we got there."

"And you think Portree is our only option? When I was living outside of Kyle, everyone told me that place was a no-go area."

Mya nodded sadly. "Our teams pretty much raided every possible house, farm and shop this side of Portree. Hell, they even went all the way up to Uig to the ferry terminal. Trust me; they weren't happy to make that journey to find little more than a few bags of M&M's and a couple of Bounty bars in a vending machine."

"Going to Portree won't be a walk in the park."

"I'm aware of that. But I'm also confident that it's our only option."

"And if you can't get fuel?"

"Then it's going to be a long walk back."

"I don't like it. I don't like the idea of such a big risk for what essentially will be a single carload of food that might last us another few days at the most."

"I've been thinking about that. There are a load of crofts in this area. I'm pretty certain we can pick up a sheep trailer somewhere along the way."

Emma nodded. "Okay. That's a little better, but it's still a huge gamble."

"If you've got another plan, I'm all ears."

Everyone turned to Emma again and she looked down at her hands. "No. No, I haven't."

"For what it's worth, Emma, I don't have a problem doing this. If we don't find food, then we're not going to last long. We'll all end up dead one way or another."

Mya's words sent a chill through everyone in the room before Emma took charge. She turned to Trish. "What's our situation as far as medical supplies go?"

"Well, the room we were using downstairs when we were last here has been completely gutted. They took everything with them. Liz and I brought our bags when we escaped from the hospital and we had five nurses on duty when we evacuated. We could do with a good resupply, but we've got a few bits and pieces to keep us going for the time being, provided we don't have to treat anything too serious."

"And the patients you had at the hospital?"

"Better since they're away from the smoke-filled air."

"Normally it would be Shaw who gave us any updates on weapons and ammunition. Jen, could you deputise someone to take a full inventory of what we're left with?"

"Yes, darling. I don't think it will take very long, considering."

"Yeah. Me neither."

Emma turned to George. "You brought tools down here with you?"

"Yep. Jack brought some of his too."

"I don't suppose there's such a thing as planning too far ahead these days, but short of a miracle, we're not going to find any weapons or ammo caches. Do you think, between the two of you, you could make us some?"

Doug laughed. "Oh, that's priceless."

"You think that's fuckin' funny?" Jules snapped.

"Olsen's army's out there, and God knows how many thousands of infected, and we're going to defend ourselves with clubs."

"Let me tell you something, you pompous wee shite," she replied, leaning forward in her chair. "This man has saved us time and time again with the stuff he's built. When Fry attacked, it was his mangonels that defeated an army much bigger than our own. He gave us a navy, for Christ's sake. All the time, you were probably sat with your feet up in some fuckin' bunker complaining that your Chateau Lafite wasn't quite at room temperature. You laugh at this man again and somebody will need to take a fuckin' inventory of your teeth."

Trish burst out laughing, holding her stomach and leaning forward in her chair. Suddenly, the others began to laugh, too, and finally, Jules and Doug joined in. Doug held his hand up. "I apologise." He nodded towards George. "I wasn't laughing at you; I was laughing at the situation."

George nodded. "I get it. I do. And I get that it feels hopeless, but I'll say this to you." He stared towards Doug then Beck and finally Trish. "There are people here who will never give up. No matter what faces them, no matter how dire it all seems, they'll keep on fighting to the end. And while they're around, I'll always have hope. You've not known them as long as I have, so you won't know what I mean yet. But you'll realise soon. You'll learn that no situation is ever hopeless with them around."

"Too fuckin' right," Jules said, suddenly re-energised by her confrontation with.

"Okay," Emma said, turning to George. "Spears would be useful. If we get any infected against the fences, that would be a good and safe way to get rid of them."

George nodded. "We can make them easily enough."

"And looking forward a little further…. I know you made the crossbow for Wren and the swords for Mila. How possible would it be to make more of those?"

George sat back in his chair a little. "I noticed there was a decent-sized equipment shed out back. That'd make a good workshop for me, Jack and James."

"Fine," Emma said. "You take whatever you need."

"We might need to find or make a bit more equipment before we can think about manufacturing crossbows and swords, but leave it with me."

"Thank you, George."

Emma turned to Raj. "I know you'd probably be heading over to the other islands right now to trade, but I think, in the circumstances, you might struggle with that."

"We could see if any of them were feeling charitable."

"Those communities are subsisting as it is. Trade is exactly that. We give them something and we get something in return. It's finely balanced, and to be honest, I don't see any good coming from sending you guys out there."

"Maybe I will be going out with a full yacht to trade soon if things go well in Portree, eh?" he replied with a smile on his face.

"Yeah. Maybe, Raj." Emma smiled too, but hers was weaker, sadder. "Okay. I think we've established that pretty much everything hinges on the mission tomorrow." She looked towards Mya and suddenly felt a little sick in her stomach. "Do you have any thoughts on who you'd like to take with you?"

Mya locked eyes with Emma. They both knew the answer, but it felt too cruel to say it out loud. "Some thoughts. I'd rather speak to the people in question first though."

Emma nodded gratefully. "Okay then. I suppose that brings us to the end of this meeting unless anyone's got any other business." She leaned back in her chair and glanced from person to person as she went around the circle.

"Well, actually, I have," Jules said.

"Okay. Go ahead."

"Like you said, a hell of a lot hinges on tomorrow, and none of us can even guess what we're going to find in Portree. The thing is, though, we don't know what the future holds. We don't know what's going to happen tomorrow, next week, or six months from now. We don't know if we're going to stay here or move on to somewhere else. But for the time being, at least, I think it probably makes sense to plan as far ahead as we can from the point of view of food, don't you think?"

Emma nodded. "I'd say that's a pretty reasonable approach, yes."

"Well, I mean it's a good time to be sowing crops, isn't it? There's a lot of land surrounding this place, and as much as I'm sure Mike would like that huge back lawn to be a cricket pitch, I think it would be prudent to try to start growing our own food like we did back in Safe Haven, don't you?"

It was like someone had plunged a dagger straight through Emma's heart. It had only been a day since they had been forced from their homes, their futures, and Jules was talking about a new future. Emma combed her fingers through her hair again. "I...." She couldn't say what she wanted to say. She couldn't get up and shout, "How dare you? What are you thinking? Safe Haven is our home, and it always will be." She couldn't say any of that. She couldn't tell them all about the promise she'd made to Mike, to herself. They wouldn't understand.

"I mean I'm guessing there are like shovels and stuff in that equipment shed. I'm not saying it won't be hard work, but as well as the fact that we'd get some food out of it, it'd give people something to do, wouldn't it? I mean they wouldn't have time to focus on anything else."

Emma still couldn't speak, and when it was Ruth who replied instead, a silent scream reverberated around Emma's head. "I think that's an excellent idea, Jules. As you say, if people have something to do, something to work towards, then they can't dwell on all the things that aren't working in our favour right now, can they?"

"That's what I was thinking," Jules replied.

Get a grip, Emma. Get a grip. She took a breath and glanced around the circle. It was obvious by the expressions on everyone's faces that they all agreed. "That's a good idea, Jules." It was painful for her to say the words, but it was easier than telling them the truth. She turned to Mya. "If you find any seeds on your travels or anything else that you think could be useful, it would be appreciated."

Mya nodded. "I'll see what I can do."

"Okay," Emma said. "I think that brings this meeting to a close. Maybe we should meet back here tomorrow night when Mya's back and take things from there."

"I think that's an excellent idea," Beck replied.

One by one, they all stood and drifted out of the room, leaving Beck, Doug and Trish alone.

"Can I have a word with you?" Mya asked as she and Muppet loitered on the landing waiting for Emma to appear.

The two women watched as the rest of the council disappeared down the stairs. "I'm pretty certain I can guess what this is about," Emma replied.

"From everything I've been told and everything I've seen, Mike's had more experience scavenging than any of the others. I'd like him to go with me tomorrow."

"It's up to him, not me," she said sadly.

"Well, I'm pretty certain he won't go if you don't want him to."

"I think you put too much faith in the influence I have over my brother."

"I think you put too little faith in it."

Emma shrugged. "We'll see. Any idea who else you want with you?"

"I'd say it's more important than ever that you stay here."

"How do you figure?"

"For a start, there's Sammy. But you handled everything really well in there. In the absence of Shaw, you can bring some stability to the ranks."

"If that's what you think, we really are screwed."

"Seriously, you need to be here. Maybe I can take Jules' brothers or Vicky and a couple of the others."

Emma shrugged. "You're the ringleader and it's your circus."

Mya laughed. "Nice analogy. It does feel like that a bit."

"You'll look after him, won't you?"

"Not that Mike needs it, but yes. I never leave anyone behind." Emma smiled weakly once again. "You do realise that there's nothing without this, don't you?"

"I'm wracking my brains trying to come up with something else, trying to remember back to every conversation I had when I lived near Kyle. I'm drawing a blank though."

"You can't magic something out of thin air."

"I really wish I could."

"You and me both."

6

It almost seemed ceremonial when George opened the doors to the equipment shed. Jack and James stood behind him and they all stared into the dim interior for a few moments before moving.

"I suppose this is the start of a new chapter," Jack said.

"I suppose it is," replied George.

"Come on. Let's get the clutter away from the windows so we've at least got some light." Jack and James stepped inside and immediately began to shift the debris that had built up over the many years of the Skye Outward Bounds Centre's existence. Pasting tables, old paint cans, moth-eaten parasols and a whole host of other useless and not-so-useless items lined the walls and blocked the windows. One by one, they shifted them out of the way.

Against the back wall of the shed was an old, dusty wooden workbench. Its surface was also littered, but as more of it came into view a broad smile broke on George's face. "That's almost identical to the one I built for my garage back at home."

"Aye," James replied. "She's a grand 'un alright."

"I can give you a hand if you'd like," Ephraim said, appearing at the entrance and making them all jump.

"You have a bloody habit of scaring the daylights out of people, don't you?" George replied, leaning on his stick with one hand while holding his other up to his chest.

"Sorry. Still haven't got used to this whole being around other people thing."

"Well, I'm not going to turn you down. We need to gut this place and turn it into a workshop. We're going to have plenty to do around here."

The shed was about twenty feet by fifteen feet and to the side of the door was parked a ride-on mower as well as an old-fashioned hand-push one. Leaning against the wall next to them were rakes, hoes, spades, forks and a variety of smaller gardening tools.

"There must be twenty years' worth of rubbish in here. We should start a big bonfire."

"There was a time when I'd have agreed with you. But nothing's really rubbish these days."

"Oh really?" Ephraim replied, walking up to one of the holey parasols. "And what use is this exactly?"

George looked at it for a moment. "The canopy can be cut up into cloths. The pole can be sharpened at one end and made into a spear and I can't think of a use for the pulley mechanism just this minute, but I can guarantee you that, at some stage, it will come in handy with a repair or an invention that's going to make life easier for people around here."

Ephraim looked at the object in his hands. It had just been an old and useless piece of garden furniture when he'd grabbed it, but he suddenly had an appreciation for what it could become and an even greater appreciation for George. The old man had a kind of mystical standing in the community when they'd been up in Safe Haven and Ephraim had never really understood it. But now he was seeing it first-hand.

George was a throwback. He was a throwback to a time when there was no waste, when nothing was discarded. *He was probably someone who used to save his yoghurt containers and turn them into pots for seedlings. He probably had a thousand jars in his garage at home, each filled with nuts, bolts, screws and nails for a thousand different just in cases.* Ephraim smirked. "Nobody likes a know-it-all, George."

The older man smiled. "I'm guessing you're speaking from experience."

Jack and James chuckled to themselves and started to sift through the piles of discarded objects in search of more treasure. Ephraim turned and looked out towards the main building. George turned too and the pair surveyed it together.

"I can think of worse places to be sent if you lost your mind," Ephraim said distantly.

"Hmm?"

"This place. It used to be an asylum."

George raised his eyebrows. "Oh, yes. I'd heard something."

"Do you think we're going to make it?"

"We've made it this far."

"True. But if they don't find food tomorrow, we might not make it much further."

"Mya's got a good head on her shoulders and Mike never leaves a stone unturned when he goes out scavenging." George pulled a pipe from his pocket and looked at it fondly. He put it in his mouth and gave it a long suck. "He and Hughes always managed to find me tobacco whenever they went out," he said with a small chuckle.

Ephraim had heard of Hughes. He'd heard what had happened to him and he knew it was an open wound for any of the people who had been close to him. "Smoking will kill you, y'know?"

George took the pipe back out of his mouth and looked at it. "I think my smoking days are over. It's been a couple of months since I used the last of my tobacco. But my point is, if there's food out there to find, Mike and whoever goes out there with him will find it."

"And if there isn't any to find?"

"Then I suppose we're all going to lose a few pounds then, aren't we?"

The two men looked back to the main building before finally getting to work.

*

"How's it going, Jen?" Emma asked as she stepped into the busy kitchen.

"The one good thing is that they've got a natural spring in the grounds, so there's that. Granted, it means we're fetching and carrying water, but it beats having to go out and look for it."

"Like you say, let's be grateful for small mercies. How's everything else going?"

"Well, we've got soup on the stove, but when they left here, they took all the plates, all the bowls, all the cutlery. We're lucky they left us with a few pans. It's going to be a nightmare getting everybody fed. We're going to have to take it in turns to use mugs, for God's sake."

Emma nodded slowly. "I'll talk to Mike. I'll get him to keep an eye out for anything useful when he goes to Portree."

Jenny suddenly felt guilty for complaining. "I'm sorry, darling," she said, reaching out and taking her friend's hand.

"You don't have to be sorry. It's not your fault."

Jenny looked down at Meg, who was sitting patiently between the two of them, sniffing at the air as the smell of soup tantalised her. "No, I mean here I am complaining about something so irrelevant when your brother's going to be...."

"Mike can take care of himself."

"Of course he can. And he'll have Mya with him."

"Exactly." It took Emma everything she had not to cry, but she couldn't dwell on what faced her brother.

"Thanks for keeping an eye on things down here. I'm going to check to see how everyone else is settling in."

Emma left the kitchen and headed along the long corridor. Some doors were closed; others were open, revealing the centre's shellshocked inhabitants. She paused outside one of the rooms and Talikha looked up from unpacking her bag. "This will take some getting used to," she said, smiling.

"I suppose it's a while since you've slept on land," Emma replied.

Humphrey broke from his exploration of the room to head across and greet Emma. She crouched down and made a fuss of him for a few seconds before the excitement of all the new smells became too much and he wandered off again.

"When we get settled, and when we have stockpiled enough to begin trading, we will be back on the yacht once more," Raj said, smiling.

"How do you guys always manage to remain so upbeat?"

"We are here. Considering recent events, that is something to be grateful for in itself."

"We need to bottle your positivity and sprinkle it around a bit."

"It is good that you have taken charge. You are someone who will bring stability."

"Ha. I don't know about that, Raj," she replied, walking into the room and sitting down on the bed. She looked out of the window to see Sammy with Daisy still on her makeshift lead, chomping away at some of the overgrown grass. "I still can't believe Shaw just disappeared like that."

Raj sat down beside her and stared down at the dark grey carpet. "I blame myself."

"What? Why?"

"I should have seen signs. More and more pressure kept piling on him and there's only so much a person can take. He did amazing things for our community. He kept us safe and he never asked for anything in return. Maybe if I'd asked him how he was feeling rather than just assuming he'd get on with it. Maybe if we'd discussed ways to ease his burden, then things—"

"Nobody ever knows what is going on in someone's head," Talikha said, interrupting him. "It was all our faults and none of our faults. If we had done things differently, there was still no guarantee that this wouldn't have happened."

"I suppose," Emma replied sadly.

"We just have to hope he is safe. We have to hope we will see him again one day."

"Do you really believe we will?"

"I believe that if we are meant to, we will."

Emma climbed to her feet. "I hope you're right, Talikha. Well, I'd better go find out how everyone else is settling in."

Raj reached out and placed a hand on Emma's arm. "Things will work out. And Mike will be fine tomorrow."

"You heard, did you?"

"I have heard nothing, but it is obvious, isn't it?"

"I guess it is." Emma looked out of the window again, but now there was no sign of Sammy or Daisy to give her comfort. "I'll catch up with you later."

She continued her journey, stopping at every open door, doing her best to make the occupants feel a little better about their situation. Most were still in denial and disbelief. Some put on brave faces, and that raised Emma's own spirits a little, but there was an air of foreboding hanging over the place.

*

"The fence is secure," Mike said as he approached Mya, who was putting air into the tyres of the Land Rover with a foot pump.

"Good."

"So, you had your meeting."

"Yeah."

"And it's you and me tomorrow."

"Yeah."

"Who else?"

"I wanted to discuss that with you. You know these people better than I do. You used to go out scavenging all the time. I was thinking Jules' brothers."

There was a time when Mike would have laughed at such a suggestion, but Andy, Rob and Jon were as worthy as most to take out. "That's one option."

"You have another?"

"Wren, Robyn and Mila."

Mya stopped pumping for a moment and looked over to the large equipment shed where George and the others were hard at work. "That'll go down well."

"Hey, look. I'm not crazy about the idea of telling George, or anyone for that matter, but the fact is we can't get into a firefight in Portree. If we start shooting, we're pretty much dead in the water. Robyn, Wren and Mila lasted a long time on the road and they're skilled with their weapons. I think they're our best chance to get out of there in one piece."

Mya thought for a moment before she started pushing down on the foot pump once more. Muppet suddenly appeared out of nowhere. He looked from Mya to Mike then back to Mya before wagging his tail and running off. They both laughed as he disappeared around the side of the building. "At least somebody's enjoying himself."

Mya thought back to when she found him on that Paris road. She thought back to all the times he'd put a smile on her face since. "I don't think I'd have made it without him."

"I think you'd be someone who could make it through anything."

"That remains to be seen, I suppose." She carried on pumping for a little while longer before withdrawing the connector and replacing the cap. "Okay, she said, nodding.

83

"Assuming you can get them to agree, they'll make up the rest of the team."

"I've already spoken to them. They're all in."

"I don't envy them telling George."

"Yeah. Me neither."

*

Beck sat at his desk with the lever arch file open in front of him. He could hear Regan and Juno outside with Mel while Trish stood at the window looking out. "There's a big part of me that wonders if we'd have been better staying here all those months back," he said, closing the file once more.

"We'll never know," Trish said, turning around and perching on the sill. The day had gone quickly. It was already late afternoon and the sun was getting lower in the sky.

"If I'd have stayed, Trill might not have left. We might not be in such a dire situation."

"Like I said, we'll never know. We can't think about what ifs. We need to think about what's next."

"Well, that's something that is most definitely out of our hands." He swivelled in his chair and looked towards his wife. "Have we heard who's going with Mya?"

"Mike, Wren, Robyn and Mila."

Beck let out a long sigh. "Jesus."

"What?"

"It's just quite jarring that a bunch of kids are our best hope of success."

"They're more than a bunch of kids."

"You know what I mean. Good grief, a few months ago, I had proper soldiers under me, and now … this."

"I told you; you need to stop living in the past. When I spoke to Mya, she was happy with the team that was heading out with her."

"I'm sure she was. Given the slim pickings, she'd probably just be grateful that she's not taking a geriatric along. But this is my point. A few months back, she'd have had a pick of soldiers."

Trish stood up and walked across the room, sitting down on the desk right in front of her husband. "I don't like seeing you like this. You need to be more positive. You need to be more upbeat."

"Maybe I could learn a couple of song and dance numbers and tell a few jokes. Would that do? Would that help me seem more upbeat?"

"I can't talk to you when you get like this," she said, standing up.

"I'm sorry," he replied, reaching out and grabbing her hand. "I'm sorry."

Regan laughed in the other room and a sad smile appeared on Beck's face. "You need to be positive for them."

"I always am."

"You need to be positive for me."

"You're the only one I can truly confide in."

"I know and I always will be. But there are good things amongst all the bad that's facing us. We've got a roof over our heads. We've got fresh water. Our daughters are laughing in the next room. And tomorrow, five brave, selfless people are heading out to try to find supplies for the rest of us. Regardless of how old they are, regardless of the fact that they haven't had military training and they don't take orders from you, that's something. That's a big thing."

Beck nodded. "You're right. You're right, as usual."

"Now, come on," she said, pulling him to his feet. "We're going to take our kids downstairs to get something to eat with everyone else. We're going to spend a little time with them and then sleep in beds underneath a roof. And tomorrow, things will start looking better for everyone."

Beck leaned in and kissed her on the cheek. "I really don't deserve you."

"Well, duh!"

*

Wren, Robyn and Mila had discussed not telling George about their mission. The chances were, though, that he'd have found out somehow and that would only have made things a hundred times worse.

He sat on the bed, a little bewildered as he processed the information. Wolf lay next to him and the three girls all stood at the window, waiting for his response.

For a few minutes, he didn't say anything, but eventually, he let out a long, sad sigh. "I suppose you're the logical choice," he said reluctantly.

The trio looked at one another with surprise on their faces. "Err … that's not the response we expected," Robyn said, half laughing.

"Well, it's not like you'd listen to me if I asked you not to go."

"Don't be like that, Grandad," Wren said.

"I'm just being truthful. You wouldn't and … you probably shouldn't. If I asked you not to go, it would just be for my own selfish reasons. You're my family, and I love you more than anything in the world, and I can't bear the thought of anything bad happening to you. But at the same time, if we don't find a supply of food then our escape from Safe Haven will have been for nothing."

A tear rolled down George's cheek and Mila went to sit next to him on the bed, taking his hand in hers. "Do not cry. I will not let anything happen to either of them."

"Getting old is hard." He gestured towards the walking stick leaning against his bedside cabinet. "There are a thousand things your mind wants to do, but your body won't let you."

"What are you talking about, Grandad?" Wren asked. "You do loads. More than most around here. I mean, God, you haven't stopped since you arrived."

"Organising a workshop is one thing, but I'd sacrifice never lifting a hammer or a screwdriver again for being able to head out with you tomorrow and actually being of some use."

"We've all got our parts to play, Grandad."

"Yeah, and I just wish mine was a different one."

"When I found you both again, it was the happiest day and the saddest day of my life," Robyn said, and suddenly all eyes turned to her. "It was the happiest because I got to hold both of you. It was the saddest because I thought I'd never see Mila again. But we're all back together, and there's a reason for that. It's because me, Wren, Mila, you, we're all fighters. And you can say what you like about getting old, but you're still fighting, and—"

"It's not the same."

"It probably feels that way, but it is, Grandad. It really is. You didn't even take a breath before getting to work on that equipment shed. You showed everyone that you're not giving up, that you're going to carry on fighting. And that's what we're doing as well. Wren, Mila and me are really good with our weapons and we've been in lots of situations on the road that most people would struggle to get out of. We don't take unnecessary risks, and I'm not denying that going to Portree will be dangerous, but in all honesty, Grandad, we've faced much worse."

"You can't possibly know what you're facing."

Robyn shrugged. "True enough, I suppose. But we've all got each other's backs, and it's not like we're going to be facing Olsen's army this time. We're going to be fighting the infected and we've been doing that ever since we left Edinburgh. I've never been good at anything in my life, but I'm really good at this."

George let out another long breath. "I wish it was something else you were good at."

"Yeah, well, it's not. And that's why we're heading out tomorrow morning with Mike and Mya, and that's why the three of us will be coming back tomorrow afternoon with Mike and Mya."

George looked up at Robyn and wiped away the tears from his eyes. "I suppose you're not my little princesses anymore, are you?" he said, letting out a sad laugh.

"Grandad, we'll always be your little princesses, but there's nothing to say we can't be something else too."

*

Shaw had almost hugged the coastline as he'd travelled. Where possible, he'd stayed in the trees and finally stumbled across a bothy that had seen many a better day, but for the main part, the roof and walls were intact. It was positioned next to a great rock by a loch and sheltered by a cropping of pines. Once, it would have been a resting point for fishermen or crofters returning from market.

Now he sat on the creaking wooden bench that sounded and felt like it could give way at any moment under his weight. He reached into his rucksack and removed a can of beans. It was hardly haute cuisine, but it was food, and it would fill a gap. He plucked the ring and peeled back the lid then grabbed a fork from the side pocket of his backpack. He had about half a dozen tins, which would probably be enough to keep him going for a couple of days or even more if he was sparing.

He grabbed the plastic bottle from the netted side pouch and shook it around a little. It had a brownish hue, but that was common for the Highlands and islands. Most streams and rivers had tributaries leading from peatland. It quenched his thirst, and that was the main thing.

It wouldn't be long before night started to close in, and as Shaw ate mouthful after mouthful of cold beans, he stared out of the crud-covered window at the loch in front of him.

Another time and I could have been happy living somewhere like this. Just here by myself, nobody to judge me. Nobody expecting anything from me. If you live a life with no friends, you live a life with no pain.

He took a drink from his bottle and scooped out another forkful of beans. *There must be a hundred old cottages close by that I could have bought for a song. Would that have been such a bad thing? Would people have thought less of me for just checking out from society?*

I could still do it. He paused with his fork half in the tin and half out. *I could still find a place. I could find a place down here.*

Somewhere next to the sea. I could fish and grow vegetables. I could swim in the lochs in summer and pick berries and make jam and.... Jesus. I really am losing it.

Shaw laughed to himself, quietly at first, then a little louder. Then a little louder still. He put the tin of beans down on the bench and stood up, arching his back a little and walking to the window.

The sun glistened on the loch as it made its descent and a sudden urge gripped him. He stepped back out into the warm evening air and continued to the narrow shoreline where the peaty water lapped against the pebbles. He sat down on one of the flat rocks and proceeded to untie his boots. He slipped them off, his socks too, and then stood, unbuckling his belt and slipping down his trousers and pants. He peeled off his jacket and shirt, and now he was completely naked.

A broad smile lit his face as he took a tentative step into the water. Even though it was a warm day, the temperature of the loch was pretty cool, and he giggled like a small child as it sent shivers through him.

He took another step and another. It had been an age since he had felt as free as this. *No responsibilities. No judgement. No consequences.*

He walked further into the loch and felt the water rise above his shins, his knees, his thighs. Shaw paused again and slowly turned a full circle. There was no one and nothing around. In the distance, he could hear the squawk of a crow and, if he concentrated hard, the gentle bristle of some of the scrub grass that lay adjacent to the bank. But other than that, it was like the world had fallen silent for him to enjoy this moment.

He spread his hands out and let the water swim through his fingers as he brushed them over the surface before finally leaning forward a little and plunging his whole body in. It was a sensory overload, and as he disappeared beneath for a moment, he couldn't help but let out a loud, excited underwater laugh. *This is crazy.*

Shaw's head exploded through the surface as he kicked his legs and settled into a comfortable breaststroke. He breathed in deeply before dipping his head once more. The freedom invigorated him, warmed him, made him smile on the inside and out. The loch was about the size of two football fields side by side, and he continued, stroke after stroke, kick after kick, until he reached the centre.

There he paused, treading water and slowly turning. He had no idea how deep it was. All he knew was that no matter how hard he tried, he couldn't feel the bed beneath his toes. He sucked in another greedy breath, still with the same grin threatening to etch on his face forever.

I'm completely alone here. Not another soul living or dead. He closed his eyes and dipped his head back using the cold water like a giant pillow. Shaw had no idea how long it had been since he'd first stepped into the loch, but as he opened his eyes again, the sun had fallen noticeably.

He still had the taste of the bean sauce on his tongue, and the exercise, using muscles he hadn't used in the longest time, suddenly made him hungry. He started his journey back, promising himself he would wake up with a morning swim tomorrow. He kept going until it was shallow enough to stand and then he slowly trudged the rest of the way to shore.

He remained smiling all the way, and as he reached the spot where he'd removed his final piece of clothing, he let out another small laugh. He turned around in a full circle and suddenly realised that this was his life now.

Safe Haven had been one chapter and this was the next. He didn't have to get up at the crack of dawn to check in with the lookouts. He didn't need to worry about resupplying the northern settlement, using too much ammunition during target practice, or running out of antibiotics at the hospital. He didn't have people asking him for advice and help. There was no one relying on him to be there twenty-four-seven. He was alone. He could do as he wished. He was responsible only for himself.

He picked the remainder of his clothes up and returned to the bothy, still dripping wet. Shaw sat down on the bench and it moaned under his weight once more. He found that funny too and laughed again. He picked up his beans and began to shovel them into his mouth. It wasn't long before his fork was scraping the bottom of the can, which he brought up to his lips. He angled it back and let the last drops of sauce run into his mouth before placing the can down.

His stomach growled. *Still hungry. That barely scratched the surface.* He reached into his rucksack and grabbed another tin. He looked at it long and hard. *One tin, two tins, what's the difference?* He cracked the ring pull and peeled back the lid before inhaling deeply. The smile was suddenly back on his face and he sunk his fork into the sugary contents of the can.

He could feel the sauce dripping over his lips and down his chin as he ate, but it didn't matter. He felt a drop hit his thigh and it was only then that he looked down and realised he was still naked. The grin turned to a chuckle, then into a belly laugh. The bench creaked and groaned as he moved from side to side and tears began to run down his face. Then he thought about what he would look like if anyone peeked in through that crud-encrusted window and saw him. This caused him to laugh even louder and even more tears ran down his cheeks. He remained there laughing for several minutes.

When he eventually stopped, he looked at himself again and started to cry, but there was no mirth in these tears, only sadness.

What's happening to me?

7

Emma stood at the entrance staring down the long driveway where the Land Rover had disappeared moments before. "Stupid question, I suppose, but how did you sleep, darling?" Jenny asked as she and Meg walked up beside her.

She turned and her friend immediately saw the black rings under her swollen red eyes. "I'm guessing I look like quite a sight."

"Err ... no ... not at all."

"Wow! You are such a bad liar."

Jenny laughed. "I'm sorry. Come on," she said, taking her friend's hand and guiding her back inside. "You're running things now. You need to exude confidence."

"Y'know, he must have gone out with Shaw and Hughes and Barnes a hundred times and I never felt like I do right now."

They walked along the corridor with Meg brushing up against Emma's leg doing her best to put a smile on the other woman's face. "I honestly can't remember a time when it was more important. That's probably got a little to do with it."

"Maybe. Maybe it's because they're heading to Portree. Maybe it's because the only stuff I heard about that place when I lived in Kyle was bad."

They entered Jenny's room and Jenny pulled a chair up to the window. "Sit down there."

Emma was a little confused for a moment until she saw Jenny with a cosmetics bag. "Seriously, Jen? I don't think this is the time for a makeover."

"Well, that's where you and I disagree. If everybody's pinning their hopes on you, it's not great to look like you've spent the entire night crying."

"In fairness, it was only from about three o'clock onwards."

Jenny smiled. "You just sit there, darling, and me and my bag of tricks will have you looking as right as rain in no time."

Emma stared out of the window as Jenny got to work. At least here she couldn't see the driveway. She wasn't reminded of where her brother and the others were going and what faced them. She caught movement out of the corner of her eye and saw Sammy with Daisy. "Y'know, I'm scared to death that if things go badly in Portree someone will think making goat stew isn't a bad option."

"Mike nearly killed Murdo just for making a joke about it. My guess is if someone so much as looks at her the wrong way, Trish and Liz will have to spend the next few months sewing them back together," Jenny said with half a smile as she dabbed something underneath Emma's eyes.

"She's part of the family, Jen. I know to most people it's just a goat, but—"

"But nothing. There's no difference between Daisy, Meg, Wolf, Humphrey, or Muppet. As you say, she's part of the family, and anybody who thinks otherwise won't just have Mike to deal with."

Emma smiled and reached out, taking the older woman's hand. "I don't know what I'd do without you. I don't know what any of us would do."

Jenny smiled, but Emma could see sadness behind the foundation and mascara. She always did her best to mask her true feelings, but the last twenty-four hours and taken a heavy toll. Shaw was more than just Safe Haven's military leader or the guy who made the trains run on time. "We'll be okay," she said. "I know it doesn't feel like it at the moment, but we'll be okay."

Jenny sniffed and leaned back. "You've got lovely eyes. I always thought you should wear a bit of liner. Accentuate them a little."

"Is that your way of telling me to shut up?"

Jenny laughed, reaching for her pencil. "Stay still. I've always found that there's something very therapeutic about applying makeup to others."

"Is it because if it goes wrong, then at least it's not you who looks like a clown?"

Jenny laughed again. "You know, you may be right. I'd never thought about it like that." Emma sat back a little and she let Jenny draw and dab and pinch until she was done. "There, she said, pulling out a small mirror from her bag and showing Emma the results.

"Y'know, you are literally the only person I know who, when told just to pack the essentials, would bring a makeup bag."

"Well? What do you think?"

Emma angled her head and blinked, bringing the mirror a little closer to her face. "Well, you can't see the dark rings anymore. I suppose I look human now at least."

"Exactly. There's no chance of you scaring the children anyway."

Emma laughed this time. "Thanks. You're doing my ego no end of good this morning."

"You're welcome, darling." Jenny put her bag away and stood up. "Now, come on, we've got false smiles to dish out like penny sweets."

Suddenly, it all made sense to Emma. This wasn't just some shallow attempt to make Emma feel better about how she looked in the face of having such little sleep and being steeped in so much anguish. This was so they could put on a façade like Jenny probably had a thousand times before. The makeup was like a mask. Behind it, you could think and feel what you wanted, but to the rest of the world, the people who didn't really know you, it seemed like business as usual.

"Right behind you," Emma finally said, looking out of the window towards her little sister one more time. All the concerns about her brother, all the fretting about food and supplies she pushed down inside and took a deep breath. *Come on, Emma. We're down, but we're not out. It's time to prove it.*

*

"Y'know, it's funny," Mike said.

"What is?" asked Mya, taking another bend at breakneck speed.

"My sisters are scared to death that we're going to come up against a huge horde and get overwhelmed when we hit Portree. They haven't even factored in that you're a complete psychopath behind the wheel and we might crash and die horribly long before we get there."

Wren, Robyn and Mila all laughed in the back seat. "Considering your reputation as a bit of a hard man, you're actually pretty wussy when it all boils down to it, aren't you?"

"Why? Because I'd rather die in battle than due to some crazy woman trying to break the world land speed record in a clapped-out old Land Rover?"

"Mike, Mike, Mike. You're old before your time. You've got to learn to live a little," Mya said, pushing her foot down further on the accelerator and making the tyres screech once more as they took another bend.

They continued along for several more minutes in silence. It was a surprisingly good atmosphere in the car, considering what they were all about to face. Occasionally, a RAM would appear in a field or from a stretch of woodland, invariably too late to reach the speeding vehicle, but it was a reminder to all of them of what they would face.

"What about that place over there?" Wren asked from the back.

Mya looked in the mirror and eased her foot off the gas a little. "Good spot," she replied and slowed down a little more.

To their right was a small farm. It was at the far end of a stretch of woodland, and without turning one's head a full ninety degrees, it would be hard to spot from the road. She slowed down a little more until they reached a galvanised steel field gate.

Without saying a word, Mike jumped out of the car and walked up to it, sliding the bolt across and pulling it open before closing it once more. There was a track by the side of the overgrown field and suddenly Mike's mind drifted back to his escape from Leeds with Joseph. They had gone through many a farmer's field back then with varying degrees of success, but this time, there was no room for failure. He climbed back into the Land Rover and glanced across at the fuel gauge. The dial looked like it was on empty. How they were still going was nothing short of a miracle, but they carried on metre by metre until Mya brought the Land Rover to a halt.

Again, Mike climbed out, opening another gate, then another, until finally they navigated a dried-out track that seemed far more used than the others. Giant tractor tyres had carved their signatures in the peaty soil for years and years, making the ride very bumpy even for a battle-hardened vehicle like the old army Land Rover.

They finally reached the main yard of the croft. A single-story white cottage sat at one end. A vehicle shed and a small outbuilding lay opposite. This was it. This was the beginning of their journey today, and they all knew it.

Wren was the first to step out of the car, immediately raising her crossbow. Robyn joined her. Mila climbed out of the other side, and Wolf and Muppet dived over the back seat and out through the open doors. Mike and Mya cast each other a knowing glance then they stepped out too.

"Okay," Mya said, "we need to—"

"Hold up!" Robyn interrupted, raising her bow and aiming towards the house.

Suddenly all eyes followed her line of sight and it was only a second before they understood why. A body exploded through the lattice window, causing glass and wood to fly through the air. The figure collapsed to the ground in a heap, but the pause didn't last long. It scrambled back to its feet and charged. The growls that emanated from the back of its throat were unmistakable. The strange, animated movement as it sprinted in their direction sent a familiar chill surging through them as the malevolent thing cast its grey, soulless gaze like a witch's spell.

Wolf and Muppet were already storming towards it when Robyn released her bowstring. The arrow disappeared into the creature's skull and the beast fell once more. The two dogs slowed to a stop before walking back to their respective mistresses. They had both been in this situation before and they knew that when the hunt was on, they stayed as a pack, only striking when one of their own was at risk.

Mike walked up to the body and it was only when he was closer that he noticed a bite mark on the creature's shoulder and a deeply furrowed channel around its neck. Further sounds emanated from inside the croft house and drifted across the yard to greet him. "Sounds like there are more inside," he said, looking back at the others.

"Wren and I will stay out here, make sure no one else joins us," Robyn said, turning a full circle with her bow still raised.

"Muppet, stay!" Mya ordered, raising her finger. She, Mike and Mila walked towards the front door while Robyn and Wren kept guard. She paused and placed her fingers on the handle. "You ready?" she asked, first looking at Mila and then Mike. They both nodded and Mya pushed down and inwards, barging the door with her shoulder and bringing her Glock up at the same time. The large kitchen gave no clue as to where the sound was coming from, but the smell of death hung in the air like fog.

"It's coming from in there," Mike said, clutching both machetes as he walked to a thick pine door. He stopped in front of it and listened as the sound from the other room seeped out through the narrow gap underneath.

"Open the door then get out of the way," Mya said, placing her Glock back in its holster and retrieving her throwing knives instead.

There was part of Mike that wanted to charge in like he usually would, but Mya was calling the shots, and for the time being, at least, he needed to stifle his usual gung-ho impulses. He threw the door open and leapt to the side, giving Mya a clear shot at anything that appeared. They all waited, but nothing did. He glanced towards Mila then Mya before smashing the handle of one of his machetes against the door frame. The growls of the creatures escalated in volume, but still nothing appeared.

He waited a few more seconds before popping his head around the corner. When he did, everything made sense. "Oh fuck."

"What is it?" Mila asked.

"Nothing good," he replied and the two women joined him as he stepped into the large living room. There was a rope uncoiled at the bottom. It was attached to a high rafter and had obviously been what the creature that had burst through the window had been hanged with. The stench as they entered was terrible and all of them covered their mouths. Laid out on the sofa was the body of a young girl, only it wasn't a young girl any longer. It had turned, and the sound from the adjacent room suggested what attacked her was still in the house.

They carried on further, and now the door they were all looking towards began to shake in its frame. "You ready?" Mike asked, walking up to it.

Mya planted her feet apart and nodded. Mike placed his fingers on the handle and pushed hard, this time diving for cover as thundering feet stormed out of the other room. In an instant, the two figures were down. One was roughly the same age as the man they had killed out in the yard. The other was quite a lot older.

"What do you think happened here?" Mila asked.

"Whatever happened, it was horrible. My guess is the guy got attacked and put his daughter down before trying to hang himself. He must have turned before he managed."

"As you say, horrible," Mila replied.

"The rest of the place seems quiet, but we'd better check it out," Mike said, and the three of them proceeded through the house room by room. When they were happy no more threats were present, they returned to the kitchen.

"All clear," Mila called out.

Robyn and Wren entered the kitchen with Muppet and Wolf behind them. "We only ever came this close to Portree once, and I never saw this place before." She turned to Wren. "Good work spotting it. We've got no idea how long these things have been like this, so let's check the cupboards."

Robyn almost ran to the kitchen cupboards and swung two doors open at the same time. The excitement and anticipation dissipated in an instant. A salt and pepper shaker stood next to a virtually empty bottle of vinegar. Behind them was a bag of flour with green mould growing all over it. "Ugh! Gross."

"Something stinks in here, and it's not just dead people," Wren said and opened the door to the small pantry. She took a step back as the smell hit her. Buckets of potatoes, carrots, onions and more had sprouted long roots before rotting away. She nudged one of the buckets with her foot and dark brown liquid made a sloshing sound. "That really stinks," she said, closing the door.

"Okay," said Mya. "So, we might not be getting any food from here, but we need to check the rest of the cupboards anyway. I'm going to go check the equipment shed and see if they've got a trailer."

"I'll come with you," Mike replied, and the two of them left the pungent smell of the house behind as they stepped out into the yard.

"I like how everything went down here," Mya said.

"What do you mean?"

"I mean everyone worked well together right off the bat. Robyn is really impressive with that bow. She didn't miss a beat before taking that thing out. Wren was covering the rest of the yard before the arrow had even struck. Everybody played their part perfectly. When we set off, I didn't know how we'd work together, but I'm officially impressed."

"I told you. If I could have anyone covering my back, it's those three … and you … at a push."

Mya smiled. "And now I'm tearing up."

They walked around to the side door of the equipment shed and Mike opened it up as Mya grabbed her throwing knives. He banged three times on the galvanised steel entrance and the pair waited for a few seconds. Mike sniffed at the air before stepping inside. It was similar to the shed Joseph had back at his farm. Skylights allowed in enough of the morning for them to be able to see a tractor, a trailer and a micro digger next to several shelving units.

Mya walked up to the double-decker trailer. "This is just what I was hoping for. We'll be able to fit plenty in here."

"We should check the tractor and the digger. I'm guessing they'll have been running them on red diesel. We should make sure it's still good before we siphon any."

Mya nodded appreciatively. "Yeah. We mix that with the little bit of fuel that's left in the tank and it's no good; then we're screwed. The problem's going to be that their batteries will probably be dead."

Mike remembered back to when Hughes had swapped a battery to get a tractor started soon after they had met Wren. When they got back to Safe Haven, he had taught him enough about vehicles to make sure that if he was ever in that position again, he could do it himself. *Thanks, Bruiser.* "Okay. We take the battery from the Land Rover to start the tractor. That way, at least we'll know the fuel's good and we won't be taking any risks."

Mya smiled. "Good. Excellent. Can I leave you with that while I get the tyres pumped up on the trailer and we search the rest of the place?"

"Yeah. No problem."

The group each went about their tasks efficiently. There was no food found, but there were tools, clothes, bedding, towels, crockery and lots more that would come in useful. Under the sink were a host of cleaning materials, including a nearly full bottle of white spirit, which Wren grabbed eagerly.

"Oh God," Robyn said as she watched her sister squirrel it away in her rucksack.

"What?" Wren replied.

"'What?' she says all innocently. You might manage to fool everyone else, but you don't fool me, pyro girl."

Wren smiled. "Hey, look. You never know when it might come in handy."

"No, course not. I never feel dressed without having a bottle of something flammable in my rucksack."

"Are we all ready?" Mya asked, appearing at the door with Muppet and Wolf. The two dogs had been exploring the locale and both sat contentedly in the entrance waiting for the next leg of their adventure to begin.

"Yes," Mila said. "We have loaded what we believe we can use into the trailer."

"Good," Mya replied. "The diesel in the tractor was good, so we've got a couple more gallons to play with. At least the dial won't read empty."

"Find anything else useful?" Wren asked.

"A few tools that might help them with their vegetable patch," Mya replied, smirking.

"You don't think it's a good idea?"

"I think it's optimistic given our current situation."

"There's nothing wrong with a bit of optimism."

"No. I suppose you're right."

They placed the last few scavenged bits and pieces in the trailer then they were on their way. They travelled a little easier, knowing that the engine wouldn't come to a spluttering stop at any moment, but at the same time, as they got closer and closer to Portree, foreboding hung heavier in the air.

Mya slowed down as the fields gave way to sparse woodland and a single row of white cottages to their left. The incline of the road headed down to a bend and more trees beyond. "This would have been a beautiful place to live once."

"Why are we stopping?" Mike asked.

"It's a while since I've been to Portree, but I'm pretty certain that if we follow this road around, it takes us to the supermarket and then into the town centre."

"Okay. So, are you wanting to check these houses out before we head in or what?"

Mya looked across at the white cottages. "It probably makes sense to use the rest of the space we've got to gather food in bulk rather than odds and sods."

"So what have we stopped here for?"

"We need to get eyes on the place and figure out exactly what we're doing before we go in."

"Oh man, I really wish we'd managed to salvage a drone before we left Safe Haven."

"Yeah. You and me both. We'll just have to do this the old-fashioned way. We'll head down through the woods and hope we don't run into too many of them."

The moment they opened the car doors, the sounds of the undead drifted towards them on the morning air. "And there I was hoping they might all have got bored and moved on somewhere else," Robyn said as the seven of them headed into the woods.

Muppet and Wolf walked ahead, alert as ever, sniffing the air, searching for danger. "I think we should create a diversion," Wren said.

"Here we go," mumbled Robyn.

"Go on," Mya said.

"Well," Wren said. "Even if they're nowhere near the supermarket, Portree's not a big place. All it would need is a couple of loud noises and they could all come down on us like a thousand tonnes of bricks. But if we create a diversion to occupy them, something at the far end of town maybe, then we wouldn't have to worry as much."

"Okay," Mya said. "What did you have in mind?"

"Drum roll, please," Robyn said.

Wren ignored her, shaking her head irritably. "Well, I've found that fire—"

"And there it is."

"—is a pretty good subterfuge. Lots of smoke, lots of loud bangs and noises. Whenever I've used it in the past, they've always been drawn to it."

Mya nodded slowly. "I like it. It's a good idea. Okay, let's hold up a minute," she said, snapping her fingers and bringing Muppet to a stop too. Wolf turned and double-backed to sit down by his mistress's side. The sound of the creatures had got slightly louder since leaving the car, and even though they couldn't see them, they had an idea of where they were. "The supermarket is that way," she said, pointing roughly to the northeast. "There's a square with a few shops and offices that way if memory serves." She pointed southeast.

"How far?" Mike asked.

"Not too far. It's not a big place. My guess is that you're looking at about half a mile between the two of them. Like I said, it's a while since I've been here."

"So, we head to the square?"

"I'd say that's our best option."

Wolf suddenly started growling and Muppet joined in a second later. The five humans immediately withdrew their weapons and scoured the treescape. Mike looked across at Mya to see her Glock still holstered. She grabbed a hunting knife from her bag and stood perfectly still like a cobra, ready to strike.

"Four o'clock," Mila said, and they all turned to see two creatures sprinting towards them through the trees.

"On it," Robyn replied, releasing an arrow. It whistled for just a second before cracking through the skull of the first.

The twang of Wren's crossbow rang out a second later, and the other beast was down.

The two dogs continued to growl and sniff at the air. "Nine o'clock," Mila called out, and they all shifted position.

A second arrow flew through the trees bringing the first of the three charging beasts down. Twang! A bolt stopped another dead in its tracks, and only when the third had reached the small clearing they were in did Mya release one of her throwing knives.

They all watched in awe as it disappeared into the monster's eye socket. The beast fell to the ground with a thud, and Mya was about to collect her knife when Wren spoke this time. "Six o'clock."

A shiver ran through them all as at least fifteen creatures weaved through the trees. Mike and Mila ran forward, staying a couple of metres apart from each other, drawing the attention of the entire pack.

Muppet and Wolf broke from their previously statuesque poses, their jobs as lookouts now abandoned as the battle got underway. A bolt then an arrow blurred on either side of Mike and Mila, each bringing down one of the attacking beasts.

Ten metres. Another arrow, another down. Five metres. A bolt. Another down. Two metres. Like it was choreographed, Mike and Mila both kicked out hard, catapulting the two beasts closest to them back into the others. Muppet and Wolf launched at the same time, taking down two more.

A loud whooshing sound threatened to break Mike's and Mila's concentration for a moment, but it quickly became clear what it was. A few more of the creatures went reeling as Mya swung a bough twice her height like a baseball bat, letting it go at the apex of her swipe.

Only one beast remained standing for the moment, and Mike lunged, bringing a machete up through its palate and cracking through the roof of its mouth.

Muppet and Wolf continued to bite and tear at the two monsters they had brought down. Arrow. Bolt. The first pair of beasts back on their feet were the first two down.

Mila's replica katana blades whooshed as she swiped and slashed. Mike concentrated on the scrambling monsters trying their hardest to get back into the fight. Hack, hack, hack, kick. Arrow. Bolt. Arrow. Mya grabbed hold of a mop of hair, thrusting her hunting knife through the monster's eye before parrying a pair of reaching arms and repeating the same gory procedure with the next.

The growls diminished until the loudest that could be heard belonged to Wolf and Muppet as they continued to rip at their targets. Mike and Mya walked up to the pathetic-looking monsters who'd had most of their necks and faces shredded by the two protective canines. Mya recalled them while Mike slashed down hard with both machetes at the same time, hacking through the beasts' skulls and rendering them still.

Robyn and Wren turned slowly with their weapons still raised. After surveying a full three hundred and sixty degrees, they finally lowered them and walked forward to join the others. "Clear," Robyn said. "For the time being, anyway."

"You see what some of these were wearing?" Mike asked.

"Wasn't really something I noticed."

"Yeah," Mya said. "I saw."

"Many of these were Olsen's people," Mila replied.

"Maybe they were the ones left over from the school where they held us. Maybe they were down here looking for Beck and got overrun," Wren interjected.

"Maybe. But we are too late to find out, though, yes?"

"I suppose." Wren and Robyn collected their bolts and arrows. Mya grabbed her knife and Mike and Mila searched the rest of the bodies for anything useful.

Within a couple of minutes, they were all heading towards the symphony of growls. They remained silent and alert, knowing that, at any second, another attack could come. Finally, the trees thinned out and both dogs began to growl once more. "Keep them here," Mya said, holding her finger up to Muppet, who immediately sat down while Wren grabbed Wolf's collar.

Mike, Robyn, and Mya edged forward, using the cover of the woodland to shield them from the mass of creatures who were producing the wall of sound that drove into the forest. They halted a few metres back from the tree line and ducked down behind a wide growth of shrubs. Their eyes were drawn to the far end of the square.

Hundreds of infected were gathered, but that was not what caught their attention. All that remained of the row of buildings to the east were burnt-out husks. "What do you suppose happened?" Robyn whispered.

"Could have been anything," Mya replied in an equally hushed tone. "Lightning strike maybe." Robyn and Mike glanced at each other unconvinced. "The row of shops over there," Mya said, pointing to the south of the square. "We need to get around the back."

"Me and Bobbi can do it," Wren said, taking them all a little by surprise as she crept up behind them.

"I think we're safer sticking together," Mya replied.

"Not out in the open. Two will be a lot harder to spot than seven."

"I suppose you've got a point."

"No way," Mike said. "I'm not having the two of you taking such a massive risk by yourselves."

"We've done this before, Mike."

"Yeah, and look how many of those things are out there."

Up until that moment, Wren had avoided looking directly towards the massive swarm that had congregated in the square. "I'd prefer not to, in all honesty."

"We'll be okay," Robyn said. "You wait for us with Mi—"

"Screw that," Mike replied. "I'm coming with you."

"We can look after ourselves."

"In most situations. What if you head around a corner and there's a pack of them waiting for you? It takes time to reload bows. I'm going with you."

Wren and Robyn looked towards Mya, knowing she was the one who was giving orders. She nodded. "Take Mike. Get in there and get out as quickly as you can. I suppose that goes without saying, but there, I've said it anyway. Head straight back here and then we'll go shopping."

Without any further discussion, Mike, Wren and Robyn began to skirt the tree line in the direction of their target.

8

Jules had been the one who had suggested that they prepare the ground for crops, and she was also the one leading the crusade. Jon was by her side as they worked with their spades, cutting segments of sod to reveal the fertile soil beneath. These were the only two spades and so, when they needed a break, they would pass them on to another pair so the work continued.

They could hear sawing and hammering coming from the workshop as George, Jack and James laboured away on whatever project they had deemed a priority.

Inside, Ruth and Richard were trying their hardest to keep the small number of children who had escaped Safe Haven occupied. Trish and Liz had set up a kind of day care room for the elderly and infirm. Rob, Andy and a few others were patrolling the fences, making sure there were no infected lured by the sudden upsurge in noise and activity.

Everyone was occupied with something. Everyone was trying their hardest not to think about what was happening to their friends and loved ones in Portree, what had happened to Shaw and all the people they had lost.

"Do you really think we can start again? Here I mean," Jon asked as he carefully etched around another square of earth.

Jules wiped the sweat from her brow as she looked up and saw a line of people transporting pans of water into the kitchen. "We don't really have a choice, do we?"

"It'll take a lot of getting used to. I mean we don't even have running water here."

"A lot of people didn't have running water back in Safe Haven. We were among the lucky ones. It won't harm us to fetch and carry for a while."

"A while?"

"I'm pretty certain if anyone can think of a way to get the plumbing up and running again, it will be George."

Jon paused and looked across to the small workshop as James appeared, leaning four freshly made spears against the outside wall before disappearing inside once more.

He let out a long sigh. "Two days ago, we had an arsenal. Soon, we're going to be fighting with sticks."

Jules stopped digging and walked over to him, placing her hand on his shoulder. "I need you to stop this. Do you have any idea how fuckin' lucky we are? You, me, Rob, Andy, we're all still together. We got out of there alive … together when so many others have lost loved ones and so many more didn't make it at all. So what if we've got to start from scratch? So what if we're going to have to use spears instead of guns? So what if we've got to fetch and carry our water? We're alive and we're together."

Jon nodded slowly. "I suppose you're right."

"Of course I'm fucking right. Now get back to work, you lazy arse." She smiled a warm smile, and despite all his misgivings, Jon did too.

"I love you, Jules."

She shrugged. "How could you not? I'm a ray of fuckin' sunshine, me." Jon laughed. "I love you too."

*

A single room had been designated to store all the supplies that had been brought from Safe Haven. The food was piled up against one wall, the weapons and ammunition against another.

"There's part of me that really doesn't want to ask," Emma said as she walked in to find Jenny and Vicky standing by the window looking at their inventory sheets. They both had grim expressions on their faces, and just taking a quick look at the meagre bits and pieces that lined the walls was enough to figure out why.

"Well, on the upside," Vicky began, "in addition to the weapons people are already carrying, we've got twelve M16s, six SA 80s, four Glocks, a couple of shotguns, six M67 grenades, and about four hundred rounds of ammo, not including what people have in their guns and rucksacks, which I'm guessing after our firefight on the way here will not be much."

"So, we could put up a battle."

"Not much of one."

"But it's something."

Vicky nudged the sports bag that had once resided in Emma's loft. It was already open and beneath the rifles could be seen an array of hand-to-hand combat weapons like knives, hatchets and crowbars. "Before long, we'll be fighting with those and little else unless George and his helpers can start manufacturing bows for us."

"Well, I still say what you've listed is a pretty good supply."

Vicky let out a deep breath. "For a one-off run-in, it's an okay cache. If we're up against an army, it's nothing. I mean Jesus, we're talking about six or seven rounds of ammunition for each man, woman and child here. You really think that sounds like a good supply?"

Emma's shoulders drooped. "When you put it like that, no." She turned to Jenny. "And what's the food situation like?"

It was Jenny's turn to exhale a long, despairing breath. "If we're careful, we can probably stretch it to ten days, maybe a little more."

"Jesus."

"We could do with him at the moment. Never mind feeding the five thousand, if he could feed the seventy-odd of us for a couple of meals it would help."

"Let's just hope Mike and the others are successful. Otherwise, I really don't know what we're going to do."

"Well, darling. That decision won't fall on you alone."

"That doesn't make me feel any better about it."

"No, me neither."

*

Wren, Robyn and Mike paused on the edge of the tree line to the south. In front of them was a road that ran straight down into the square. For a few seconds, they would have to abandon the relative safety of the trees in order to reach the other side.

"I'll watch the road while you two head across," Robyn said. They stared over to the other side. A car park lined with a single row of trees led around to the rear of the buildings they were going to set aflame.

"Be careful," Wren said.

Robyn shrugged. "We don't really have a choice. I'm the best shot and we don't want to be using guns right now."

"Okay. On three," Mike said. "One. Two. Three!"

*

Growls started in the back of Wolf's and Muppet's throats once more. A few seconds later, three infected were charging through the woodland towards them.

A throwing knife brought one down before it even reached the small clearing. Mila ran forward, driving both swords outwards. The blades disappeared into the necks of the remaining two creatures.

Mya watched as the heads spun in the air before disappearing further into the woodland. The bodies collapsed in useless heaps and Mila carefully wiped off both blades while the older woman retrieved her knife.

"The sooner we are away from here, the better, yes?" Mila said, returning her swords to the crisscrossed scabbards on her back.

"Yeah. There isn't any part of this I like."

"Wren and Robyn will be successful in their mission. You do not need to worry."

"I have no doubt. It's the rest of it that I'm concerned about."

Mila looked down at the bodies. "These were more of Olsen's people. She must have sent a lot of them down here looking for Beck."

"Yeah. More than I anticipated."

Mila studied her for a moment. "You are worried."

"About what?"

A small smile crept onto Mila's face. "That when Olsen and her people get to Safe Haven they will find Beck is not there. They will come looking."

"She'd have no reason to think that we'd return here. Even if she did, she'd have a lot to think about before sending her people out on scouting missions."

"And if she does?"

"Hopefully, by that time, we'll be in a much stronger situation and we can give the bitch what's coming to her."

Mila smiled. "You sound like Mike."

"Mike and I have a similar ethos."

"The best form of defence is attack?"

"Not quite."

"What then?"

"Cross us and we'll tear your world apart."

"Ah, I see. You hide your psychosis well," Mila said with a crooked smile.

"I've had lots of practice."

*

In her life, Robyn could never remember a time when she had felt so nervous crossing a road. She paused in the middle, raising her bow, checking in both directions while Mike and her sister made it across to the other side. Not a single creature saw her as she continued over with her weapon still raised and ready.

We made it. We made it. Her celebration was short-lived as the sound of running feet made her glance across to the car park. A line of five beasts was charging towards Mike and Wren before they even hit the tarmac on the other side.

Robyn glanced in the direction of the square, making sure none of the undead had broken ranks, before she ran over to the verge and to the others. She released her bowstring before even coming to a stop.

*

Click. A bolt disappeared into the skull of the beast furthest to Mike's right as the others charged towards him. An arrow seemingly appeared from nowhere, cracking another monster's skull. The other three came at him in a straight line, and without pause, he pivoted, cannonballing at their feet, not giving them time to react.

He felt a tangle of legs shake his frame before all three bodies went splaying over the tarmac. As the creatures scrambled to their feet, a bolt stopped one. An arrow took down another, and the last hellish, pallid-skinned ghoul lunged for Mike as he stood. He brought one of his machetes around and down, cracking through the monster's skull. It collapsed to its knees, and as he withdrew the blade, it fell forward onto its face.

Mike wiped his weapon clean before returning both machetes to his rucksack. "That was a bit of a mental move," Robyn said as she and Wren walked up to him.

"It's worked for me before."

"Yeah, but … y'know."

Mike shrugged and looked around for any more signs of infected before turning in the direction of the line of buildings. The constant noise of the horde from the square accompanied them as they walked down, but for the time being, it was just the three of them.

"If we break a window or anything, some of them might come looking," Wren said as they passed building after building with no sign of an easy entry.

"That one's got a window open," Robyn said, looking up to a thin horizontal gap on the third floor.

"Yeah. As much as I like a challenge, Bobbi, I don't fancy climbing up there, do you?"

"I wasn't thinking about climbing it. I could fire an arrow through."

"Actually, that's a pretty good idea," Mike said.

"Why do people sound like that whenever I come up with something? You mean that's a pretty good idea *for me?*"

"That's not what I meant."

"Calm down, Bobbi. Do you really think you can make the shot?"

Robyn stood back a little and brought her bow up but didn't nock an arrow. She practised the shot in her head, finally releasing the bowstring. Her eyes watched an imaginary missile rise and disappear through the window. "Yeah. I can make it."

"You understand what happens if you miss, Bobbi?"

"I've got plenty of arrows, and I saw that bottle of white spirit. It's not the end of the world if I miss."

"That's not what I'm talking about. If you miss the window, that arrow will keep travelling up. That horde will see it, and I know they're not the brightest creatures on the planet, but they'll come looking.

Robyn's face suddenly turned a shade paler. She looked back up to the window and nodded. "I can do this."

"Good then," said Mike, who turned and ran back towards the five creatures that had attacked them when they'd first entered the car park. The sounds of the horde from the other side of the row of buildings continued to send chills through them all. He grabbed and cleaned the arrows and bolts protruding from their bodies then crouched down and carved strips from jackets and shirts before returning to the two sisters.

Robyn handed Mike an arrow and he proceeded to wrap and tie a thick width of material below the head. He held it out and Wren poured white spirit over the cloth. "Are you ready?" she asked, turning to her sister.

Robyn looked up towards the narrow horizontal gap once more. "Ready," she replied.

Wren grabbed a lighter from her rucksack and flicked the flint wheel, immediately igniting the material. A weak orange flame spread, but as Mike rotated the arrow from side to side, it got brighter. He carefully handed it to Robyn, who nocked it and angled the upper half of her body a little while keeping her feet planted firmly apart.

"Good luck," Mike said.

"Thanks," Robyn replied as her eyes zeroed in on the aperture, which was just a little wider than the average letterbox. Wren and Mike glanced towards the arrow then looked at each other nervously.

Robyn took a deep breath as the flame continued to consume the thick strips of material knotted below the arrowhead. Her body seemed frozen and her eyes unblinking like a statue before she finally released her bowstring. The three of them watched as the burning missile climbed. The flame disappeared to nothing more than a flicker as the wind rushed over it. Then a sense of elation swept over them as it vanished through the window.

"Holy shit!" Mike said.

"You did it, Bobbi," Wren said, throwing her arms around her too. "That was like a one-in-a-million shot."

Robyn exhaled deeply and then looked back up at the window. Seconds passed, then a full minute, and as no sign of a spreading fire came, their excitement diminished. "We've got no idea what's beyond that window. I mean it could be an empty room with tiled walls and floors for all we know."

"She's right," Mike said. "Do you think you could make the shot again? Maybe if you can lodge an arrow in the ceiling it'll set fire to a beam or something."

"I can try," Robyn replied, looking at her bow as if asking it to perform one more miracle.

"Wait a minute," Wren said excitedly. "Look." They all stared up again and dancing shadows could be seen in the room. "You did it, Bobbi. You did it." They remained there a little longer until the moving, glinting orange impressions on the walls gave way to flames. Grey and then black smoke followed as the room quickly became consumed.

"It's spreading," Mike said. "Let's get out of here."

The three of them ran through the car park pausing at the single line of trees and crossing the road as they had before, with Robyn covering. When they had all made it across to the opposite, thicker tree line, they let out relieved breaths but didn't come to a stop again until they had retraced their steps back to the others.

"Oh my God. What happened here?" Wren asked, looking around at all the bodies.

They had come under attack several times since the trio had left, and when they had heard them returning, they were convinced they were about to enter battle once more. It was only when Wolf's tail began to wag wildly and he started trotting rather than charging towards the approaching sound that Mya and Mila relaxed.

"This place is crazy. We need to get out of here as soon as possible," Mila said, looking down at the carpet of bodies in front of her. "You were successful, yes?"

"Bobbi made the most amazing shot I've ever seen," Wren said proudly. She desperately wanted to kiss Wolf, but blood coated his teeth and fur, and she knew he would need bathing before she could do so safely. Instead, she lovingly scratched behind his ear as he leaned into her.

"Good," Mya said. "Let's get out of here. My guess is that when the smoke starts rising, those things will be heading this way from all over town, and that means they'll come through here to get to the square."

The seven of them ran, reaching the Land Rover in a fraction of the time it had taken them to make the initial journey. As they all climbed in, a hollow boom erupted into the air from the direction of Somerled Square.

All their heads turned in the direction of the sound as plumes of thick black smoke rose up. "This is good," Mila said. "They will all be drawn there. We will have time to get the supplies without worrying about an attack."

"Let's hope," Mya said. "We're going to give it a few minutes and then set off. I want as many of those things to be out of the way as possible by the time we head into that car park."

"Ja. This makes sense."

*

Shaw woke up slowly. His head ached like he'd been drinking into the early hours, but the only drink that had passed his lips was water. He felt the dried streaks of tears that had made his cheeks tighten a little as memories of the previous evening came back to him. He sat up slowly and the old wooden bench creaked beneath him. It had been a warm night, but he had slept in his clothes as he had no sleeping bag and no bedding.

He climbed to his feet and stared out of the cruddy window once more. The loch was like a mirror, but now all the excitement he'd felt the evening before for his newfound freedom was gone. He turned to look at his rucksack, knowing all that awaited him for breakfast was a cold tin of beans. *I could make a fire.* He discounted the idea as soon as it came into his head. Replacing a cold tin of beans with a hot one would do little to improve his temperament.

Shaw walked outside and went across to the water, crouching down and cupping it up to his face. With each cool scoop, he could feel the dried tears melt away, and suddenly he felt better. He looked back at the small hut.

I could live here. I could find some supplies and maybe a wood burner. I could fish and forage in the forest. I could live here.

He looked back out over the water and his mind drifted to those he'd left behind. Jenny, Mike, Emma, Jules,

Ruth, Richard and all the others who had depended on him and whom he had depended on. He loved them, but at that same moment, he never wanted to see them again. He wanted to remember them not as the hopeless refugees who had made the journey down here in boats but as the members of a thriving community back in Safe Haven.

If he decided to believe the latter, then Barnes would still be alive. Saanvi and Prisha and all the other people they'd lost would still be alive and the guilt and pain would be gone. He could just live out his days here by himself, knowing that he'd done everything he could, knowing he'd given Safe Haven his all.

Jack never saw any bodies at the northern settlement. What's to say Barney's not alive? What's to say he didn't get to the boats, and instead of coming across to the island, he and his people went north? Maybe they went up to Ullapool. Maybe they're up there starting a new life too. It's time for all of us to start again. It's time to forget about Olsen and Safe Haven.

Maybe one day I'll run into Barney and the others. Maybe one day I might go back and visit Emma and Mike. Maybe one day, we'll look back at Safe Haven as the biggest mistake we ever made. Maybe we'll laugh and joke over a campfire and talk about the bad old days, knowing that if we'd left the place sooner, we could have saved so much heartache. He remembered back to the gunfire from the day before. *That needn't have been them. It could have been anyone.*

Maybe one day, Lucy and Hughes and Beth and David and John and Jake and Annie and all the hundreds of other people we lost in order to keep that small stretch of coastline will forgive us.

He turned back to look at the bothy and suddenly realised tears were pouring down his face again. "Please forgive us."

9

Pops, crashes and bangs accompanied the climbing tower of smoke as it rose higher and higher into the air. From their position, Mya and the others only saw a small handful of creatures cross the road in the direction of the square.

After a full ten minutes had passed, Mya turned the key and started the engine. The Land Rover moved away slowly and all of the occupants remained alert. Their eyes searched out every corner, every ginnel, every gap in every fence, looking for movement, searching for the infected.

For once, Mya did not drive with her usual gusto. The sheep trailer in tow was old and rattled with every pothole, every bump in the road it struck. They all started to breathe a little easier as they entered the car park, but the respite didn't last long.

"What the fuck is this?" Mike asked, horrified. He was the first to see it, or at least the first to acknowledge the horror of what he was seeing.

Mya brought the vehicle to a halt at the entrance and the temperature in the car noticeably dropped. "What have we become?" Wren whispered, barely able to believe what she was seeing.

Infected had been tied to each of the four pillars of the canopied entrance. Judging by the array of stones, rocks and other objects strewn on the ground around them, they had been used for target practice. Rows of empty beer cans and bottles stood to attention, and pallets, crates and empty boxes formed a mountain of debris along the wall next to the doors.

"Two of them are still moving," Mila almost gasped.

Mike and Mya opened their doors and climbed out. In the open air, the stench of the beasts drifted towards them. The pair slowly moved forward, and suddenly, a third beast roused. A large part of its skull had been smashed and its brain was visible through the jagged hole.

"Jesus," Mya said.

In all the time Mike had known her, he had never seen her on edge, but at that moment, he could sense her unease. He withdrew both machetes and walked up to each of the creatures. One after the other he drove a blade through their skulls, rendering them still.

His foot hit one of the objects on the ground as he turned around, and he looked down as it rolled away. *Tinned prunes. Nice.* The tin was dented and part of the label was stained dark red with blood. He looked back towards the figure he'd just put out of its misery.

In life, it had been a young woman. Her blouse had been ripped open and a dozen or more pockmarks where the barrage of missiles had struck her breasts, rib cage, and abdomen told a sad tale about how long the sick game had gone on. Her nose was crushed and broken chunks of flesh were ripped from her face by the sharp edges of whatever objects had hit.

Mike felt a presence by his side and turned to see Mya. Her expression mirrored his. "As disturbing as this is, there's something else that's slightly more troublesome," Mike said, gesturing towards the mountain of boxes, pallets and discarded shrink wrap.

"Yeah," Mya replied, heading towards what remained of the double doors.

"Jesus!" Robyn cried as she, Wren and Mila exited the Land Rover with Wolf and Muppet behind them. Her horror went unacknowledged by Mike as he followed Mya into the supermarket.

"Fuck!" Mike hissed.

"Yeah," Mya replied, flicking her torch on as the pair continued down one of the aisles. The only signs that food had ever been present were gnawed packets and containers. Rodent droppings carpeted some of the shelves while others were empty but for the dust patterns showing that tins had once resided there.

The freezer doors were still firmly shut, and for that the pair were grateful. The rotting contents of the spoiled food had inflated some of the plastic bags like balloons and they could only imagine the smell of what lay within.

"What does this mean for us?" Wren asked, breaking Mya's quiet contemplation as she joined her and Mike.

"Nothing good."

"Bit of an understatement," Mike replied.

The group continued their search of the store in silence, hoping that they would find a crate, a pallet, a box … something that wouldn't render the mission a total write-off. They pushed through the PVC swing doors at the rear of the shop floor and entered the small warehouse and loading dock area. They all shone the beams of their torches around the racking. A small head popped over the side of one and let out a squeak before disappearing just as quickly.

"This place has been gutted," Wren said, turning to Mya. "What are we going to do?"

Mya shook her head slowly and continued to follow the torch beams. "I suppose while we've got the infected occupied by the fire, we check out the houses in the area."

"That's it?"

"It's all I've got at the moment."

"This is so, so bad," Robyn chimed in.

"Mya's right," Mike said, finally abandoning his search and turning to the others. "It's all we've got at the moment. Let's not waste any more time here."

The group retraced their steps back through the store. "This was Olsen's people, yes?" Mila asked.

"That would be my guess."

The two dogs walked by the side of the four of them and their body language echoed the defeat the others were feeling. Wren opened the rear door and Wolf was the first to leap in, then over the back seat. Muppet immediately followed before the rest of them climbed in. They each took a second's pause to look back towards the store before slamming the doors shut behind them once more.

Mya started the engine and the Land Rover left the car park. She brought the vehicle to a stop outside the row of cottages they had parked in front of earlier. Mike exited the vehicle before the engine had even stopped and the others quickly followed.

The overgrown hedges provided good shielding from anyone or anything on the road, but it didn't matter because the pops, cracks and bangs that continued to make the morning air vibrate told them all that the fire was still spreading and that would be enough to keep the attention of the infected for some time.

It was only when they all approached the front door that they noticed the lock had been jimmied. A sliver of painted wood lay on the doorstep and they cast nervous glances at each other before Mya pushed the door inwards.

Ignoring all other rooms, they headed straight towards the kitchen. "Craaap!" Robyn said as they entered. The cupboard doors were all open and the storage spaces behind were empty.

Muppet and Wolf both brushed up against their mistresses, sensing the air of desperation that hung heavy in the room. Mike walked to the back door and swung it open, revealing the small enclosed garden. At the far end was a shed with a door that had clearly been forced open. He walked the cracked and overgrown path to it and looked inside. Cobwebs covered the ceiling and window. Lawn furniture was stacked neatly in one corner, but whatever else had resided within was now long gone. He looked behind the shed and found a pile of neatly stacked sacks. He opened one up to see it was full of split logs.

"Out here," he called to his four companions, who were still standing in the kitchen in a state of disbelief. One by one, they stepped outside and joined him.

"They're logs," Robyn said.

"Yeah. I managed to figure that out already. We need to load them into the trailer."

"You've got to be kidding me. People are expecting food. They're really going to be over the frikkin' moon if we show up with a load of wood, aren't they?"

"Mike's right. We've done all the hard work. We've got to go back with something," Mya said.

"You can't be serious. We need to check the other houses. We need to—"

"We will check other houses, but what makes you think for a second we're going to find anything different? Whether it was Olsen's people or someone else, Portree has been turned over. The fire in the square that gutted those other buildings ... they used exactly the same method as us, and my guess is it was to meet the same ends. We'll check the other houses out, but I'm pretty certain we're not going to find anything. There are five of us. If a well-equipped army came into town, they could gut it in a fraction of the time it would take us to cover a couple of streets."

"So what? We just pick up the scraps of whatever and hope that keeping warm for a couple of extra nights will make people forget that they're starving? I don't know if you noticed, but there are trees all over the grounds of the centre. I wouldn't say this is a priority."

"No, it's not. But it's something," Mike replied, hoisting a sack onto each shoulder and heading back down the garden.

Wren's head dropped and Wolf let out a small whine as he looked up at her. Her sister placed an arm around her. "We're finished. It's all over."

*

By mid-afternoon, the sun was high in the sky. Jules had coordinated a growing army of helpers all morning and a sizeable patch of ground had been prepared. Sweat was pouring down her face as Emma walked up to join her.

"I didn't see you at lunchtime," Jules said to her friend as Emma offered her a bottle of water. Jules unscrewed the top and gulped several mouthfuls before handing it back.

"No. I was talking to Jen about our supplies."

"I bet that was a comforting conversation."

Emma laughed. "Yeah."

"So, how bad is it?"

"Didn't you elect me the leader so you didn't have to think about stuff like that?"

"You make a good point. Seriously though. What are we looking at?"

"About a week to ten days … ish."

"Well, let's hope Mike and the others managed to find a big trailer then."

"Yeah. Raj and Talikha want to take a small group out to forage. That's what I was coming to see you about."

"Out? You mean out of the gates?"

"Yeah. Not far, but we're surrounded by forest here and they both think we could find quite a bit to supplement the supplies."

"Is that sensible? I mean shouldn't we just wait until Mike and the others get back and see what they bring with them?"

"The thing is that whatever they bring back, it's going to start dwindling the second we put it in the pantry."

"We've got a pantry?"

"Of sorts. But my point is it's only going to be a short stopgap. That's all it was ever going to be. We need to become self-sufficient as quickly as we can and only use that stuff as a last resort."

Jules looked across the expanding vegetable patch as others continued to work. "I suppose you're right. So, are you wanting me to go with them?"

"Well, I was thinking that I'd go if you could help Jen keep an eye on things here."

"Is that a good idea? I mean it's more important than ever that nothing happens to you now."

"Sammy's going, so I need—"

"Sammy's going?"

"She and Wren go foraging all the … used to go foraging all the time back home."

"But … I mean … it's not exactly safe around here. I told you what we found the last time we came down."

"Given a choice, I'd rather we didn't have to think about it, but I don't have a choice, Jules. We don't have a choice."

"Shite." She looked across at Jon and then turned back to Emma. "Take Andy and Rob. I know they're not the brightest bulbs in the pack, but they'll have your back out there."

"I was going to ask them. If anything happens here, you've got Darren, but we won't be going far."

"How many people are you taking?"

"I don't know. A dozen or so."

"I suppose this goes without saying, but please be careful."

"I won't take any risks."

Within twenty minutes, Emma had her team together. All but Andy and Rob carried empty rucksacks for whatever they might find. Instead, Jules' two brothers had rifles slung over their shoulders and each held spears that George and his team had made for them.

The group stepped out of the gates with trepidation. They turned to see Kat and Ephraim close to them once more.

"We'll be here when you get back. Don't worry," Kat said as Emma turned to look at them.

"Thanks. We're not going to venture far, so I guess it all depends on how much we can find and how quickly."

"Be careful."

"I wish people would stop saying that."

Kat let out a small laugh. "Sorry."

The Skye Outward Bounds Centre was set in woodland, so just by turning left or right, they would be in foraging territory. "Okay, you guys, which way?" Emma asked, looking at Sammy and then Raj.

"This way," Sammy answered, pointing to the right.

"Okay. You're the boss." Raj and Talikha walked by Sammy's side as Humphrey brushed up to one and then the other. Emma went to join them, looking around nervously as they headed away from the road and further into the woodland. They followed the fence for a while before turning to the west and walking a little further into the forest.

Emma glanced behind her to see Rob and Andy bringing up the rear while the other six foragers all looked around nervously as they continued.

"Don't worry, my friend. If there are any infected around, Humphrey will let us know in plenty of time."

"That's not what I'm worried about. When Mike finds out that I let my little sister out into the woods, he's going to go spare."

Raj smiled. "He will understand."

"I'm not so sure about that."

"You're in charge," Sammy said. "That's what everybody's saying anyway. And this is my choice. I used to go foraging all the time with Wren."

"Yeah, but that was back in Safe Haven, where … y'know … it was safe."

"If it was so safe, why are we down here now?"

"You know what I mean."

"Mike keeps saying we have to keep fighting. Well, that's what this is, isn't it? We're not fighting infected right now, but we're fighting just the same, aren't we? We're fighting to find food. And he and Wren have gone off to Portree, where there are hundreds of those things, so why shouldn't we be out here fighting too?"

"Nobody likes a know-it-all, Sammy. I've told you that before."

A smile appeared on the young girl's face briefly and she took hold of her older sister's hand. "Nowhere is safe. Not anymore."

"Your sister speaks with the wisdom of age," Talikha said.

"Doesn't she just?"

*

"Hello," Beck said, taking Jenny completely by surprise.

Even Meg let out a quiet yap as he appeared in the doorway.

"I swear to God. I'm not going to last the week out," Jenny replied, pressing her hand against her chest.

"Sorry."

"What can I do for you, Prime Minister?"

"I was just coming to see if there was anything I could help with."

Jenny looked around the shelves of the pantry. Everything they had brought down with them from Safe Haven had been counted and catalogued. "Wanted to see if you could help or wanted to see first-hand just how desperate our situation is?"

Beck smiled. "A bit of both actually."

"Well, get a good look because this isn't going to last long."

"In all the time I've known Mya, she's never let the people who are depending on her down."

129

Jenny shrugged. "That may be so. But she's not a miracle worker. If she and the others come back with a trailer load of food, it will only last so long before we need another, then another."

"Hopefully, we'll be able to get some fast-growing crops in the ground and that will make the situation a little less demoralising."

There was still plenty of light left in the day, but in the confines of the pantry, Jenny needed a small dynamo lantern to help her see when making entries on her inventory sheets. She turned this off and went across to join Beck in the doorway. "We both know that's just a band-aid. The polytunnels were one thing. They couldn't fall victim to the climate up here. All you need is one summer of bad storms or a prolonged period of dry weather and your crops are ruined. And it's not like we can go out hunting deer, is it?"

Beck remained silent for a moment. Deer had once been a common sight in the Highlands, but while in government, he had ordered massive culls to bolster the country's food reserves. Before the virus had struck, the UK had imported over fifty percent of its food from abroad, and with the situation changing virtually overnight, drastic measures needed to be taken. As a result, the wild deer population, particularly in Scotland but the rest of the UK too, dwindled to such levels that seeing one was rare, if not miraculous. "Yes, well—"

"Oh, don't get me wrong. You did what you had to do. I dare say if we didn't have someone with your foresight as our prime minister, we wouldn't have lasted half as long as we did. But it means our options are a little more limited now."

"We've still got a couple of fishing boats."

"And we're a few miles inland with our remaining drops of fuel in the tank of a Land Rover that's on a last hope mission to try to give us a little bit of a breathing space before things get really bad."

"I … err.…" In all the time Beck had known Jenny, he had never seen her so pessimistic, so down. She had always been the one to buck everyone else up. She had been the one to find solutions, not dwell on problems.

Jenny took a deep breath. "I'm sorry. You've caught me at a bad time."

"I don't suppose there are many good times at the moment."

"It all feels like it's unravelling right in front of my eyes. I always believed. Always."

"Believed?"

"Believed Mike. Believed Shaw. Believed in our idea. Believed in Safe Haven. I always believed that we had right on our side and while ever we stuck together and worked towards a common cause, we'd be okay." As she spoke, Beck could see the sadness welling in her eyes. "And then we lost Lucy and Jake. Then Barnes. Now Shaw. It's all come tumbling down on us." She gestured around the small pantry. "This is what we're left with. This is the sum total of the time we spent in Safe Haven." She closed the door behind her and began to lead Meg through the large kitchen towards the exit.

"No. It isn't."

Jenny stopped and turned. "Do you know something I don't know?"

"Since I joined you, I think I must have heard a hundred stories or even more about how you all made it up from Yorkshire. I heard about Fry, and I heard about Webb, and I heard about Troy and everyone in between. Nobody can take away what you've been through together. Nobody can take away the bonds that you built. Your council.… I've never come across a group of people more in tune with one another. You're like a family … but, y'know … pleasant to be around."

Jenny laughed. "We were on our best behaviour with you there."

Beck smiled. "There's a way out of this."

"There was a time when I'd have agreed with you. Hell, on the journey here yesterday, I was saying practically the same thing to Shaw. I was trying to convince him, but I suppose there's only so long you can carry on deluding yourself." She turned and started walking to the door again.

"What about Mike and Mya?"

"I'm sorry?" Jenny replied, turning and causing Meg to come to a halt too.

"What about Wren, and Robyn, and Mila? Are they all deluding themselves too? Are they out risking their lives on a fool's errand? I understand Sammy is out foraging. Sammy. She's just a little older than my girls and she's out there with Emma. I'm guessing they're delusional too?" Jenny cast her eyes down to the floor.

"It's okay to get down about stuff, Jenny. It's okay to clench your fists and punch the wall. Hell, I do it all the time. Somehow, Trish always manages to pull me back. She always manages to give me hope when I think there's none left. I know you were close to Shaw. I wish I'd got to know him better, but you still have people here who will literally risk their lives for you ... for us. We don't have the luxury of defeat."

Jenny brought her eyes back up to meet Beck's. "The luxury of defeat?"

"Yes. When you've lost, when there are no moves left to make, when there's nothing left to fight for, then you can just get down on your knees and wait for the end to come. But you've got people here who love you, Jenny. You've got people who depend on you, too, and people who are looking to you and the rest of the council to give them that hope that they need so badly. Safe Haven was more than a place. You should know that as well as anyone."

Jenny continued to stare at Beck for several seconds before finally breaking her gaze and looking down at Meg. "They are my family."

Beck stood with a confused expression on his face for a few seconds before replying. "Who?"

"Earlier, you said that the council were like a family. They are my family. And so are Mike and Wren and the others." She brought her eyes up to meet Beck's once more. "I don't want to lose any more of them, but I know I will. I don't know how I'll cope with more loss, but you're telling me now that I have to, that I have to keep going on, no matter what."

"Yeah. That's right, Jenny. Because you and I don't get to give up. Whatever else happens, we don't get to throw in the towel."

"What's so important about me?"

"I don't know."

Jenny laughed. "Thanks. You really know how to make a girl feel special."

"It's the truth. I don't know what's special about you. But if I'd have known you when I was back in Westminster, I'd have loved to have had you as my chief whip. You have this disarming way about you that no matter what you're asking people to do, they do it without hesitation because, ultimately, it's always the right thing for them and everybody else. That's what makes you special, Jenny, and that's why you can't give up, not now, not ever."

"Not ever is a long time."

"I know. But you are the difference here. You are the one who can make people feel that little bit better about themselves no matter what else is going on. You're tuned in to people. You look after people. You're there when they need a shoulder to cry on, a friend to talk to, or a worker to roll up her sleeves. I don't think there's a single person here who is more pivotal when it comes to the success or failure of this community."

Jenny shook her head. "You put too much faith in me."

"No. I'll let you in on a big secret, Jenny. When I was the PM, a lot of the time I was winging it. But the one thing I was really, really good at was identifying qualities in others and knowing who to trust. You have the qualities this community needs. And I know, without a shadow of a doubt, you can be trusted to help everyone through this time."

"I don't know how you can be so sure about that."

"I can be sure because that's who I am, and I can be sure because I know that's who you are too."

10

The atmosphere in the Land Rover was grim as they made their return journey to the Skye Outward Bounds Centre. The battery had died on their radio even before they had reached the farm, so there was no way to contact Emma and prepare the others for what they had or, more importantly, hadn't found. They had visited a few houses around Portree, making sure that they gave the infected horde a wide berth. The results had been beyond disappointing. Each place they had searched had clearly been visited previously and not a scrap of food had been found.

They had, however, scrambled together more clothes, bedding, cutlery, crockery and a few other items that would make life a little more comfortable for the former Safe Haven inhabitants. All in all, though, the mission had not accomplished its primary objective and thus was a failure.

"What are we going to do?" Mila asked, eventually breaking the stony silence that had hung in the car since they had set off.

"I suppose we let the council know and then come up with another plan," Mya replied, putting her foot down a little harder on the accelerator.

"Another plan? Like what?"

Mya just shrugged. "I wish I had an answer for you."

"There is no other plan," Wren said. "This was our only option. If we can't get food, we can't live here. We need to go somewhere else."

"Somewhere else? Like where?" Mila asked. "This was our last best chance."

"Maybe we can go to one of the islands. Maybe they'll show us a little charity."

"We don't need charity," Mike replied.

"Oh no, of course we don't, Mike. We're in such a great position. We've got sixty-odd people back at the centre. I suppose once we've figured out how to make food out of thin air we'll be all set."

"We'll figure this out," Robyn said quietly.

"This was us figuring it out, Bobbi. Heading into Portree, risking our lives like that was us figuring it out. It was our sticking a plaster on an amputated leg solution to the mess we're in. There is no more figuring it out. It's a simple equation. People plus no food equals death and starvation." Wolf leaned over from the back and put his head on Wren's shoulder.

"Robyn's right. We'll figure it out. There's always a solution," Mike replied.

"Oh yeah. Tell that to Lucy and Jake." It was as if all the air had suddenly been sucked out of the car, and even as the words came out of Wren's mouth, she couldn't believe she was saying them. A breath caught in the back of her throat for a second. "I'm sorry," she said. "I'm so sorry. I didn't mean that. I'm sorry, Mike." He didn't respond and Wren's eyes filled with tears as Robyn squeezed her tighter.

Mike stared out of the side window, looking across the fields and to the trees beyond. If Wren had plunged a dagger into his heart it couldn't have hurt more than those words. "You've definitely checked the rest of the island out?" he asked, refusing to address Wren at all.

The tension in the car eased a little. Denial was a useful tool. "Trill and his people were pretty thorough. I mean, hell, there might be the odd croft house off the beaten track that we never searched, but given our fuel situation, we can't really afford to start doing that."

"Looks like we're going to be doing a lot of foraging then."

Wren wanted to scream. She wanted to shake Mike and tell him to get a grip on reality. *There's optimism and then there's just being delusional.*

Mya looked at the fuel gauge. "With the diesel we found at the farm, we've probably got enough fuel to get to the boats and back a few times. "We could get a few hauls of fish. We could go along the coast and collect mussels and … stuff."

"Ja. This would help a little, but it is not a long-term solution, and what happens when the fuel runs out? We cannot walk to the coast and back every day with buckets. It is not possible."

"Okay. Maybe we do need to think about finding somewhere else. Maybe we don't all live in the same place. Maybe we find a small settlement by the coast or something."

"We had a small settlement by the coast."

"Yeah, well, maybe we find a different one."

"Until we get forced out of this, as well, yes?"

"Look. I don't have all the answers. I'm as punch drunk as you are by what we found in Portree."

Mila let out a long sigh. "I am sorry. I take my frustration out on you. You do not deserve it."

"We're all frustrated. We're all anxious. We're all pent up. Let's take a breath because when we drive through those gates and show what we've come back with, it's only going to get worse."

*

"I thought we'd have found more than this," Sammy said sadly as the group reached the road. They had been out for a couple of hours and, thankfully, had not run into any infected. But at the same time, they had only found some hawthorn, dandelions and alexanders.

"Yeah," Emma said distantly. She had gone out with the foragers with the aim of returning with rucksacks full of hope. She looked around at the other faces and saw equal tones of sadness in their expressions.

"It is alright," Talikha said. "I saw much to be thankful for in these woods. Sadly, not all fruit can be picked just when you want it, but there are blackberries, wild strawberries, elderflowers. There is rosehip, and there are beech trees, oak trees, and this is to say nothing of the mushrooms that we may see."

"You're talking about the future," Emma replied, "and I'm worried about right now."

"The burden does not rest with you alone. Raj and I will come out again tomorrow. Maybe we will go in the other direction and have more luck."

"Do you honestly think that will make a difference?"

"One of the many beautiful things about nature is that it is unpredictable. We have no idea what we might find."

"I wish I shared your wonderment and faith. Right now, I'm not feeling either."

"Things will get better, Emma."

"I don't see how they can get any worse."

They carried along the lane until the gates of the Skye Outward Bounds Centre came into view. "The happy wanderers return," Ephraim announced loudly as they approached.

The gates swung open and the group entered one by one. Emma lingered back while the others continued towards the centre. "Have you been on duty all this time? Nobody's come to relieve you yet?"

"We're fine," Kat said.

"Oh yes. We're just having the time of our lives here," Ephraim added.

The two women gave him a glare before turning to look at each other. "How did it go?" Kat asked.

"Well, if you like hawthorn and dandelions, it was a resounding success."

"Oh."

"Yeah."

"Well, at least when Mike and the others come back, that's going to give us a bit of a breathing space."

Emma looked down at the radio on her belt. "The battery died on us soon after we set off. If you haven't seen anyone, I'm guessing we don't know how things have gone down there."

"Sorry," Kat said. "I've only had the pleasure of Ephraim's company since I got here."

"I think I'd have preferred to go to Portree."

Kat laughed. "Oh, very witty," Ephraim replied. "I'm sure you were just the life and soul of every party before this whole apocalypse thing got in the way of your burgeoning comedy career."

"Don't sulk," Emma replied. "You know I'm only kidding."

All three of them suddenly raised their heads as a familiar sound travelled towards them. "That's an engine."

The trio stared down the lane as the noise got louder and louder. Finally, the Land Rover and trailer appeared from around the bend and Emma felt genuinely happy for the first time that day. Mya brought the car to a stop in front of them. She rolled down the window and the smile on the others' faces soon dissipated.

"What's wrong?" Emma asked.

"It wasn't exactly what we were hoping for," Mya replied.

"What does that mean?"

The passenger door swung open and Mike climbed out. "I'll tell you all about it."

The two siblings watched as the Land Rover continued up to the house. "I'll get someone to take over from you as soon as I get back to the centre," Emma said to Kat and Ephraim before turning to her brother. "So, are you going to tell me then?"

The pair started to walk. "Someone had beaten us to it. Probably Olsen's people. Whoever it was, they were well-organised and there were a lot of them. The supermarkets and houses in the area were all picked clean."

"Are you winding me up?" she asked with a hopeful half-smile on her face.

Mike stared towards her as they walked and she knew in that instant that he wasn't. "I really wish that was the case."

"What's in the trailer then?"

"Logs, bedding, clothes, crockery, tools, a tractor battery, engine oil, scraps of whatever we could find."

"Oh, God."

"Yeah."

"We went out foraging and found just slightly more than fuck all." They carried on in silent contemplation for a few moments. "What the hell are we going to do, Mike?"

"I suppose you need to call a council meeting."

"Ha!" She didn't mean to laugh, but it came out anyway. "A council meeting? What possible good will that do?"

"Err ... aren't you the new council leader?"

"Oh, so all of a sudden I'm meant to have all the answers?"

"We'll figure something out."

Emma let out a deflated sigh. "I didn't expect to be having to do this shit. I can't believe Shaw left us."

Mike reached out and took his sister's hand. "We will get through this."

"I know." There was a time when her frustration would have been too much for her to cope with. There was a time when she would have done exactly the same as Shaw, and indeed, she did do exactly the same as Shaw, but not again. She had made her brother a promise and it was one that she had no intention of reneging on. "I want you there."

"Me where?"

"In the meeting."

"Bollocks to that. I don't do meetings anymore."

"Hey, look. Do you really think I wanted this responsibility? I need you in there."

"Why?"

"Because you're my brother."

It was Mike's turn to let out a long sigh. "Okay."

*

"I'm really, really hungry, Billy," Gummy said.

Billy's shoulders slumped. It was late afternoon and they had finished the last of the potatoes at breakfast. They were all hungry and had spent the day searching for food and anything else that might help them. Eventually, they had found a small village, which had been gutted, but in the sheds and garages they had been able to take a pick of bicycles, which, after tyre inflation and a quick service, they now rode southwest to Skye. Whenever they had seen signs of infected, they had either hidden or outpaced them until they were out of danger. Only twice had they had to fight.

"We're all hungry, Gummy," Billy replied eventually.

"I can hear my stomach growling."

Billy applied the brakes and came to a stop prompting the others to do the same. "Look. We're not far from Kyle of Lochalsh now, mate. We'll try to find something when we get there, okay?"

"But what if we don't find anything?"

Billy's shoulders sagged a little more. "Why don't we cross that bridge if we come to it, eh?"

Gummy's bottom lip slipped out, overlapping the top one, and Billy couldn't help but smile. It was a subconscious thing he always did and it made him resemble a small child. The quartet set off once more and Decko increased his pace to join Billy at the front.

"Not for nothing, but I'm bloody famished too."

"Yeah," Billy said. "Let's just hope we can find something soon, shall we?"

"Bloody hell, Billy. We must have checked twenty or thirty houses today and we haven't found a thing."

"I'm aware of that, Decko. I was standing right by your side."

"Well, all I'm saying is—"

"What? What are you saying? Have you got some plan to get us food that I've overlooked?"

"Alright. Calm down. Don't get your knickers in a twist."

The pair carried on side by side for a moment before Billy spoke again. "Look," he said, gesturing towards the steep hill in front of them. "When we get that out of the way, it's all downhill into Kyle. We'll find somewhere to kip for the night and hopefully scramble together some mushrooms from the woods or something, and then tomorrow we'll be able to stuff ourselves until our hearts are content."

"It's going to be a long fucking night if we don't find something to eat."

"Tell me about it."

The hill was far steeper than it originally looked and on several occasions they climbed off their bikes, preferring instead to walk them up the more severe stretches of incline. The pine forest to either side was thick and unrelenting. They kept their conversations to a minimum as they all knew that at any second an attack could come from out of nowhere. It took them the best part of half an hour to climb the hill and the relief they all felt as they reached the brow was palpable.

It wasn't quite levity but certainly relief. A sheen of sweat painted all their foreheads. "Please tell me it's all downhill from here," Galli said.

"If memory serves, when we get past this bend, it's all downhill to Kyle and we'll be able to see Skye. Now remember, there were a lot of infected around Kyle at one time, so keep your eyes peeled."

"That's reassuring." Galli and Billy shared a smile. It had been a long, long day and they had barely had the chance to spend any time together. The prospect of resting for the evening, empty bellies or not, lit a small candle of happiness inside them both.

As the road levelled out, they all stared in wonder for a few moments as the towering trees around them seemingly reached up to the sky. "It's something, isn't it?" Decko said, reading the minds of the others.

"It's crazy beautiful," Galli replied. "Y'know. Every holiday I took, it was out of the country. Spain, Portugal, Greece, I couldn't get enough of them. I really wish I'd spent time getting to know my own country a little better."

"Well, we'll have plenty from here on in," Billy replied.

The pair shared another smile. It was true. Yes, they were living through the apocalypse, but they had survived thus far, and if they could carve out a quiet corner of existence for themselves, then maybe there was a little hope for all of them.

Ahead, they could see the gradient of the road change to a downward trajectory and they all climbed back onto their bikes and started pedalling. They followed the curve of the trees around and, suddenly, there was the Kyle of Lochalsh with its bridge stretching over to Skye and their future.

On the hillside to their right, a white cottage was set beyond the trees overlooking the bay below. "I say we check that place out," Galli replied.

Billy shrugged. "Seems as good as any," he replied and the four of them were on their way, brimming with the hope that they might find something to satiate their hunger before they lay down to sleep.

11

The council meeting had several extra faces as the rumours and scaremongering spread around the Skye Outward Bounds Centre like a flesh-eating virus.

In addition to the usual members, Beck, Doug, Mya and Mike were all present. "Okay. So, I think it's safe to say it's been a mixed day," Emma said, starting the meeting.

There was no polite laughter. There were no smiles. "Yeah, shite mixed with piss and vomit," Jules replied.

"Nice. Nice image," Mike said.

"Look," Emma began again, "we know why we're all here this evening." She looked out of the small window. The sun still had at least an hour before it disappeared, but there was a part of her that thought they'd be in Beck's office brainstorming long after it had gone down. "We need ideas. Portree was a complete bust. The houses north of it have pretty much been gutted of anything useful, and I know when I lived in Kyle, we exhausted virtually everything to the south."

"Surely there must be some places left on this side that haven't been raided," Doug said, looking at Mya.

Mya shrugged. "Trill was a thorough man. Sure, there might be the odd one off the beaten track, but finding them will require time and fuel, neither of which we really have."

"Mya's right," Emma replied, taking over once more. "They managed to track down a little red diesel today and we need to make sure we take full advantage of that. If we're going to use it, it needs to be for a sure thing, not a Hail Mary."

"Life is just one long Hail Mary right now, isn't it?" Doug replied.

"Says the man who Satan comes to for advice," Trish said under her breath. This time, a ripple of laughter did go around the room.

"Well, looking at the positives," Emma said.

"Ooh yes, let's," Doug replied.

"Look!" Emma swung around towards him. "We're in a shitty situation. Things are grim. The last thing I need right now are snarky little put-downs every time I open my mouth."

"Ignore him," Beck said, giving Doug a sideways glance. "Please, go on, Emma."

Emma took a breath before continuing. "The scavenging group we sent out came back with a good supply of wood, tools, bedding, clothing, and, as I mentioned earlier, a little more diesel. George and his team sorted out the workshop and manufactured about thirty spears," she said, looking at the older man with a smile.

"We don't really have the facilities to manufacture anything using metal at the moment, but we're going to have a crack at making some bows tomorrow. Jack drew up plans for them this afternoon while James and I worked on the spears."

"That's brilliant. Thank you, George," Emma replied before continuing. "Jules did a fantastic job today. I think everyone here will agree that she prepared far more ground at the back than any of us thought possible in such a short space of time. I went out with a foraging group this afternoon, and although we didn't come back laden exactly, we returned with a few delicacies that you no doubt enjoyed on your dinner plates this evening."

Doug was about to say something but suddenly thought better of it.

"Talikha and I will take another group out tomorrow and head in a different direction," Raj said.

"Are you hopeful that you'll yield better results?" Beck asked.

"It is hard to say. It is not the best time of year for foraging. From here on, the forest will become more bountiful, but we must be patient."

Beck let out a long sigh. "Patience isn't really a luxury we can afford at the moment." He turned back to Emma. "So where does all this leave us?"

Emma glanced at Jenny. They'd had a long discussion earlier about what remained in the pantry. "I honestly don't know. Well, that's not true. I do know, but I don't really have any idea about what to do."

"Mya had an idea earlier on," Mike said.

"Oh?" Emma replied, turning to look at the pair who were sitting side by side.

"She suggested we try to find a place on the coast. Maybe a few houses, so we could still use the fishing boats."

"Says the vegetarian."

"Yeah, well, me, Raj and Talikha will eat whatever we can forage, won't we?"

"So, all that was just busy work that we did today?" Jules snapped.

"Hey, look," Mya said. "It was just an idea. We might not even be able to find anywhere suitable."

"I don't like it," Emma replied. "A coastal settlement's all well and good if you've got a way to protect it. We had cliffs to the back of Safe Haven and all other approaches were well-manned. There's nothing like that on Skye. We could wake up one morning and find out we're overrun by infected."

"Isn't it worth a look at least?" Mike asked.

"And piss away the little diesel we've got left?"

"We could sail around the island."

"Mike. We've got a few days' worth of food left at the most. We don't have time for this. We used fuel and resources to get here. Uprooting everyone and trying to set up somewhere else completely untested would be a disaster."

"Emma makes a good point," Beck replied. "This place isn't perfect, but it's defendable against the infected, and that's something."

"So, what's the answer then?" Vicky asked, beating Ruth to it.

Beck looked towards Doug, who gave him a barely perceptible nod. Then his eyes crossed to Trish, who did the same before he finally turned to the others. "There's not anything about this that I like."

"That sounds ominous."

He walked across to his desk, which had been pushed up against the wall beneath the window. He bent down and opened the bottom drawer revealing a half bottle of Glengoyne and the lever arch folder that he had brought with him from Safe Haven. He grabbed the folder and shut the drawer. "Before everything went to hell, we made plans just in case everything went to hell," he said, perching on the desk with the file in his lap.

"What's that supposed to mean?" Jules asked.

"It means that we prepared a foundation to build back if the virus ever reached these shores. The problem was everything spiralled out of control way too quickly. We were going to have this network of underground bunkers where tens of thousands of people would be able to live for a few years, scientists, government, military and a broad cross-section of skilled workers from the general population in order to start again. Our hope was that the infected would simply die out or that we'd find a way to eradicate them en masse."

"What happened?"

"Well, to the best of my knowledge, the one just outside of London is still up and running ... or at least it was when we escaped."

"Escaped?" Jules was not the only one to be shocked by the word, and now all those who were not a part of Beck's entourage were glued to their seats, hanging on his every word.

"That's a story for another time. What I'm telling you now is something pertinent to the future, which I think you'll agree is a little more important. We had three of these places almost ready to go and one up and running, but it fell to the infection."

"How?"

"How does anybody fall to it?" Doug asked. "Each site had its own research labs. Each site had thousands of people all lost in their own little worlds, their own little denials, their own little self-obsessions."

"Ha. Finally, something I know you're a fucking expert in."

"Whatever the reason. However it happened, whether it was tainted water, an outbreak from one of the labs, or soldiers getting attacked when sending one of the drones out ... it doesn't matter. The fact is we lost contact with them," Beck stated sadly.

"Okay," Emma said. "Why are you telling us this?"

"Because the one in Scotland wasn't finished. We were just a matter of a couple of weeks away. All we needed was a couple of weeks," he said, shaking his head sadly.

"Okay. And this helps us how?"

"It was a fine balancing act. We knew that as soon as it was ready, we had to have the supplies to hand to stock it for the long haul. So we made sure they were to hand."

"Okay. I'll repeat the question. How does this help us?"

Beck let out another long sigh on a day when he had already exhaled so many. "Because a vast amount of those supplies, and we're talking food, medical equipment, weaponry and ammunition, seeds, polytunnels, lab equipment, you name it, are just lying there in trailers ready to be driven away."

Even Mya raised an eyebrow. She had known about the bunkers and the varying states of readiness, but this information was new to her. "And where in Scotland is this vast supply reserve exactly?" Emma asked.

Beck's left eye twitched before he looked towards Trish and Doug. "Glasgow."

"Okay," Emma replied. "I'm guessing you're talking about the outskirts of Glasgow somewhere."

"No. I'm talking about bang in the middle of Glasgow."

Emma let out a huff of a laugh and shook her head dismissively. "Then it may as well be on the moon. What was the point of even bringing it up? For a start, we haven't got anything like the amount of fuel we'd need to get down there. And that's not even taking into account the fact that the whole place will be swarming with infected. I mean Jesus. Inverness was an absolute death trap and that had a population of just over forty thousand. Glasgow must have ten times that."

"Fifteen and a half, actually," Doug muttered.

"What?"

"Fifteen and a half. It had a population of just over six hundred and twenty thousand."

"Oh, right. Thanks, Doug, 'cause it's important to be accurate when we're talking about figures like this." She turned back to Beck. "Even if we could get down there, it would be suicide."

"Where are the supplies?" Mya asked and all eyes moved towards her before returning to Beck.

"Before Glasgow's subway was opened, a station had originally been planned for Hope Street, adjoining Central Station. The tracks were never laid, but the construction itself has been there since eighteen ninety-six. It provided safety for officials and their families during World War II and helped safeguard mountains of equipment and ammunition in case Hitler was successful and his forces managed to invade. Glasgow was going to be one of the springs from where we took the country back."

"This is a fascinating history lesson, Prime Minister, but what does it have to do with us?" Emma asked.

"Well, rather than a railway track, a road was constructed leading through a tunnel from the station to the river. Or, more specifically, an underground parking complex that was bought via a compulsory purchase order in the sixties when we thought nuclear annihilation was all but inevitable."

"Underground parking garages don't exactly have a lot of headroom. You wouldn't be able to get an artic in and out of one," Mya said.

"This one was adapted. In the nineteen eighties, soon after the Soviet Union invaded Afghanistan, all the plans for Hope Street were dusted off again with a view to actually making it a fallout shelter once more. When the virus struck, a survey was carried out and we found that massive amounts of asbestos had been used in the original construction of the administration and residential quarters.

"In the end, it was deemed more expedient to build something new from scratch after several million had already been spent reinforcing the tunnel and adapting the garage. And although we chose to construct a new bunker, Hope Street was the obvious choice for a secure supply hub. We could just keep everything there until the bunker was ready to go."

"So, you're saying that we can just head into that car park and drive those artics out of there?"

"It's not quite that simple. Although the backup batteries will probably have kept the security systems running for some time, entry via the car park will be impossible now."

"So, how do we get to the station?"

Beck turned to the relevant page in his file. From where Mya was sitting, she could see copious notes alongside a small colour map that had been taped to the page. "You take the underground tunnel from Saint Enoch's to Buchanan Street. After four hundred metres or so, you'll see a door to your left. It leads to a room where they used to keep tools and equipment for line and signal repairs. Behind the racking, at the back, there's another door. This one has a combination lock. You head through that and it will bring you out at the Hope Street station."

"And we have the combination?"

Beck nodded. "We have the combination."

"This doesn't sound like the kind of information you would normally handle, Prime Minister. It's a little too hands-on. Where did it come from?"

"Before we fled the bunker, we gathered a lot of intel. We weren't quite sure where we were going to end up."

"This all sounds very James Bond and very exciting, and I'm sure Q's going to walk through the door any minute and give you a watch that fires laser bolts at the zombies, but it doesn't make a blind bit of difference," Emma said, more than a little irritated. "We don't have the fuel to get down there, and even if we did, it's still a suicide mission. As that arse pointed out earlier, there'll be over six hundred thousand fucking zombies just waiting to chow down on anyone who's stupid enough to try getting into the city."

Beck nodded sadly. "That's the downside."

"Do you think? Pretty big downside."

"Maybe we can—"

"Don't even think about it, Mike," Emma said, interrupting her brother. "This is a no-go from the start. We've got enough problems to think about without using our last remaining fuel and losing more people on some bloody mental mission."

"But what if—"

"I said no." This time, her eyes bored holes through her brother. She turned back to Beck. "That's it? That's all you've got in that little magic file of yours? That's what you were prepared to defend with your last breath?"

"That's not all that's in there," Beck said as calmly and as reasonably as possible. "But it's everything that's pertinent to our current situation."

Emma let out a shriek of a laugh. "Are you kidding me? Pertinent to our current situation. It's close to two hundred and fifty fucking miles away. How is that possibly pertinent to our current situation?"

Beck closed the file. "It's all I've got at the moment."

"It's all you've got at the moment?" She shrugged irritably. "You think some more information is suddenly going to appear in it tomorrow or the next day?"

"Emma. Darling," Jenny said, reaching across and placing her hand on Emma's arm.

Emma looked around the room at all the faces staring towards her and suddenly coloured up. "I'm sorry," she said; then she turned to Beck. "I'm sorry. I didn't mean to shout like that."

"Everybody's stressed at the moment, and you've got more responsibility than anyone. It's only to be expected," Beck replied softly.

"I suppose this leaves us back at square one then," Jules said.

"Well," George began, and all eyes turned towards him. "I'd say when we were on that island across from Safe Haven, we were at square one. Today hasn't gone as we'd hoped, but we won't have to worry about tying people up chopping wood for a while. We won't have to worry about people getting cold at night because we've got extra bedding. We've got a good patch of ground dug over, and when we've found some seeds, and trust me, we will, we'll be able to sow them. Like I said, today didn't go as planned, but we're a long way from square one."

"Well said, George," Trish replied and Emma suddenly felt even guiltier. She was meant to be the one leading people, helping people, reassuring people, and instead, she'd been the one to interject anger into the meeting.

"Look," Jenny said, "why don't we bring this meeting to an end? I think we should reconvene tomorrow morning after we've all had a good night's sleep."

"That's probably sensible," Emma replied. "I've still got a few things to do before I can call it a night. For a start, I need to find a few volunteers to be lookouts. I don't want a couple of people doing it all night. I want several splitting shifts so they'll always be fresh." Beck smiled appreciatively. "Okay, everyone, we'll meet back here after breakfast tomorrow morning."

Vicky and Ruth were the first to head to the door and the others followed. "Emma, can I have a word?" Beck said.

Emma glanced longingly towards the exit before turning back to the PM. "Of course." They both waited and watched as the rest of the council exited the office. When Doug and Trish left, closing the door behind them, Beck reached into his drawer and pulled out the bottle of Glengoyne and two mugs. The bottle was just less than half full, but he poured generous measures into each mug before returning it to the drawer. He handed one of them to Emma and sat in one of the chairs. She pulled another around and sat opposite.

The sun continued to fall and sleep couldn't come soon enough for Emma. "I'm not quite sure what I'm going to do when that bottle runs empty," he said, taking a drink.

Emma took a drink as well and winced a little. "I'm not really a connoisseur, but I'm guessing that's the posh stuff."

Beck smiled. "You could say that. Listen, I wasn't trying to usurp your authority or—"

"Please," Emma said, holding her hand up. "It's me who needs to apologise. You were trying to help and I blew up at you for no reason."

"It wasn't for no reason. You made good counterarguments. They were ones that I'd already come up with myself. The only reason I brought the whole thing up is because … it doesn't matter." He took another drink from his mug.

"No, please. Go on."

"How can I put this?"

"Just say what's on your mind."

Beck took a deep breath. "I think we've walked into the Last Chance Saloon and the barman is taking final orders."

Emma looked at him blankly. "You might need to clarify that a little," she said with a polite smile.

"If we don't make this work, then there is nothing else, Emma. We've got old people and children downstairs, and yes, everybody, and I mean everybody, has been doing more than their fair share, and yes, people will be going to sleep tonight with food in their stomachs. But when the food runs out, this place will stop looking like a sanctuary from what we escaped in Safe Haven and start looking like a prison."

"I think I preferred your vague metaphors."

Beck took a drink. "Yeah. Me too. But my point is that's why I brought Hope Street up. You said it yourself; we can't use our last drops of fuel running fools' errands, searching for scraps of food in abandoned croft houses or scouring the coastline for a miniature Safe Haven that probably doesn't even exist. We've only got one chance left, and when we decide what that's going to be, we need to go all in."

Emma sat back in her chair and sniffed loudly, wiping her eyes before the tears even had a chance to appear. "Shaw picked the right time to walk out on us."

Beck shook his head. "In all honesty, Shaw being here wouldn't make a difference. You're handling things just as well as he could."

"I'm not sure about that."

"I am. Shaw's talent was having the right people in the right places to make things run smoothly. You don't have that luxury. You don't have Mary and her team making the meals anymore, but still, everyone was fed. You don't have Barnes by your side, but you're making sure the grounds will be secure tonight. You're doing well, Emma, so don't think for a second that if things go bad from here, it's on you because it isn't."

"Who is it on, exactly, then?"

"Olsen and her people. You're doing everything you can, but all I'm saying is that the next decisions that are made need to be decisive, and they need to be winning ones, otherwise we're finished."

"No pressure then."

Beck smiled. "I'm here to give you counsel if you need it, but these are your people. They trust you, and justifiably so."

Emma let out a long sigh and finished her drink. "Thank you, Prime Minister. I'm not sure quite what for yet, but thank you anyway."

Beck laughed. "You're welcome, Emma. Remember what I said now. I'm here if you need me."

Emma placed the empty mug down on the chair next to her and walked to the door. She smiled politely before closing it behind her and leaving Beck alone.

He looked at the remaining whisky as it swilled around the bottom of the mug then knocked it back. He closed his eyes as the rich, liquid luxury ran over his tongue and down his throat, and then he too climbed to his feet and walked up to his desk. He stood in front of it and stared out of the window.

There was still a little time before the sunset, and as its light hung over the trees, sadness befell the prime minister. This wouldn't be the final dusk he would ever witness, but he wasn't sure how many more would be left for him and his family. He had met presidents and kings. He had danced with princesses and dined with sultans. He had partied with some of the biggest names in Hollywood and he had even jammed with his idols.

But now he was just a man like any other. He had no power, no influence, and fear gripped him like a vice. He wasn't scared for himself but his family. Trish, and Regan, and Juno. They were looking to him, depending on him, and he could do nothing. Not now. Probably not ever again. He reached into his drawer and pulled out the bottle, pouring himself another good measure before returning it to its resting place.

He took another drink and closed his eyes, but this time when he opened them, he felt the sting of tears. The trees blurred in the sun's glow as he looked towards them. *It's all over.* "It's all over."

12

It had been no surprise to anyone, especially his sister, that Mike had volunteered to be one of the first lookouts. He had taken himself to the main gate and, every ten minutes or so, walked up and down the surrounding fence line. Two other volunteers were positioned elsewhere in the grounds patrolling their own sections of fence. There was enough moon and starlight for them to see what they were doing and, more importantly, see any movement from the other side of the fence.

Puzzlement gripped Mike when he heard the sound of feet wandering down the road from the Outward Bounds Centre towards him. *I've only been out here about an hour. It's nowhere near change-over time yet.*

When the silhouette of Wren's figure appeared, things made a little more sense. They hadn't really spoken since they'd arrived back, despite her trying to make conversation a couple of times.

"Hi," she said.

"Hi," he replied, wanting nothing more than to be left alone.

"I brought you this," she said, handing him a travel mug.

He leaned one of the homemade spears up against the gate and opened the lid. "Coffee?"

"Jenny said you deserved it."

"Jenny?" he asked, taking a tentative sip. "Too bad. I thought it might be spiked if Jenny had something to do with it."

Wren forced a laugh. "It'll probably be a while before we get to taste booze again."

"Yeah," Mike said, offering Wren the mug.

"Thanks," she replied, not really wanting a drink but hoping her acceptance of it might ease the tension a little. She took a small gulp of the hot, bitter liquid and handed it back to Mike. "I don't want to drink too much; otherwise I'll be bolt upright like an owl all night."

"I don't think there's much chance of me getting any sleep, so I might as well have something warm inside me."

The pair stood for a moment, looking out through the gate. "Grandad told me what went on in the meeting."

"Yeah. Well, y'know what they say about the best-laid plans. I'd like to get the full story one day."

"What do you mean?"

"About Beck and the others escaping from London."

"Oh, that. Yeah. Makes you wonder what the hell went on."

"Yeah."

"This is a bit stilted, isn't it?"

"What is?"

"Our conversation." Mike didn't reply this time. "I'm really sorry about what I said, Mike. I didn't mean it."

"You did," Mike replied. "And you were right."

"No. No, I wasn't. It just came out of my mouth before I even thought about it."

"That's usually when most truths are spoken."

"I'd give anything to take those words back." He looked towards her, and even with just the light of the moon, he could see a glint in her eyes that suggested they were full of tears.

"Look. Let's put this behind us. Everybody was stressed. Everybody was on edge. It was said, and now it's over and done with. We're good."

"Do you mean that?"

"Yes. I mean that." He placed his arms around her and gave her a hug. "We're family, Wren. We'll piss each other off on occasion. It doesn't mean anything."

"Thank you," she said, reciprocating the embrace.

"There's nothing to thank me for," he said, kissing her on the cheek and pulling back. "Now, go get some sleep. I get the feeling it's going to be an even longer day tomorrow." It was only then that Mike realised she was alone. "Where's Wolf?"

"Robyn and Mila fell asleep on the couch and he was draped over them."

"Couch? You have a couch?"

"We got one of the staff apartments."

"Talk about bloody favouritism." They both smiled.

"Meet you for breakfast?"

"Sure." He watched as she disappeared back into the night then he turned his attention to the road beyond the gate once more. It was just a couple of minutes before he heard footsteps again and a smile crept onto his face. "I told you, we're all good. Get some sleep."

"I must have missed a conversation," Mya said.

"Ah. I thought you were someone else."

"Evidently. You and Wren made up now?"

"How do you know it was Wren?"

"I saw her heading back to the centre."

"You just know everything, don't you?" Mike felt something against his leg and looked down to see Muppet at his feet. "Where did you come from, fella?"

"He's my wingman. He was on the flank while I walked down the road, probably looking for rabbits or something."

"So, I'm guessing you couldn't sleep either."

"You figured that out all by yourself? I underestimated you." Mya's teeth shone in the moonlight.

"So, what, have you just come here to take the piss?"

"That was one of the reasons, but not the only one."

"What are the other reasons?"

"Hear me out before you immediately pooh-pooh the idea, okay?"

"Pooh-pooh. What are you, like eighty?"

"Do you want to ask me that again with your arm pinned behind your back and your face pressed up against the railings?"

"Nah. I'm good."

"Good then."

"Okay, so let's have it."

"There's a way we can get those trucks."

It was the only thing Mike had been thinking about since the meeting. Their situation was desperate, and no amount of local scavenging or foraging would help them. This was an eventuality he had never planned for. He had never envisaged a time when Safe Haven could have fallen, and now that it had, it was too late to take anything but desperate measures. "I'm listening."

"I worked in Glasgow on and off for five months. I know the city pretty well."

Mike's brow creased. "You worked in Glasgow? Why would somebody like you be stationed in Glasgow?"

Mya smiled. "It was my life's ambition to work as an usher at the Royal Concert Hall, Mike. They were the happiest few months of my life."

"Don't tell me then."

"Don't ask stupid questions. The point is we can get down there without using a drop of diesel."

"Okay. How exactly?"

"The Clyde runs right through the heart of the city. Jesus, the George the Fifth Bridge leads onto Oswald Street, which will take you right to Hope Street."

"You're a bit of a nerd, aren't you?"

"When your life hangs in the balance of making one wrong turn, Mike, it pays to know your surroundings inside out."

"I suppose." Mike unscrewed the top from his mug and was about to take a drink when Mya grabbed it from him and glugged a mouthful instead. "By all means. Help yourself."

"Thanks," she replied, handing it to him once more.

He took a drink, too, before screwing the lid on. "Say we sail down to Glasgow and get to the trucks without half a million plus infected descending on us. They'll have been sitting there a long time. The batteries will be dead. The fuel could be useless for all we know. Even if we manage to survive, and that's a big fucking if, it could be a complete waste of time, and that's something we don't have."

"What are the alternatives, Mike? We use the last of our fuel scavenging, hoping we can find a few scraps to feed people? We go out with our rucksacks every day foraging in wider and wider circles? How long before we run into a pack or a horde, and for what? You saw what they came back with today. We've got about a week's worth of food left, maybe a little more if we're careful and we keep sending people out. But after that, it's going to get very bad very fast."

"You think we can do this?"

Mya shrugged. "Like you said; there is so much that can go wrong it's scary. But I think it's our one last best chance to save the people here."

"And us?"

Mya shrugged. "People like you and I will always be okay, Mike."

"When we're not heading out on a suicide mission."

"Yeah. When we're not heading out on a suicide mission."

"Who'd go?"

"You can drive an HGV, yes?"

163

"I don't have a licence, but yes."

"I know Darren can too. And I make three. Three drivers for three trucks."

"That's it. You want just the three of us to head into Glasgow?"

"Given a choice, I'd like people who were good with weapons that didn't go bang too."

"You've got to be kidding me. The chances of us actually pulling this off are like a million to one. You want Wren, Robyn and Mila thrown into that mix? Without us, without them, this place is finished if there's any kind of trouble."

"This place is finished anyway, Mike. Heading down to Glasgow is the one thing that could save us."

"Jesus, Mya."

"And what about Raj and Talikha?"

"Raj and Talikha will be fine. We can't afford that mast to be seen where we're going, so we'd let them take us a good portion of the way up the Clyde then row the last couple of miles or so. There won't be any danger for them."

Mike turned to look at her. The potential dangers from the road seemed irrelevant now. "Tell me you've thought this through. Tell me you've thought about every aspect of this."

"I have. Whether you go or Raj goes, or Darren goes, or the others go, it doesn't matter. I'll find a way down there and I'll try to find a way back. I'd just feel better if I had backup. So, y'know, yes, I've thought about it, but it's not up to me whether you go, it's up to you."

"It'll probably take a couple of days to get there."

"Yeah."

"And then we've got no idea how long it might take to get back. We might find that roads have disintegrated or trees have come down. We might run into all sorts of problems."

"That's assuming we actually make it to the return journey," Mya said, her teeth glinting once more.

Mike shook his head. "This really is our only option, isn't it?"

"It's not the only one, Mike. But you and I have got a date with Olsen and this is the best one to make sure we get to it."

"What time is it?"

Mya looked at her watch. "It's eleven thirteen."

"Kat's due to take over from me at two. Do me a favour. Go get her now. Then get Em, Beck, Raj, Talikha, Darren and the council together."

"What, now?"

"The sooner we set off the sooner we get back."

"Or not as the case may be."

"Yeah. Or not."

*

"What's all this about, Mike?" Emma asked.

The centre wasn't exactly a hive of activity, but enough people had been awoken for tired mutterings and rumours to be abound. Rather than heading straight to the former PM's office, where everyone was undoubtedly awaiting their appearance, Mike had led Emma into the kitchen, where they now looked at each other in the light of a lantern. "I need you to hear me out before you flip."

"All the best conversations start like this. I can't wait. Go on."

"Mya came to see me while I was on lookout duty."

"Okay."

"She said that there's no need for us to go by road to Glasgow. We can sail right into the heart of it. She said that we could pretty much hop off the boat within spitting distance of Hope Street."

Emma didn't speak for a moment. She just stared at her brother. "I think I've already figured out why you asked me not to flip before you finished."

"Maybe I should have started at the end and worked my way back," he replied with a weak smile, and Emma let out a small laugh too.

"I haven't been able to think of anything else since that meeting," she admitted. "We're screwed every which way. If we don't do something, we're going to wither away and die. There's a good chance that whoever goes down there isn't going to come back and we'll still wither away and die. But if they succeed … then there'll be something that looks like a future."

"Exactly. I thought you were going to rip my head off."

"I hadn't thought about sailing down there. That actually gives the whole thing an air of plausibility. Rather than being a billion-to-one chance, it's much more like a million-to-one chance this way."

It was Mike's turn to let out a small laugh. "See. I knew I'd bring out the optimist in you one day."

Tears began to fall down Emma's face. "There's no other way, is there?"

"Well, there is. You, me and Sammy could go off now, just the three of us. We could take a satchel of food and head further down the coast. We'd survive … just the three of us. We'd live. We might even find a new settlement."

"And we'd be leaving our friends to die."

"Pretty much. But they'd have the same options, the same chances. A few of them would survive. Wren, Robyn, Mila. Mya, Jules and her brothers, Darren, possibly Vicky."

"And the others?"

"Not everyone can fight, Em."

"We have to protect them, don't we?"

"We started Safe Haven. We founded it with a view to looking after people, with a view to making sure no one went hungry. The community looked after everyone and vice versa. It would be the easiest thing in the world to look after ourselves. It's what people have been doing since the dawn of man, but that doesn't mean it's the right thing. It doesn't mean it's the decent thing. Before the outbreak, society was more polarised than ever. But we built something amazing in Safe Haven. We could walk out of here, you, me and Sammy. But we'd be saying that everything we did there was a lie."

Emma nodded and stepped towards her brother, wrapping her arms around him and pressing her head against his shoulder. "I'm so scared, Mike."

"Look. I've got no intention of dying."

"As opposed to all those other people who have every intention of dying?" she replied, holding him a little tighter.

"Exactly."

"That's not funny."

They both heard the hinge creak on the door and turned to see their little sister standing there, looking at them both. "How long have you been there, Sammy?" Mike asked.

"You're going to Glasgow?" she asked disbelievingly. Tears were already running down her face as the words came out of her mouth.

"Yeah," Mike said, beckoning her across. There was a pause before she started moving, but when she reached her siblings, she threw her arms around them both.

"Is it because we couldn't find much when we went out foraging today?"

Mike kissed his little sister on the head and held her tighter. "What you did today actually helped, Sammy. What I did was come home with a trailer full of nothing."

"It wasn't your fault. Nobody thinks it was your fault," she said, her voice quaking a little.

"It's not about fault, Sammy Bear. It's about doing what we need to in order for us to stay alive. Me going down to Glasgow gives us the best possible chance of doing that."

"Why does it always have to be you?"

"When there were more of us, we could share the responsibility around. But Hughes and Barnes and now Shaw's gone too. Em and you have to stay here to keep things ticking over."

Sammy pulled away from him and the streaks of silver on her cheeks shone like mirrors in the lantern light. "Don't patronise me."

Both Mike and Emma let out a short laugh. "What do you mean?" Mike asked.

"I heard Jenny say it to Shaw and I asked what it meant. It's what you're doing now."

"Hand on my heart, I'm not, Sammy. I'll be heading down there with Raj and Talikha, and with them gone and Wren gone I don't think there's another person here who knows more about foraging. I don't think you appreciate just how much you've learnt since we moved to Safe Haven."

The indignant look on Sammy's face dissipated. "Do you mean that?"

"You're damn right I mean it. We only have a few days' worth of food left, and if we're delayed getting back here, foraging could make all the difference. And with Em running things now, it looks good that you're contributing in such an important role too."

"Mike's right," Emma said, pulling back from her. "You've heard of the term leading by example?" Sammy nodded. "Well, that's what we need to do. You, me, Mike. We need to lead by example and show everyone that we're not giving up, so they shouldn't either."

Sammy wiped her face with the sleeve of her top. "But I don't want you to go."

"I know I made a promise to you, Sammy. But if I don't do this, then it's going to end badly for everyone."

"You said that the three of us could survive together. You said we could go down the coast and carry on."

Mike crouched down in front of Sammy and nodded. "That's true. The three of us would probably be okay if it came to it. And right here, right now, if you tell me that's what you want to do, then that's what we'll do."

The young girl was taken aback and her mouth dropped open a little. "You mean that?"

"I mean that, Sammy. If you want us to go, then we'll pack a bag tonight and go."

"It's true," Emma said, perching herself on one of the countertops. "Tell us you want us to go and we'll go, just the three of us."

A small flame of excitement flickered inside the young girl for a moment. "And Wren and Robyn and Mila?"

"I can't speak for them, but they're survivors. They'd stand just as good a chance as us."

A smile crept onto Sammy's face and her eyes began to dance a little. But then it was gone in an instant as her thoughts drifted to others. "And what about Jenny and Meg?"

"We'd be leaving everyone behind, Sammy. We couldn't take some and not others."

"But how would they survive?"

Mike fixed Sammy with a sad stare. "She probably wouldn't. And Ruth and Richard and Jack and Ruby and Tommy and the children we brought down here probably wouldn't either."

"So, we could live but it would mean others dying?"

Mike nodded. "The only way this works is if we all pull together. Everyone has a place and everyone has a skill set. It's just that sometimes those skills don't include foraging, or scavenging, or fighting. Sometimes it's knowledge. Sometimes it's knowing how to make a bow or getting an engine to work."

"We couldn't do it. We couldn't leave them."

Mike took hold of Sammy's hands. "So, you're telling me right here, right now, that we're staying, that we're going to do everything we can to make a go of this?"

"Yes." Mike flung his arms around her again. "I'm so proud of you."

When she pulled back, her tears glistened in the lantern light once more. "You'll be careful, won't you?"

Mike smiled. "I'm always careful."

*

There was a tap on the door and it took Mila a few seconds to realise that it wasn't part of a dream. She fumbled with the dynamo lantern at the side of her bed, finally finding the switch.

"Ugh. What are you doing?" Robyn asked. "It's the middle of the frikkin' night." They had heard George leave earlier on after someone had come to the door, but they simply assumed it was something that needed fixing as usual. Now, though, someone was knocking on their room door.

Wolf let out a short, sharp bark. "Settle down, boy," Wren said, barely awake and hoping beyond hope that Mila was mistaken.

"There was a knock on our door," Mila said.

"You were dreaming. Go back to sleep," Robyn whined.

Tap. Tap. Tap.

Wren's eyes slowly opened and she shuffled up. It was a twin-bedded room, but they had dragged another one in so they could all sleep together. "Hello?" she called out.

"Are you decent?"

"Mike?"

The door slowly opened inwards and Wolf jumped down and walked up to greet their visitor. "Hello, boy," Mike said, crouching down to stroke him.

"Err … what's going on?" Robyn asked, sitting up a little further in bed.

The lantern that Mila had put on threw out enough light and Mike turned his own torch off. "You might want to put some clothes on. I'll be waiting in the living room when you're done." With that, he closed the door, leaving the three girls alone.

"Oh, I so don't like this," Robyn said.

"Do you think it's something to do with Grandad?" Wren asked, jumping out of bed and sliding her jeans on.

A look of panic swept over the others' faces and they started to get dressed with equal haste. It was a matter of seconds before the three of them, closely followed by Wolf, were barging back out of the door and into the living room.

Mike had lit another lantern and was sitting down in the armchair while they all took seats on the couch. "It's Grandad, isn't it?" Robyn said, any thoughts of sleep long forgotten.

"What is?" Mike asked, confused.

"What do you mean what is? Why you've woken us up in the middle of the frikkin' night."

Mike shook his head. "No. They're about to start a council meeting upstairs. George is fine."

"Well … no offence, Mike. It is lovely to see you. But why have you knocked us all up in the middle of the night?" Mila asked.

There was a pause of a few seconds before the other three laughed. "Err … I wasn't aware I had."

A look of confusion swept over Mila's face until Robyn grabbed her arm. "Knocking a girl up means something different over here."

Mila shrugged. "I do not understand. You were there too. We were asleep and he knocked us all up."

Robyn and Wren laughed again. "I know a bloke who got arrested for that."

"It's a euphemism for getting someone pregnant," Wren said.

"Ah. You English. Nothing is ever simple with your language. I think I might have heard this before but had forgotten." She turned back to Mike. "So, why did you wake us?" She turned to Wren. "Wake is alright. I can say this without you getting the gigglies, yes?"

"Wake is fine," Wren replied.

Mila returned her gaze to Mike. "Why did you wake us?"

"Because I've got something to ask you."

"If it is did we sleep well, I may kill you."

Mike smiled. "I really wish it was something that inane."

171

"Okay, Mike," Wren said. "You haven't woken us up at this time for nothing. What is it?"

"Mya and I are heading down to Glasgow."

"What?" all three of them replied in unison.

"She's figured out that we can actually get into the heart of the city by boat."

Wren let out a nervous laugh. "You're kidding me."

"No. She says we can sail straight up the Clyde and the—"

"I don't mean you're kidding me about that. I mean you're kidding me about actually contemplating doing this."

"No. It's our last best chance."

"You call this a last best chance? What about the six hundred thousand plus infected who are going to be waiting for you down there?"

"Mya reckons there's a place we can moor that's not that far from where we need to be."

"And what about getting back out again? You're just going to drive the trucks through an infested city with no problems at all and head back here?"

"I doubt we'll be that lucky."

"So, this is why you've got us all out of bed. You're here to say your last farewell. I'm guessing Emma and Sammy aren't actually talking to you, so you thought you'd find someone who would."

"Emma and Sammy are on board with this."

"Yeah, right."

"They know it's our only hope."

"It's not our only hope," Wren replied irritably. "We could try scavenging elsewhere."

"Ja," Mila said. "When I was living by myself, I had to go further and further afield, but I did not go hungry. I survived. We will just need to adapt. We will need to—"

"There's a big difference between feeding yourself and feeding seventy-odd people, Mila."

The German woman's shoulders sagged and she leaned back on the couch.

"You're wanting us to go with you, aren't you?" Robyn said. She had remained quiet, just watching Mike and listening to his words as he spoke to the others, but now all the pieces had fallen into place.

"Mya would like you to come with us."

"And you don't?"

Mike gulped, doing his best not to get emotional. "You're family to me. I love you. The last thing I want is for any of you to be in harm's way. I don't want you anywhere near Glasgow, but at the same time…."

"At the same time what?" Wren asked.

"I think our chances are greatly improved if you come. You're all adept with your weapons and practically silent. You're quick, you're smart, and you've spent more time out on the road than anyone."

There was a long pause before Wren spoke again. "What do you think our chances of doing this are?"

"Better than our chances of everyone here surviving if we don't."

A sudden bang made them all jump, and a few seconds later, George appeared in the doorway to the living room. "Get out," he shouted, looking at Mike. "Get the hell out of here."

"Grandad!" Wren cried, jumping to her feet.

George ignored her and marched across to Mike, grabbing him by the arm and pulling him up. "George," Mike said, standing and shaking his arm free. "I'm—"

"You're getting out; that's what you're doing. Get out of here and don't come back."

"Grandad, stop!" Wren pleaded as George took hold of Mike's arm once more and started guiding him to the door. Wolf let out a disconcerted whine as the tension in the room notched up another level.

Mike turned back to look at his three friends. "We'll probably be heading out within the hour," he said, and this time George punched him in the back, forcing him out of the door. He used his stick to slam it shut behind Mike and then he turned to the girls. "The last time you ran out on me, I was in no fit state to do anything about it, but I'll be damned if I let you go on some bloody suicide mission."

"Mike was only telling us about it, Grandad. We haven't even discussed it yet."

"And you're not going to. It's bloody madness."

"So, you're saying it's okay for Mike and Mya to go and risk their lives for all of us but not us?"

"That's exactly what I'm saying. I would hope Mya would have known better. I don't know. Maybe she just wants a way out. Maybe she wants to go out in a blaze of glory, but Mike…." George tapped his temple several times. "He's always been a bit strange in the head, that one. Don't get me wrong. He's got us out of a lot of scrapes, but it was just a matter of time before something like this came along … some mad mission that would finish him off."

"How can you say that, Grandad?" Wren asked, horrified.

"Because it's the truth. And him coming here to try to coax you three along. I'm not having it. I'm not having any of it."

"Heading to Glasgow is the only way we're going to survive this, Grandad. It's the only way we're not all going to starve to death." It was Robyn who spoke now, standing with Wren shoulder to shoulder.

"No. It's the only sure-fire way you three won't survive. Look. We'll figure something out. There've got to be more places to scavenge around here to give us a stopgap until we've got something more permanent sorted."

"Mya said that if we could—"

"I don't give a damn what Mya said," George yelled, cutting Wren off and making all three girls go rigid with shock. They'd seen him disappointed, sad, and frustrated, but they'd never seen him raging like this.

The atmosphere in the room was so thick, so heavy; it was like they were all trapped in lava. "You don't get to choose for us," Wren eventually said.

"Like hell I don't. If you want to stay under my roof—"

"It's not your roof. We're not in Inverness anymore. We're not even in Safe Haven. This is no more your place than it is ours and there are plenty of spare rooms that we can move into. We haven't decided if we're going or not. We're going to discuss it quietly and rationally, just the three of us. It will be our choice, our decision. You might like to think we're all just your little girls, Grandad, but the world's changed a lot since we used to visit in the school holidays. People depend on us. People need us. You're my grandad, and I love you, and I always will, but there are bigger things at stake here than you just having your cosy little family life."

"I…." George didn't know how to respond. Wren had never raised her voice to him like that before.

"Now, we may decide that you're right, and we choose to stay. On the other hand, we may decide that it really is the only option, in which case we'll be heading out with Mike and Mya. Either way, it will be up to us, and no amount of threats or blackmail, emotional or otherwise, will sway us." Wren tapped her leg, and Wolf, who had been standing off to one side, more than a little distressed as this family drama had continued to unfold, went after her.

Even in the lantern light, Robyn and Mila could see how heavy George's eyes were as they walked past him in silence and followed Wren out of the living room.

When the door closed behind them, George collapsed into the armchair and started to sob.

CHRISTOPHER ARTINIAN

13

It was like something out of a gut-wrenching nightmare. Emma and Sammy had clung to him like koalas holding on to a branch for dear life. Eventually, he had broken their grasp and held hands as they'd walked him out to the Land Rover. They had clutched each other tightly one last time before he'd climbed in. When it moved away, they were still standing there watching and waving sadly as if it was the last time they would ever see him, which, given the circumstances, it might very well have been.

"So, this is nice. I've been meaning to go on a cruise for the longest time," Mya said as she walked up to Mike. Humphrey gently nudged Mike's leg, a little unnerved by the early morning adventure but happy to have so many friendly faces on the yacht at the same time. Muppet remained glued to Mya's side. They had been travelling for over an hour and Mike had been just on the verge of heading below deck to get some sleep before Mya had appeared.

"Yeah. Shame there's no casino or bar."

Mya reached into her rucksack and brought out a large hip flask. "I keep this in case of emergencies," she said, unscrewing the top before handing it to Mike.

He grabbed it gratefully and took a gulp too. "Thanks," he said, giving it back to her. They both stood by the railing, looking out over the moonlit sea. "How is everyone down there?"

"The girls were still just about awake when I came up here. Darren was out like a light."

"Is he okay?"

"He was freaked at having to leave Beck and his family, but he understands that if we don't do something, it's going to end badly for everyone."

"He does know that he's not still on the payroll, doesn't he?"

"He knows, Mike. It's all about duty with Darren and L—dammit." She was about to say Les's name when it caught on her tongue. Everything had happened so quickly that it was hard to take it all in. "Dammit," she said again, chastising herself.

"Are you okay?"

"If we get this done, I will be."

"And if we don't?"

"Then I'll probably be a long, long way from okay, but chances are that I won't notice."

"What was all that stuff you did with the batteries before we set off?"

"Don't ask me, ask Darren. It was something about wanting them both to have as much charge as possible, so we took the Land Rover battery out and replaced it with the one that we scavenged from the farm. Then he gave it a push to start it and we ran it for about twenty minutes or so before setting off."

"Yeah, but to what end?"

"Like I said, ask Darren. All I know is that my rucksack and his are really heavy. We're each carrying a car battery and a load of jumper cables."

"I'll take it for you."

"That's sweet. I'll manage though."

"Yeah, until we run into a horde."

"Well, aren't you just Mister Lightness and Joy?"

Mike let out a small laugh. "I forgot how much I need to be thankful for right now; heading into the centre of the most populous city in Scotland on some crazy mission that's probably going to put us all in the ground. I should be at the top of the mast singing 'Hallelujah'."

"You agreed to come."

"Well, it's only polite, isn't it? If your friend says she's going to commit suicide by zombie horde, it's just the decent thing to join her."

Mya took another drink and then handed it back to Mike. "Joking aside. We can do this. I wouldn't have suggested it if there was no chance."

"And how much of a chance do you give us exactly?"

"Some."

Mike laughed and took another swig before giving the flask back to Mya. "Keep talking. You're making me feel so much better."

"It's not like we had any kind of choice, is it?"

"I suppose not. But ... I mean ... is there anything that scares you? Is there anything that fazes you at all?"

"Some things."

"Like what exactly?"

It was Mya's turn to laugh. "You'll see soon enough."

"What the hell's that supposed to mean?"

Mya handed the flask back to Mike. "There's one other person in the world that I've ever confided this to."

"Okay. Now you've definitely got my attention."

"Tunnels."

"What?"

"I have a thing about tunnels."

"Err...."

"I know."

"But—"

"I know, Mike."

"Mya. I've got your back. You know that. I'll do whatever I have to when we reach our destination. But we're going to be heading down into the deepest, darkest depths of the underground beneath the city."

"I know, Mike."

"And you're only bringing this up now?"

"You did ask."

"In fairness. Yeah. I did. I was hoping it was going to be sock puppets or nuns or something."

"Well, now you know."

"Yeah. So——"

"Look. Don't dwell on it. I hate them, but I'll do my job just like always. One of my last missions was in the Paris underground, funnily enough. And I'm here to tell the tale, aren't I?"

"So, you're not going to freak out on us when we're down there?"

"Let's hope not."

"Like I said, I always feel so much better when I speak to you."

"Oh, so you're scared of nothing?"

"I'm scared of not seeing my family again."

"I mean anything physical."

"Sharks."

"Sharks?"

Mike shrugged and handed the flask back to his drinking companion. "Yeah. You got a problem with that?"

"Err ... no. But...."

"But what?"

"Have you come up against many sharks?"

"No. Never seen one."

"And yet they're your biggest fear?"

"Hey, look. A tunnel is just a tunnel. It's a route underground, that's all. It can't hurt you; it's just a passageway. Sharks can swim twenty-five miles per hour. They can smell blood in the water from a quarter of a mile away. They've got teeth like razors, and they don't have eyelids, so even when they're asleep they're monitoring everything that's going on around them. I'd say that's plenty to be scared of, wouldn't you?"

"Okay, okay. Chill. I was just making conversation. And FYI, it's not really the tunnel; it's what lies in the darkness beyond it that freaks me out."

They stood in comfortable silence for a few moments before Mike spoke again. "So, who was this other person that you confided in?"

"Hmm?"

"The other person you told your deep, dark secret about tunnels to."

Mya took another drink before handing it back to Mike. "My partner … kind of. We worked together a few times. He was my friend too. And you don't build many friendships in my business."

"Did he die before the outbreak?"

"No. It was soon after it had started."

"I'm sorry."

"What for? You didn't kill him."

Mike handed the flask back to Mya. "I know, but it's never easy to lose friends. I've lost plenty."

Mya let out a long sigh. "I've never had that many to lose." She screwed the top back on the flask. "Well, all this talk about tunnels, sharks, losing friends, and impending doom has made me tired. I think I might head below and grab some sleep."

"Yeah. I think I'll join you. Something tells me that when we hit Glasgow, it's going to be a long, long time before either of us gets any rest."

"Not necessarily. We could end up having the longest rest we've ever had."

"You've got a really twisted sense of humour, y'know that?"

"Who says I'm joking?"

*

Sammy had drifted off in Emma's arms. It had been a long time since she had done that, and when they both woke up, there was a brief and wonderful moment of confusion before the reasons leading up to them crying themselves to sleep while holding each other close came flooding back to haunt them.

Muted sounds from the kitchen came drifting towards them and they both slowly rose from the bed they had shared.

"Are you okay?" Emma asked.

"I'm thirsty," Sammy replied.

"Go into my rucksack. There's a bottle of water in there."

There was a knock, and a ripple of unease shivered through the two of them. Emma stood up and walked to the entrance, opening the door slightly to see who it was. Jules was standing there with a forced smile on her face. "I thought we could all eat together."

"Yeah. We've only just woken up. Come in," Emma said, beckoning her friend into the room.

Jules walked past her and went to sit on the bed that was still made from the previous day. "Kat's organising everything in the kitchen. She's not exactly Mary, but she's doing okay. She's got Ephraim helping her."

"Ephraim?" Emma asked, walking back to the bed. She and Sammy had both slept in their clothes, other than socks, which Emma slipped back on as she continued to get a morning roundup from her friend.

"Yeah. Things are a little better since they came back with all the extra cutlery, crockery and pots and pans yesterday. People won't have to wait as long to be fed and watered."

"What's the mood like? I'm guessing people have heard what happened last night."

"You'd be guessing right." Jules shrugged. "The mood's pretty good, all things considered."

"Good?"

"Yeah."

"I suppose they can afford to be in good moods when it's not their family out there, can't they?"

"Actually, maybe good isn't the right word. Maybe hopeful is what I should have said."

"Hopeful?"

"Yeah. I mean, y'know, look who's gone down there. They've all seen those people pull miracles out of their hats before, so—" Jules stopped herself and her shoulders sagged as she realised what she had said. She looked towards Sammy. "I'm sorry. I didn't mean it like that. It's not a miracle, of course, it's not, because your brother and Mya will—"

"I'm not a baby, Jules. I know what's going on," Sammy said.

"No.... No, of course you're not. I'm sorry, Sammy. Anyway," she continued, turning back to Emma, "you've got more volunteers who want to head out foraging with you today and—"

"I'm not sure that's a good idea considering Raj and Talikha aren't here," Emma replied.

"Why?" Sammy asked.

"It's just a lot of responsibility, Sammy. I mean, yesterday, it took all three of you to monitor what people were picking, making sure they were doing it right and not digging up something that was going to make us ill. And if more people want to go out today, it will be even harder. Maybe we should just wait until—"

"I can do it. I did it plenty when we were back in Safe Haven."

"I know, but it's just—"

"I want to do it."

"Sammy, I—"

"I want to do it. Mike's had to go because there isn't enough food for everyone. Well, if we can find more, it gives him more time, doesn't it? It gives him and Wren and Mya more time to search for what they're looking for and get back here. If I can help find us more food, then it's better for everybody, and things might not get as bad as quickly." It was clear that the young girl was on the verge of tears as she spoke.

"Okay, okay, Sammy. You're right. We'll go out again after breakfast, okay?"

Sammy nodded, seemingly placated by Emma's answer. "Okay."

"Now, do me a favour. Go see if you can rustle up a cup of tea for me, will you, while I wake up?"

"You are awake."

"We've had this discussion before. Adults can be physically awake, but their heads can still be asleep. That's why we need caffeine."

Sammy let out a long sigh. "Don't think I'm not aware that this is so you can talk without me here," she said, walking across the room and disappearing out of the door.

"She's got an old fuckin' head on her shoulders has that one," Jules said.

"Tell me about it. So, what's really going on down there?"

"It's pretty much what I told you. There are a lot of nerves though. I think people were so preoccupied with getting here that they didn't actually think about what would happen when they arrived."

"I get that."

"Beck and his kids are in the kitchen helping out."

"Beck?"

"Yeah. He's doing pretty well too. I think the fact that he's mucking in is making people feel a little better about things. Everybody wants this to work, Emma, but there's like a dark cloud hanging over the place."

"Have you seen George? Apparently, he struck out at Mike last night."

"He was in the workshop when I got up this morning. I don't know if he's been in there all night or what."

"I should probably speak to him."

"I'd say you're best leaving him alone for a while."

Emma shrugged. "You know him better than I do."

"I was thinking maybe Andy, Rob, and Jon should head out with you if a bigger group is going foraging today."

"I really don't think it's a good idea at all, given everything that's going on I'd prefer them here to keep an eye on things."

"Words I never thought I'd hear in my fuckin' life."

Emma laughed. "Who'd have thought, right?"

"Then I'll come with you and maybe I can get Vicky to go too."

"What about our vegetable garden?" Emma asked with half a smile.

Jules' shoulders drooped. "You and I both know that unless your brother and the others come back with the goods, there's about as much point to us digging over that ground as there is to ... well ... I don't fuckin' know what. But it's pointless anyway."

"Well, Jules, if there are any people who can get us out of this mess, it's Mike, Mya and those girls.

"Amen."

*

Shaw froze. He'd seen movement up ahead but wasn't sure what it was exactly. In fact, he wasn't sure of much anymore. His head was a giant jumble. He'd heard Mike talk once about how his brain was sometimes like a million different Christmas tree lights all flashing on and off in no pattern. That's what he felt like at the moment. Everything was so confusing. One minute, he'd be planning a future for himself, and the next, he'd be thinking about swallowing his gun. One moment he'd be laughing with genuine happiness; the next, he'd be sobbing.

It was overwhelming. *Shit!*

Two creatures broke from the trees and charged into the clearing towards him. *I knew it was a mistake to come into the forest ... and yet I did it anyway.*

He slipped the rifle from his shoulder and grabbed his hunting knife. They were both on him at the same time. Shaw kicked out hard, forcing one back while he brought his knife up through the palate of the other. It dropped like a rock and he readied himself for the first creature once more. *How many times have I done this? How many times will I have to do it again? It's an endless, pointless cycle.*

The monster pounced, and this time, Shaw swung his left fist, smashing it in the jaw and sending it flailing to the ground. It had been an age since he'd punched anybody or anything. He wasn't quite sure why he'd done it now, but there the creature lay. It began to scramble and Shaw pushed his foot down on its back. Its nose cracked as it mashed into the dried earth of the forest floor. Shaw dropped down, placing one knee on the monster's back. He thrust the knife up through the base of the creature's skull and in a split second it stopped struggling.

He remained there for just a breath before wiping the blade off and returning the knife to his belt. He walked across and collected his rifle then looked back at his two victims. It was only then that he realised they wore the uniform of Olsen's soldiers. Hatred jolted through him like electricity. "Fuckers!" he hissed, and for the first time in quite a while, all the lights in his head stopped flashing. His contempt for Olsen and her people was the one thing he was sure of. It was the one thing that made sense to him.

His mind drifted to Lucy and Jake, then to Barnes, then Mary and Shona and Prisha and Saanvi. Their faces and the hundreds of others they had lost flashed in front of him as if they were on a cinema reel.

What am I doing? What am I doing here?

*

It was late morning when Billy proposed they stop for a break. They had been cycling continuously since leaving the house overlooking Kyle at about six a.m. Although they had been able to fill their water bottles, they had not eaten.

Gummy had complained more or less continually that he was hungry, but when he was struggling to pedal he became a lot quieter, so setting off on the bikes was infinitely preferable to remaining in the house. Although they had seen signs of a few infected in Kyle, they had not run into any. When they had gone over the bridge to Skye, they had done so with trepidation. But they were a long way into their journey, and as they skirted the north of the island, they had only seen the remains of infected from some previous battles. One thing had weighed heavily on them though. A vast tower of smoke in the distance was a sure-fire sign that they were not alone on Skye.

"Y'know, not for nothing, but I have to agree with Gummy. I'm starving too," Galli said as she stole a moment with Billy. She glanced back to the others, who were both examining their bikes.

At that exact moment, Billy's stomach rumbled. "I know. Hopefully, we'll stumble across somewhere soon enough and we might find a few bits and pieces in their cupboards that will keep us going."

"And if we don't?"

"I don't know." He took hold of her hand and they both looked out over the shimmering sea.

"I suppose we could fish."

"I suppose. When we find somewhere, we'll check to see if there's any tackle."

"What are we going to do, Billy?"

"What do you mean?"

"I mean long term."

"I think we need to concentrate on the short term for the time being. We need to find somewhere and lie low for a while."

"For how long?"

"I don't know. Long enough for us to come up with a better plan. Maybe we go further south. Maybe we can find other communities because God knows there's nothing left to the north."

"Other communities? And how long before we run into Olsen again?"

"I don't know, Toni. What do you want from me? All this has only just happened."

"I'm sorry," she replied, squeezing his hand a little tighter.

A sinking feeling began in Billy's stomach. None of this had been thought out. It was a rushed decision to head down here and the reality of it was starting to catch up with them. "Look. One thing's for sure. We're not going to find any food or more permanent shelter while we're standing here like a couple of teenagers on a first date, are we?" he said, turning towards her with a smile on his face. He leaned in and kissed her on the cheek. "We'll be okay. Trust me." A smile lit her face, but behind her eyes he could see doubt.

14

A string of expletives rose from the galley, much to the amusement of those waiting to be served their evening meal. Mike and Wren finally emerged with two trays and placed them down on the table of the dinette.

"I'd know that smell anywhere," Robyn said.

"Let us guess. Vegetable chili," Mila said with a smile.

"You know me well," Mike replied.

"I will eat mine with Raj," Talikha said, grabbing two of the bowls and heading above deck.

"I don't think those two have slept a wink since we set off," Darren said, standing up and helping to distribute the bowls around the table.

"In all the time I've known them, they've never let us down," Mike replied.

"Certainly two of the nicest people I've ever met. Sorry, three," Darren said, giving Humphrey a stroke as he sat down at the table. "Here you go, boy." He gave a cracker to the salivating Labrador Retriever; then he fed one to Muppet and Wolf, who were sitting patiently by his side. The dogs lay down and began to chomp on their snacks.

Mike dished out the chili into bowls and placed them down one by one. Robyn didn't wait for the others. She immediately grabbed her spoon and shovelled in a mouthful of the steaming food. "Hor! Hor!" she said, fanning her mouth wildly and taking a drink of water.

"What is wrong with you?" Mike asked, finally taking a bowl for himself and sitting down.

"If anybody could figure that out, they'd have been able to make a million in private practice," Wren said, and the others laughed politely.

Robyn glugged down half a glass of water before doing the same again, causing the others to laugh once more. "This is really good," she said, eventually composing herself long enough to speak. "Different."

"From someone with such a discerning palate, I take that as a huge compliment. Thank you," Mike replied, smiling.

Robyn grinned, revealing bits of food still stuck in her teeth.

"You are such a pig, Bobbi," Wren said, shaking her head.

Mila shook her head. "We lived in close proximity to pigs for some time. They are loving, sweet and intelligent animals. To compare them to Robyn is most unfair."

"Actually, this is really good," Mya said, scooping a mouthful using one of the crackers.

"No need to sound so surprised," Mike replied.

"I just didn't have you down as a chef, that's all."

"I can't cook much. But this was a staple for me back at home. I used to make a big pot that would last for days."

"You did all the cooking at home?"

Mike spooned in a mouthful of food. He chewed it for a while before swallowing then took a drink. "Not all the cooking. We split a lot of duties. When Em was down in Portsmouth, I pretty much did it all. Alex finished later than I did, so it was only fair that—"

"Alex?" Darren asked.

"My stepdad. Well ... actually ... my dad. The only one that counted anyway. Yeah, well, before Leeds went into lockdown, I did a lot more and then we started splitting the duties. But I always tended to make my own meals anyway, being a veggie, and this was something I could make for a few days at a time."

"It's good," Robyn said again, shovelling in another mouthful.

"Normally, I finely chop a lot of veg as a substitute for the mince. There is some chopped veg in there, but the bulk of it is lentils. It gives it a different consistency." Mike looked down at his plate for a moment and let out a short laugh.

"What is it?" Mya asked.

"We're here, the six of us, sitting around this table talking about food and our lives as if it's just any other day, any other mealtime. It's like…. It doesn't matter."

"The last supper," Mila asked.

"Well. Yeah," Mike replied.

"Dwelling on what's facing us tomorrow will do absolutely no good. Trust me. I know of what I speak. Forgetting all about it, having a good meal, and spending time in the company of friends is the best possible thing we can do."

"Amen, sister," Darren said, raising his glass of water.

"I suppose you're right," Mike replied. "Plus, I always wanted to go sightseeing around Glasgow. It could be fun."

"Somehow, I doubt that," said Mya.

"Yeah. Me too. But we can live in hope."

They finished their meals, forcing good humour all the way through. They laughed louder than they should have at jokes that didn't merit it. They smiled more than was comfortable. They stroked and hugged and fussed Humphrey, Wolf and Muppet more than they had been in some time. When all the crockery, pots and pans had been cleaned and put away, Darren made his excuses and turned in while the others returned to the table.

"Shame we haven't got any booze," Robyn said.

"I'm sure Raj and Talikha have an emergency supply around here somewhere," Mike replied. "But in fairness, we should probably have a clear head going into tomorrow."

"Fair enough, I suppose."

"We should play a game, yes?" Mila said, doing her best to keep the artificially buoyant mood afloat.

"I spy," Robyn said enthusiastically.

"We are not playing I spy," Wren replied. "Maybe Raj and Talikha have got some board games around here somewhere."

"How about book, film, music?" Mike asked.

"What?" the others all asked in unison.

"You choose your favourite book, your favourite film and your favourite piece of music."

"How is that a game?" Robyn asked.

"It's just a bit of fun."

"I like it," Wren said.

"Ja. I also think this would be interesting."

"It's not a game though," Robyn replied.

"It is better than I spy."

"But I like I spy."

"Ja, and snap and *Hungry Hungry Hippos*. You have the mind of an infant."

"Rather have the mind of an infant than the arse of an elephant."

"Now, now, children. Play nice," Mya said.

"I will go first, yes?" Mila said, clapping her hands.

The five of them remained at the table for well over an hour, revelling in one another's company and reminiscing. Mila's selections took her back to her childhood, where she spoke of family life, growing up. Wren came to an epiphany that her choices were all from the time she received the letter saying that she had been selected for the Commonwealth Games squad.

Mya came to a similar revelation. For all the hardships she had encountered growing up, her favourite book, film and music were all born out of the final year she spent at home, the final year she had a minimal amount of responsibility.

There was a time when Robyn would have dreaded these questions. Up until her imprisonment by the crazy vegan chicks who wanted to turn her into human bacon, she had never picked up a book for entertainment. Since then, she had not exactly become a voracious reader, but she had read a lot more than she had ever thought possible.

"Okay, Bobbi. Your turn now," Wren said, looking up at Mike. "This was a great idea. If I'd known Mya was a Cher fan, I'd have been far less intimidated by her."

Mya laughed out loud. "One song, girlie. One song. I'll gladly go head-to-head with the rest of our music credentials."

"We are all waiting, Robyn," Mila said, stroking Wolf's head. The dogs had somehow managed to position themselves on the seating so they were all lying across someone's lap. Despite the laughter and levity, they continued to laze and slumber.

"Okay, okay," Robyn said. "You've all got to promise not to laugh."

"We can make no such guarantees. Come. Tell us."

"Okay. Book has to be *The Fault in Our Stars*."

"I've never heard of that," Mike replied.

"You really need to read it. It's this beautiful, heartbreaking, romantic—"

"I'll stop you there."

"Oh, I've read that," Mya said. "It really is a tear-jerker."

"I know, right?"

"I am impressed," Mila said. "I was expecting *Green Eggs and Ham* or *The Adventures of Winnie the Pooh*."

"Film has to be *The Blair Witch Project*."

"Really?" Mike asked. "I mean it's an excellent horror movie and very clever, but your favourite?"

"Yeah," Robyn replied.

"My sister has a thing about witches."

"You name another film where the cast actually dies.... I mean in real life, not pretend."

Mike suddenly looked confused while Wren folded her arms on the table and placed her forehead down. "Not this again," she mumbled.

"Err ... the cast didn't die in real life," Mike said, still not sure whether Robyn was joking or not.

"I'm not talking about the remake. I'm talking about the original."

"Yeah. It was a movie. It was a very well-done movie, but the cast didn't die."

Robyn shook her head. "I was a member of the Real Blair Witch group on Facebook, and I'm telling you, there were people on there who were actually from Burkittsville itself and they told me that they met Heather and the others before they all went out. The whole thing was so totally real."

"You think it's real because people on social media said so?"

"I did my own research."

"Oh God," Wren muttered again.

"I totally checked these people out. I was friends with some of them. They offered to send me real-life artefacts and stuff, but ... y'know, they were pretty expensive and I was saving up for this Rebecca Minkoff bag at the time, so I couldn't really afford it."

"What's a Rebecca Minkoff bag?" Mike asked.

"Seriously? What century are you even from?" Mike raised his eyebrows. "Anyway, one of them sent me footage of the spot where Josh went missing. And what's so sad is they were nearly back at their car by that time. If that idiot, Mike, hadn't thrown the map away, they'd probably have been able to figure it out."

Mike continued to look at her in disbelief. "You can't blame him. The Blair Witch might have possessed him and made him do it."

Wren giggled a little, keeping her head buried in her arms and shaking it a little. A look of dawning swept over Robyn's face. "I never thought of that. Y'know, I really hated that dick for what he did, but that's a good point. It might not have been in his control."

"You are a dummkopf," Mila said. "It was so completely make-believe."

"You're just ignorant. That's the problem. People aren't willing to look into things like this. They all live in their own little worlds and think that there's nothing beyond. Well, there is totally something beyond this."

"Okay," Mya said, trying to stop a full-scale argument from breaking out. "And music? What's your favourite piece of music?"

Robyn paused for a moment, still on edge from the mini-confrontation. "Queen – 'The Show Must Go On'."

Wren brought her head up from the table and looked at her sister. "Really?" she asked.

"Yeah."

Wren reached out and took her sibling's hand before turning to the others. "That was our dad's favourite song."

A thin film of tears formed in Robyn's eyes. "I played it on a loop after he and Mum…." She couldn't bring herself to finish the sentence. "Whenever I think of them now, that song plays in my head. It's silly, isn't it? How a piece of music can be a soundtrack to something or someone in your life."

"It's not silly at all, Bobbi," Wren said. "If Dad was here now, he'd be so happy that all those years of musical indoctrination had paid off."

Robyn laughed and wiped her eyes. "Yeah. He's probably up there now, peeing himself."

"Your vater had excellent taste," Mila said.

"Yeah," Mya added. "I suppose it's an incredibly apt song for what's happening at the moment too."

"I suppose it is," Robyn replied, looking up at the ceiling briefly, almost as if she was searching for a nod of approval from above, before wiping her eyes and turning to Mike. "So, come on," she said, smiling through her tears. "Book, film, music."

Mike took a deep breath. "It's funny. When I did this all that time back with Em, Luce and Samantha, I—"

"Sammy?"

"No. Samantha was a nurse we lost on the journey up here, thanks to Fry."

"Oh. I'm sorry."

Mike nodded. "Considering no music, no books and no films have been released since, I thought my choices would always remain the same."

"And they're not?" Mya asked.

Mike shook his head. "One of them is. *Seven Samurai* is still my all-time favourite movie."

"Ah. Sehr, sehr gut," Mila said. "It is a true classic. Possibly Kurosawa's finest."

"*Seven Samurai*?" Robyn asked, wiping the final traces of tears from her face.

"It is an epic Japanese black-and-white film by arguably the most influential director in modern cinema."

"Never heard of it."

"Yes. This surprises me in no way whatsoever."

"I'm just not into artsy-fartsy stuff." A crooked smile broke on Mike's face as he and Mila shared a look.

"But your other choices have changed?" Mya asked, turning in her seat to look at him.

Mike let out another long breath. "You could say that."

"Now I'm intrigued. Come on then. Let us have them."

"Favourite song, Guns N' Roses – 'Paradise City'. Favourite book, *Charlotte's Web*."

"Okay. I get 'Paradise City'. *Charlotte's Web* is definitely going to need some explanation."

Mike was about to speak when Wren took over. "I heard this story." Everyone's eyes turned towards her, including Mike's. "Lucy told me." She turned to look at Mya. "Lucy had a daughter called Charlotte … Charlie. They used to read it together. She treasured that book, and when she made her escape from Leeds, she was forced to leave it behind. It nearly broke her heart."

Mike looked down at the table, and now it was his turn to try to hold back the tears. "So, that's why it's your favourite book?" Mya asked softly.

"We haven't got to the best part yet," Wren said. "A horde was about to descend on them when one of their vehicles got a flat during the escape. Mike led them away and they all thought they'd never see him again. He showed up the following day. Not only that, he'd found a copy of *Charlotte's Web* and he gave it to Lucy, so she'd always be able to keep her little Charlie with her."

A stream of tears rolled down Wren's face and she looked up to Mike, whose head was bowed. She glanced at Mya, then Robyn and finally Mila. All of them were crying while the dogs continued to slumber happily. "I have never heard this before," Mila said. "This is a most beautiful story."

"I thought this was going to be fun," Mike said eventually, wiping his eyes and coaxing laughter from the others. "Never let me pick the fucking games again."

They laughed a little more this time. "Well," Robyn said, wiping her nose on her sleeve, "if we're still alive this time tomorrow, I say we play I spy."

"Seconded," Mya said.

"The motion carries," Wren added, and they all forced laughter once more before falling into quiet contemplation.

"I think we should all get some rest before tomorrow, yes?" Mila finally said.

"I could definitely do with some kip," Robyn replied.

"Yeah," Wren added, rousing Wolf and forcing the German Shephard from her lap. She climbed to her feet. "See you bright and early." She led the way with Wolf by her side. Robyn and Mila said their goodnights too and then followed.

"It's probably a good idea that we try to get some sleep," Mya said.

"Probably," Mike replied.

"Come on, Muppet," she said, rising from her seat. Muppet jumped down with his tail wagging, not sure if they were going to bed or heading out on some new adventure.

"We're not all going to make it, are we?"

Mya's bottom teeth clamped around her upper lip for a moment. She thought back to the Élysée Palace. She thought back to braving the tunnels of the Paris underground. She thought back to Seb, her partner, her friend, lying in the overturned van, dead. "I don't have a crystal ball, Mike. I don't know. As far as missions go, this one probably has the worst odds of any I've ever been on. But I'm going to give it everything I've got, and that's all I can do." She started walking away.

"Mya."

"Yes?" she said, turning back around.

"Thank you for everything."

"What do you mean?"

"I mean thank you for everything you've done for Safe Haven, for me. I wish you'd joined us sooner. I doubt very much if we'd be in the mess that we're in now. Maybe Lucy and Jake would have still been alive."

"You really can't think like that, Mike. Things happen, and second-guessing can drive you to the edge of insanity. Things could have gone the other way just as easily. With Beck and us in Safe Haven, we could have painted an even bigger target on your back much quicker."

Mike shrugged. "I suppose we'll never know. Safe Haven aside, thank you for always having my back. I'll never forget that you were there when I needed help the most."

"You've got a long line of people who would have been there if I wasn't."

"Maybe. But thanks anyway."

She tapped her leg and Muppet followed her back to the table, where she sat down opposite Mike. "I don't like this. It sounds like you're making peace. It sounds like you're saying goodbye. That's not a good frame of mind to adopt to go into a situation like we're about to go into. We need to be positive. We need—"

"I just wanted to thank you. That's all. I just wanted to tell you that all our lives are better for having you in them, that my life is a lot better for having you in it. I wanted you to know that you've got people now, that you're not alone anymore."

Mya leaned back from the table, surprised. "I.... Thank you."

"You're one of us. The same way Jenny or Wren or Jules or Raj are. You're family now, Mya."

Mya gulped and suddenly she felt the heat behind her eyes once more as her tear ducts threatened to open. Her family life had been a car crash. She had always been a loner, occasionally building the odd bond here or there, but nobody had ever said anything like this to her. She let out a small laugh. "You don't really know me that well. I mean—"

"I know you better than you think. You're devoutly loyal. Hence the fact you're still guarding a thousand secrets for Beck that you'd take to your grave with you rather than spill. You're incredibly compassionate, as I've experienced first-hand. You're funny, you're bright, you've got a good head on your shoulders, and you care about what happens to the community. Whatever you've faced in your past, whatever secrets you still hide in your heart, it doesn't matter. We all have secrets. You're one of us, Mya. Remember that. When we're out there tomorrow, you're one of us. Whatever happens, you'll always have a place, and you'll never be by yourself again."

A high-pitched sound caught in the back of Mya's throat and her eyes widened. This was the kind of acceptance she had longed for but always believed to be out of her reach. She remained like a statue for a few seconds, just staring at Mike, until finally her body beat her and two shimmering streams cascaded over her cheeks. "This is the second time tonight you've made me cry, you bastard," she said, trying to make a joke of it as she blotted the tears with the heel of her palm.

Mike climbed to his feet, grabbing his rucksack. He walked around the small table and placed an arm around Mya, gently kissing her on the top of her head. "Get a good night's sleep," he said before leaving her there sobbing. Humphrey finally jumped down and followed him.

Mike climbed up onto the deck and immediately the Labrador Retriever wandered off to find Raj. Mike reached into his backpack and pulled out the portable CD player he had taken from Lucy's bedside cabinet the day they had made their escape. He put the buds in his ears and advanced through the tracks to number six. He had not heard this since before Lucy had died. Even after all this time, he remembered the track listing. They would sometimes have an earbud each and listen to it before finally closing their eyes. *I really hope there's enough battery left just for one more play. Please. Please let me hear it one more time.*

The gentle but dirty guitar sound from the intro began to ring in his ears and a smile lit Mike's face and his heart. He looked out over the moonlit sea and breathed in deeply. Before he had climbed out of bed that fateful morning, he had kissed the back of Lucy's head while she slowly woke up. He remembered the smell of apples. Jenny had given her some apple shampoo, and, as impossible as it was, that's what he smelt now.

The song continued and a thousand more memories flooded his mind with each note played. He remembered how sometimes he would catch Lucy with an upturned hairbrush singing the song desperately out of tune when she thought no one was watching. He remembered how they once hooked the CD up to a set of mini speakers and they had played it over and over, gradually getting drunker on his gran's blackberry brandy. He remembered tasting Lucy's lips and tongue as they had fallen into a passionate embrace and made love. He remembered how he would sometimes find her alone in the bedroom listening to the CD while looking out over the waves like he was now.

The smell of apples got stronger and the smile broadened on his face. He turned to his right, and there she was, wearing jeans and a white shirt. It's what she had worn on the day of the Christmas party when they had their first dance as a married couple.

'Paradise City' continued to play, and even though he knew all this was in his head, Mike could almost sense that the magic wouldn't stop until the song was over. He reached out and he felt her hand slide into his. He felt their fingers entwine. He felt that reassuring rub from her thumb, the one that told him everything would be alright, no matter what they faced.

She leaned across and they kissed. All the time, Mike kept his eyes open even though she closed hers. He wanted to hold on to this moment as long as he could. Even though he knew it was an illusion, a mirage, it didn't matter. It was the closest he'd felt to her in a long time. She leaned back and stood looking at him before her eyes returned to the sea.

"It's a beautiful night," she said, squeezing his hand again.

"It is now," Mike replied.

"You might not see me tomorrow, sweetie. But I'll be with you every step of the way."

"If you were still here, I don't know whether I'd be doing this at all."

"You would. You know you would. It's the right thing to do. Our people need this."

"This is different to any other scavenging trip we've ever been on."

Lucy laughed. "And then some."

"I miss you so much, Luce."

"I keep telling you. There's no need to miss me." She pulled Mike around to face her. "I'll always be here." She touched his temple gently. "And I'll always be here." She touched his heart.

The music stopped, and in that instant, Lucy disappeared too. It was like a dagger had been driven through his rib cage where her gentle hand had been just a moment before. He closed his eyes and shook the CD player, hoping he could coax it back to life. The music did not restart, and when he opened his eyes again, Lucy did not reappear.

Dammit. He unplugged the buds from his ears and wrapped the cord around the player, shoving it back into his rucksack. *I really hope I can get some more batteries on this trip.* He cast one final look out across the waves before heading below deck.

15

Meg's frantic barking didn't just wake Jenny but also the occupants of the neighbouring rooms too. Emma and Jules almost collided as they burst through their friend's door. They both carried torches and shone them into Jenny's face to see she looked just as startled and bewildered as they did.

"What the hell's going on?" Emma demanded as Sammy ran into the room too.

"I don't know," Jenny said. "I was fast asleep and then—" Meg let out another series of barks, staring towards the small opening in the window as the night air seeped into the room. "Quiet, girl." Jenny took hold of her collar and dragged her away as the distant sound of panicked shouts travelled towards them.

"Shite!" Jules cried. "I'll get my brothers." She disappeared out of the room in an instant.

Emma's mind had been awash with a thousand thoughts before she had finally drifted off. When sleep had come, she was still fully dressed, and now it felt like she had never been to sleep. "Come on, Sammy." She grabbed her sister's hand and led her back out into the dark corridor.

The pair ran into their room and Emma grabbed her rucksack. It had been emptied of clothes and personal items. Now it contained a hatchet, a screwdriver, four spare magazines for her Glock Seventeen and a bottle of water. It wasn't exactly a bug-out bag but a go bag for a situation just like this one. She opened the drawer to the bedside cabinet and pulled out the Glock and holster, slipping it on as if it was just another piece of clothing.

"Is it the infected?" Sammy asked.

"I don't know what it is. But until I do, I want you to stay here. When I leave, you need to push that chair up against the door and just wait, okay?"

Meg's barks continued, waking even more people as was becoming increasingly evident by the sound of opening doors and tired but bewildered exclamations of fear.

"No. I'm coming with you."

"This isn't a time for arguments, Sammy."

"I'm coming with you. If we are about to be attacked, I don't want to be shut in a room alone."

She makes a good point. How the fuck would I feel if it was just me locked in a room surrounded by infected?

"Okay, but you do as I say. Do you understand me?" Sammy nodded and grabbed her crossbow.

A shiver of breath left the young girl as they headed back out of the room. "I ... love you," was all she managed to say, catching a sob in her throat before it fully manifested.

Emma reached out and grabbed her sister's hand as they entered the long hallway.

"What's going on?"

"What's happening?"

"Are we under attack?"

These questions and a dozen more like them murmured through the virtual darkness. "We're going to find out," Emma announced confidently.

Her powerful torch beam cut a path down the corridor. People instinctively shuffled back as if somehow getting caught in it would drag them into whatever trouble was heading their way.

The footsteps in the hallway got louder as Jules and her brothers then Jenny joined her at the front door. "What the hell's going on?" Vicky asked as she appeared with a rifle slung over her shoulder and a spear in her hand.

"We heard shouting," Emma replied. "And Meg's completely freaked about something."

More torches clicked on as they continued to the grand foyer. "What is it? What's happening?" George had been virtually silent since his granddaughters had left. Even Jules hadn't been able to coax him out of his sadness, but with what remained of the community under threat, he was ready to pitch in. He followed them with his stick in hand, not sure what he'd be able to do exactly if this was an attack, but refusing to let his friends face it alone nonetheless.

The night air was warm for this time of year, but as they all stepped outside, a chill ran through them as they heard Denise's frantic screams. It was lighter outside than in as the moon cast its rays across the courtyard, but nonetheless, they all raised their torches as three fast-moving silhouettes came into view.

A growl began in the back of Meg's throat and more black figures appeared behind the trio. "RAMs!" Andy yelled. "How the hell did they get in?"

"Good question, but not really our top concern at the moment. Everybody spread out," Emma ordered before placing a hand on Sammy's shoulder. "You stick with me."

The door to the centre burst open once more and all their heads turned to see Ephraim, Kat, Jack and James appearing with spears in hand. "Infected!" Jules shouted, giving them all the only heads-up they needed.

They formed a shallow semicircle as Denise, Rory and Finlay, the three people entrusted with the task of guarding them for the night, tore towards them.

Emma reached into her bag and grabbed her hatchet. "We don't know how many more could be out there, so guns are a last resort," she called out. The tension mounted with each second that passed. She looked at her little sister, who was down on one knee with her crossbow raised. A click followed by a familiar twang rose above the sound of panicked breaths and drumming feet as Sammy released her first bolt.

The attacking pack was fourteen-strong, but in the darkness it looked like an army. The lead creature suddenly collapsed to a skidding stop causing several more to tumble behind. "Jesus! Nice work, Sammy," Jules said, admiring the young girl's aim as the three guards finally came to a halt and joined the line of defence between the beasts and the centre.

"Alright. Everybody get ready," Emma ordered as the first wave of beasts closed in.

*

Meg suddenly broke rank, and for all her years, for all those extra treats she had downed from Shaw, Mike, Jules and a dozen more, she had just one focus. Her pack was under threat and she would fight to the death before she gave in. She launched, clamping her teeth around the thigh of one of the beasts and jerking her head with the ferocity of a hungry tiger.

The monster immediately went down, and as five more surged towards the semicircle of protectors, a fresh battle commenced.

*

Spoilt for choice, the creatures split, and Andy, Rob and Jon ran to greet the first of them, raising their spears like medieval pikemen, expertly shattering skulls and penetrating eye sockets, bringing the fearsome growls of the attacking beasts to an immediate halt.

*

Jenny was less out of her element than she once had been, but facing these monsters was the last thing she wanted to do. Her hands shook as she held the long-bladed hunting knife that Shaw had given her after one of his scavenger trips. *Oh God, oh God, oh God.* The beast leapt, diving out of the night towards her like something from a blood-freezing graphic novel.

In a blur, the monster went tumbling as Emma shoulder-barged it. It crashed to the ground in a hail of gravel, and before it had even come to a stop, the blade of Emma's hatchet glinted in the light of the moon as it rose into the air before cracking through the beast's skull.

*

Another click, another twang and another creature fell as Vicky, Jules and Rory jumped forward, taking on the next trio of monsters. Andy, Rob and John, keeping formation, advanced once more.

*

Emma pulled the hatchet out of her victim's head, releasing it with a slurping slosh. The blood looked like black oil in the glint of the moon. She sprang back up and charged towards the next attacker.

*

Jenny looked down at the body of the beast Emma had killed, and as if waking up to what was happening for the first time, she jolted into action, running forward. Meg had torn a large sliver of muscle from her victim's thigh. The smell nearly made Jenny sick as she approached, but her fear was quickly giving way to anger. She screamed as she brought the knife down, plunging it into the embattled creature's eye, rendering it still in a heartbeat.

*

Denise and Finlay, desperate to make up for dropping the ball on what had been their guard duty, intercepted the two creatures that were heading towards George. Finlay speared his target, but Denise, lacking his confidence, swung her spear like a bat, smashing it over the head. Stunned, the monster fell to the ground giving her the brief pause she needed to move in for the kill. She finished it off with a short, sharp jab through the temple. When she looked up again, the battle was over.

*

"What the fuck happened?" Emma demanded, stepping over the corpses of the fallen creatures towards her. "Do you understand what lookout duty means? You don't raise a fucking warning by running down the road shouting, 'They're coming, they're coming,' with an army of infected behind you."

"I'm sorry," Denise replied, on the verge of tears.

"It was my fault," Rory said, walking across. He couldn't see Emma's face clearly in the moonlight, but he could grasp the full depth of her anger from her tone and demeanour.

"Okay. I'll repeat the question. What happened?"

"I was at the gate while Finlay and Denise checked the perimeter. I thought I heard something in the trees on the other side of the fence. I watched for ages, but nothing showed, so I thought it was just an owl or something. Then all of a sudden it was like the ground was moving and I didn't understand what it was. The moon had shifted behind a cloud for a minute, and I … I … couldn't see. I'm sorry."

"What happened?"

"I flicked my torch on. There must have been thirty rabbits all running towards me at the same time. I could hear Denise and Rory by this time, and I don't know why I did it, but I screamed like a kid. I thought they were rats at first, but the ones at the front were just baby rabbits. It was like a carpet of them just sweeping out of the forest and under the gate and railings. Well, Denise and Rory flicked their torches on, and I suppose my scream scared them because they were shouting too now, asking me what was wrong. There must have been some infected in the area. Maybe that's what the rabbits were running from. I don't know. But all of a sudden, they started making a beeline towards us."

"Okay," Emma said. "I get it. You were scared; you made a noise; infected found you. There's a bloody big gate in between you and them. How the hell did they get in here?"

"It started as half a dozen. Then a dozen." His voice trembled as he spoke. "We did what you told us to do. We speared them through the gaps, and it was working. Then more came. We carried on, but then we heard this crack."

"Like a gunshot?"

"No. The next thing we knew, the gate was toppling inwards."

"What do you mean?"

"What do you think he means?" Denise said. "The gate collapsed."

"You mean there could be a fucking horde of those things marching towards us right now?"

"Jesus wept," Jules hissed.

"I don't think so," Denise said. "We didn't see anymore."

"Christ," Emma said, looking towards the long drive that Denise and the others had emerged from moments earlier. Her mind began to motor as muttered conversations continued all around.

"This could be it if those things get in here," Jules said. "What are we going to do?"

Emma ignored her comments as she tried to process everything. She looked down at her little sister, who reloaded her crossbow. In her life, she had never been prouder. If it hadn't been for that remarkable first shot, the confrontation with the creatures could have ended up very differently. As it was, they were all safe. When this was over, she would make people aware of what Sammy had done while most hid behind the sturdy wooden doors. "Okay. Jules, head back inside. Make sure everyone arms themselves. I want guards on that front door. Tell Beck exactly what's going on and get him rallying the troops. When you're done, get anyone who you think can hold a spear without peeing themselves and meet us down at the gate."

"No problem," Jules said, heading off.

"George. I need you, Jack and James to get your tools. We need to jerry-rig that gate until morning when you can do a proper repair."

"Leave it to us," he replied as he and his small team immediately marched off in the direction of the workshop.

"Jen, I'm going to need you with us. Meg's an early warning system. She could be the difference between those things getting the drop on us or not."

"Of course, darling," she replied.

"Everybody else," she said, turning around to make sure the small group who had been ready to fight the invaders could hear her, "we're going to the gate. Keep your eyes and ears open. There could be infected in the grounds. If you see or hear anything, let me know. Now come on." She squeezed her little sister's arm as she, Sammy, Jenny and Meg led the way. She glanced behind to see Andy, Rob and Jon were just a matter of feet behind them. Once that would have heightened her anxiety; now it gave her comfort.

"When we get that gate on, we'll need to do a proper sweep of the grounds," Andy said.

"First things first," Emma replied. "We don't know what we're going to face when we get down there."

"That was some shot, Sammy," Rob said.

"Yeah, Sammy," Andy echoed, "in the moonlight too. That could have gone differently if it wasn't for you."

The young girl looked down, a little embarrassed. "I had a good teacher and practised a lot, that's all." Since they had arrived at the Skye Outward Bounds Centre, she had practised more than she ever had done. The disappointment she had felt at not being able to make a substantive contribution in the battle on the trek from the boat had nearly crippled her, but she had vowed to do something about it.

"No, it was more than that, Sammy," Emma said. "That was real skill. You've got an aptitude for the crossbow. I'm so proud of you."

The young girl reached up and took her sister's hand as they continued to the gate. The journey seemed to take an age. Every sound, every leaf that fluttered in the wind drew their attention. When they finally arrived, Andy, Rob and John leaned their weapons up against the supporting pillar and hoisted the tall gate up again while the others scoured their surroundings for signs of movement.

When the wrought iron structure clanged against the brick pillar, everyone stopped dead. It was as if a loud bell had been rung. "Oh crap!" Vicky cried as five creatures broke from the woods further up the road.

Emma lifted the bolt on the left gate and swung it open. "Get ready with the spears," she ordered.

Vicky, Denise, Rory and Finlay all advanced, stepping over the bodies of the creatures that had been killed prior to their defences falling. Emma grabbed one of the spears Jules' brothers had discarded and joined them while Rob, Andy and Jon continued to secure the once sturdy barrier back in position.

*

"The gate hinges have snapped off. The wall fittings are still in place though," Rob said.

"What are we going to do?" Jon asked, looking out to the road and the charging beasts.

"I'm thinking."

*

"Get ready," Emma said. "Spread out a little bit and make sure you don't get in one another's way. Jen, keep hold of Meg. I don't want her getting hurt. Kat, Ephraim, Sammy, you're our eyes and ears. If you see any more heading towards us, give us a time."

"What do you mean?" Kat asked.

"A time," Sammy said. "Three o'clock. Nine o'clock. Use the face of a clock to give them directions."

"Oh. Okay."

"And keep checking behind you, too," Emma said. "We don't know if any infected got into the grounds."

"I have to say, my Isle of Skye odyssey is going to get a terrible write-up on Trip Advisor," Ephraim quipped.

"Humour. That's good. We'll all need a good laugh when we've scooped your entrails up and put them in a plastic bag."

"Point made, Captain Fletcher."

"NOW!"

*

It seemed like the worst thing they could be doing, but as Emma broke into a run towards the advancing creatures, it suddenly made sense. Denise, Rory and Finlay felt more confident as the momentum drove them forward. Strike! Strike! Strike!

Finlay and Denise watched as the crudely fashioned spears disappeared into the skulls of the creatures, causing them both to drop in unison. Rory mistimed his thrust, and the head of his weapon collided with the beast's rib cage, knocking it back a few paces but not stopping it. Fear shuddered through him as it opened its mouth and bit into the air, almost as if it was rehearsing what it would do when it reached him. In the cold light of the moon, its skin looked ashen, its lips unnaturally dark. "Oh God," Rory cried, not like a man but a boy.

*

Emma and Vicky, both more seasoned in hand-to-hand combat with these beasts, swung the spears around and forced the butts against the sternums of their two attackers, deliberately rather than accidentally forcing them back and interrupting the flow; then, as the creatures gathered themselves, they leapt forward again, shifting the spears around the right way and using the extra second they had afforded themselves to aim properly. Both sharpened points vanished into the eyes of their targets, causing them to drop.

*

Finlay and Denise both jabbed at the final creature as Rory tried to find the sweet spot. But then it lunged, taking them all by surprise. Rory toppled back, letting out a fear-filled scream as the ghoulish beast fell on top of him. Its head smashed against his shoulder and desperation consumed him as he tried harder than ever to push it off.

Denise and Finlay each grabbed one of the creature's shoulders in an attempt to free Rory. "This thing's built like a fucking brick shithouse," Denise cried out as she pulled with all her strength.

The beast was unresponsive. It just had one goal. Its eyes looked black in the moonlight as it got closer to its prize. A small sob left Rory's throat. Despite Finlay's and Denise's best efforts, the creature's mouth was closing in. "Please!" he cried out.

"Quick," Emma shouted, only just realising that a battle was still going on. She and Vicky started to run back to help when suddenly—Click. Twang.

*

It was a dangerous shot. Sammy had been holding her breath long before she squeezed the trigger. It had taken all her concentration. The distance was minimal, but the fact that the figure was moving and all she had to guide her was the moonlight made it a thousand times harder. She could have killed one of her own, but she knew that if she didn't act, then one of her own would die for sure.

The growls, the screams, the pleas, she had fallen deaf to all of them at that moment. She had brought the sight up to her eye, and when she was sure there was no chance that Rory could escape, she fired.

Now all the sounds came flooding back as if an unmute button had been hit. The beast's body was almost flung to one side by Denise and Finlay as Rory crab-walked backwards, getting as far away from his attacker as he could.

*

"Are we clear? Are we clear?" Emma shouted, seeing what her sister had done and turning towards the road.

"All clear," Kat said.

"All clear," Ephraim confirmed.

213

"Definitely clear," Jenny added, finally letting go of Meg's collar.

"Okay. Everyone back inside."

"Sorry," Andy said. "This thing is heavier than it looks. We overcompensated and it just hit the pillar."

"Make it up to me by securing it somehow, would you?"

"Wait up," Rob said. "The cavalry's finally arrived." They all turned to see George, James and Jack carrying ropes and tool bags, heading towards them. Behind, Jules followed with a handful of men and women armed with spears.

"The fitting on the gate's snapped off," Andy said as George arrived.

"Thought that might have happened," he replied, like his old self again and not the man who had become a sad and bitter shadow in the absence of his family.

"Can you do something, George?"

He nodded. "We can rig something alright. We'll get it secure enough for tonight and then do a proper repair in daylight."

Emma let out a breath of relief. "You're a lifesaver … literally."

"Okay," Jules said. "How do you want to do this?"

It was obvious that *this* referred to the search of the grounds. "I don't," Emma replied.

"Okay. Now I'm confused. I thought we were going to do a sweep."

Emma turned to look back at George. "Do you think we'll be able to chain the gates?"

She could see George's teeth glint as he smiled, reaching into one of the bags of tricks they'd brought with them. "Found these in the shed when we were cleaning it out. Not sure what they used them for, but I figured they'd be quite handy given our current situation."

"Have I mentioned you're a lifesaver? When you've jerry-rigged the gates, chain them and lock them, please."

She turned back to Jules and the others, who were all now listening intently. "Chances are there aren't any in the grounds. We made plenty of noise earlier and that would probably have flushed them out, but we can't be sure. We're going to secure the gates tonight and hope nothing gets in and nothing finds a weakness or a hole in one of the fences. Tomorrow, at first light, we're going to head out in teams and give this place a proper going over. We're going to do that before we do anything else. There'll be no one working in the grounds, in the workshop or on guard duty until we have checked every inch of ground. Understood?" Mutters of agreement circulated through the assembled crowd.

"So, what now?" Jules asked.

"We're all going to stay here until George and his crew are done. Then we're going to head back to the centre together. I'm not taking any chances and I'm damn sure that I'm not going to risk losing anyone tonight. Jen, it's going to be an early start tomorrow. We're going to need Meg."

"I'm fairly certain I'm not going to get a wink of sleep for the rest of the night, darling, so you just say the word."

Emma nodded. "Alright, everybody. Stay quiet and stay alert. We'll be back at the centre before we know it."

People split off into smaller groups while George, James, Jack and Jules' brothers worked on the gates. "Emma, can we have a word?" Denise asked.

Emma walked across to where she, Rory and Finlay were standing. "What is it?"

"Look. We know we let you down. I'm really sorry but—"

"There wasn't a lot you could have done. Hopefully, you all learnt a lesson tonight. Silence is our friend, especially in the dark. I know I went off on one. That's just my way. You'll get used to me. We all had a pretty good scare, but nobody got hurt, so that's a victory as far as I'm concerned. I trust you three will be the first in line tomorrow morning when we do a sweep of the grounds."

"I can promise you that."

"Good. We're okay then."

The trio nodded respectfully as Emma departed.

"All done," George announced, pulling the chain one final time.

"You're sure it'll hold?"

"Nothing's getting through there short of a tank."

"Good. Thank you, George. Thank you," she said, looking towards the silhouettes of the others as they gathered around. "We're going to head back to the centre. Everybody stay alert."

The group began to move slowly. Jenny and Meg walked by Emma's side. "You handled that magnificently, darling."

"I just did what needed doing."

"Exactly. I thought with Shaw gone, what was left of our little society was going to crumble. Seeing you in action, I think we're going to be just fine."

"That's nice of you to say, Jen, but if Mike and the others don't come back with those supplies, it won't matter how well I can lead. This whole place will go to hell."

16

Shaw's head was still a jumble when he woke up. He had finished the final tin of beans for breakfast and washed in a nearby stream. He was feeling lost and emotional, not just because he had eaten the last of his food but because nothing was making sense to him.

He was out there by himself, but why? *Why did I leave the people who were essentially my family?* He had thought he could just walk away and that would make things better for everyone. Well, maybe it had made things better for them, but things certainly weren't better for him.

The wild thoughts of living off the land in some magical bothy by a loch had long since been abandoned, and now he was just a ronin with no master searching for a meaning to life, although, in his heart, he knew he'd never find one. *I had a meaning and I flushed it away.*

When he saw four figures on bikes coming over the brow of a hill up ahead as if they were riding straight out of an Enid Blyton book, he thought the madness that had been threatening to consume him had finally come.

His instinct to hide was beaten by his curiosity and the sheer strangeness of the image. *This is it. I've lost it. Timmy's going to come dancing over the hill behind them.* He suddenly thought back to Meg and Humphrey and Wolf and Muppet. He'd always loved dogs. His father had never let him have one, but in Safe Haven there was never one far away. No matter how bad a day it had been or was going to be, seeing one of their faces always made him smile. *I miss that. I miss the soft sound of their panting. I miss the feeling of a head resting on my thigh, looking up at me when I'm eating. I miss them all.* Only he knew his thoughts weren't just restricted to dogs anymore.

Shaw remained on the verge, and as the four figures got closer, he realised this wasn't some illusion. He realised Timmy wasn't about to appear behind them. *You fucking idiot.* He hadn't given up on living just yet, but what he was doing the old Shaw would never have done. The old Shaw would have run into the trees. The old Shaw would have ducked behind a rock. It was too late for any of that now.

*

"What do you think?" Decko asked as they continued towards the lone figure.

"I don't see anyone else," replied Billy.

"I don't like it. He's just watching us."

"In fairness," Galli said, "four hapless bastards out for a bicycle ride on the Isle of Skye in the middle of the apocalypse must be quite a sight."

"I didn't think about that."

They slowed down and finally stopped ten metres away from the figure. Their eyes shot in every direction. If this was some kind of ambush, it was way too late to do anything about it. "Hello," Galli called out as the four of them laid their bikes on the ground.

"I thought my eyes were deceiving me when I first saw you," Shaw responded.

"Where are you from?"

"I've been travelling since it all started."

"That's a lot of travelling."

"It's been a long time."

"That it has."

"Have you got any food? We're starving," Gummy blurted.

"That's one of the reasons I'm on the road so early. I finished the last of my food this morning. Going to be a long day if I don't find more."

Gummy's shoulders dropped and his eyes looked to the ground. "I'm starving," he mumbled to himself this time.

"Which way are you heading?" Billy asked.

"The way you've just come from."

"You're not going to find much that way, my friend. We've checked every house, every barn, every shed."

Shaw nodded slowly. *Who the hell are these people?*

"You say you've been on the road since all this started," Decko began. "You must have had a lot of luck scavenging. The few scavengers we've come across who've been in small groups have looked like rakes."

"Come across a lot, have you?"

"Enough."

Shaw nodded again. "Where did you say you four were from again?"

"We didn't."

"Forgive Decko," Galli said. "He's naturally suspicious of ... well ... everyone."

Shaw smiled. "I get that."

"I'm Antonia—Toni. This is Billy and that's Gummy."

"I'm Jim."

Galli smiled. "Nice to meet you, Jim. You're obviously not Scottish. Is this as far north as you've got so far?"

"Yeah. Talk about a stranger in a strange land."

Galli smiled. "Tell us about it. There were more of us when we set off. We came up from Newcastle originally.

219

Thought the further north we went the safer we'd be. We settled in a place called Garve. Been living there ever since, scavenging in and around the area. Then we ran out of fuel. Then we got attacked. So now we're on the road."

"Attacked?"

"Yeah. Took out a lot of us. There are some bad types out there."

Shaw nodded slowly again. "Seen a few myself." *They're fucking lying through their teeth. Garve is a shell.* He immediately remembered back to Mike leaping out of the top floor of a doctor's surgery. *We gutted that place. We gutted every single village from Safe Haven to Inverness and back again.* "Spent a while in Troon. Got raided by pirates. Can you believe that?"

One of the men smiled as if he'd heard the story before. The other two looked towards the woman who had done most of the talking. "Pirates? That's a new one."

"Don't you rem—"

"Pirates of the apocalypse," the woman said, smiling and interrupting Gummy. "I suppose anything goes now."

They knew. Why are they trying to cover it up? They can't be Troy's people. We took care of them.

"Where did you get the rifle from?" Decko asked.

Shaw stared towards him for a moment then looked at the rifle on his shoulder, then to the one on his friend's and finally the woman's. "Probably the same place as you did. They're pretty easy to scavenge these days. I keep expecting to see a deer or something. I've only got about a couple of bullets left, but I live in hope."

"I'd kill for a venison steak," said Gummy, causing his three companions to chuckle a little, and suddenly the tension eased. "We saw one in Wick, but that was pretty much the only one we've seen. Dodged bullets like it was made of smoke. That's what you said, isn't it, Billy?"

Wick? Olsen's people raided Wick.

"He means Berwick," Billy said. "It wasn't Wick, Gummy. It was Berwick."

Gummy looked confused for a moment. "But the castle. That was—"

"Berwick," Billy said more firmly this time.

Gummy looked troubled for a moment but then turned to Shaw, shaking his head. "I get muddled sometimes."

Shaw looked at him briefly then glanced towards Billy and nodded. "Used to come to Scotland as a kid. The place used to be swimming with deer. Since the great cull, it's all changed."

"I know, right?" Billy replied.

Shaw sensed a change in the atmosphere as if suddenly they felt they'd all been caught out in a lie. "I was thinking about maybe giving Contin a try," he said.

"Is that on Skye?" Billy asked.

"Apparently, it's only small, but it used to get a lot of tourists, so there might be some holiday homes that still have something worth grabbing."

"Sounds good," Galli replied. "Do you know where it is? Do you mind if we tag along?"

"Not at all," Shaw said, reaching into his rucksack. "I'll have to check my map, but I think you'll need to backtrack a little if you don't mind a bit of a trek."

"If there's food at the end of it we don't mind."

"So where is it?" Decko asked.

"It's right next to Garve." The smiles disappeared in an instant. BOOM! BOOM! BOOM!

"BILLY!" A look of pure horror hung on Galli's face as she watched Decko, Billy and Gummy fall. They hadn't even tried to make a grab for their weapons. Shaw's Browning had been drawn out of nowhere and now it pointed at her as tears began to roll down her cheeks. "Why?" she cried, looking at him in dismay and confusion.

"You're Olsen's people."

"No … no," she said, shaking her head and looking down at Billy as he lay there on the road. "We got out of there. We left her. We escaped."

"When?"

"What?"

"When did you escape?" he demanded, still pointing the pistol directly at her.

She shook her head, baffled as to why that would matter. "A couple of days ago. You killed him. You killed my Billy."

"A couple of days ago. So, you were there with her a few months ago when you attacked Safe Haven. You were with her when one of my best friends was murdered. You were with her when another of my friends witnessed the brains blow out of the back of her little brother's head."

Tears rolled down Galli's cheeks. Despite still having the rifle slung over her shoulder, revenge was the last thing on her mind. As she spoke, thin strands of saliva hung from her lips. She gestured to Billy and her dead friends. "We were trying to start afresh. Does this settle the score? Do you feel better? Does this make up for it now?"

"Not by a long shot. But it's a start." BOOM!

Shaw observed his handiwork for a moment before something drew his attention to the brow of the hill from which he had first seen the four of them appear. A single figure was heading in his direction. He looked around. More would come, attracted to the sound of gunfire.

Suddenly, all the confusion, all the depression, all the bewilderment, all the madness was gone. *I should never have left. I should never have left my friends … my family. What was I thinking? This is my focus. This should always have been my focus. I was an idiot to walk out on the people I love. I was an idiot to forget what brought us to this point.*

He looked back towards the strangely animated figure as it tore down the hill towards him. It was still early. With a bit of good detective work and a lot of luck, maybe he could be back with his friends by the end of the day. Maybe he'd get to hug Jen and Mike and Emma and Jules. Maybe he'd get to go to sleep knowing that he belonged somewhere. He thought back to the gunfire he'd heard on that first day. *It could have been anyone. Mike, Emma, Mya, Wren, Robyn.... They're all survivors. They'll have made it. Nothing's surer.*

He looked at the bodies once more, not as the confused drifter he had been when he'd woken up that morning but as the self-asserted black sheep returning to its herd. He grabbed the weapons, knives and anything else they had on them that might be of use. The bike that the one called Billy had ridden was equipped with a rear rack. He bundled the items together in one of their jackets and tied it tight with laces from their boots then secured it in place.

The creature continued towards him, and more had appeared at the top of the hill, but Shaw was confident he had enough time to make a comfortable escape. He cast one final look towards the bodies, climbed onto the bike and began pedalling. It had been a long time since he had done this, but it was true what they said. It all came flooding back to him, and before long, he had picked up a good pace.

He looked behind and saw the monster had lost a lot of ground in just the few short moments he'd been travelling. He turned back to the direction he was pedalling and smiled. A thousand doubts, a thousand heartaches, a thousand questions still screamed in his head. But there was one thing he was sure of now. He needed to go home, and wherever his people were, that was home.

*

Mike joined Raj and Talikha at the helm. Humphrey was bolt upright by their side as if it was he who was captaining the vessel. It seemed foreign to them all sailing up the Clyde rather than being out on the open sea.

They had seen infected along the banks of the river that had followed them as far as obstacles would allow. Buildings, car parks, monuments, and chain-link fences had all presented barriers to stop the RAMs' hungry pursuit of this sailing tray of hors d'oeuvres.

"Are you guys going to be okay getting back?" Mike asked.

"There is no need to worry about us, my friend. It is we who worry about you. You are about to head into the most heavily populated city in Scotland for what must surely be our last hope."

"There's no such thing as a last hope, Raj. I'll never give up ... well ... y'know ... as long as I don't die horribly that is."

"Ah, yes. It is good that you make jokes about impending doom. This makes everyone feel so much more positive," Mila said, seemingly appearing out of nowhere.

"Jesus fucking wept. It's true what Robyn says. You're like a phantom. You could clear your throat or something, so we know you're there."

"What does it matter if we are all going to die horrible deaths?"

"I didn't say we were all going to die horrible deaths. I said it was a possibility."

Mila nodded. "This makes all the difference. Thank you."

"How is everybody down there?"

"I think I have finally begun to understand the term cabin fever. The sooner our feet are on land, and we can face our fate, the happier everyone will be."

"Yeah, I'm not sure I'd use the term happier."

Mila shrugged. "What happens happens. At least we will be doing something rather than waiting."

"Okay," Raj said, consulting the chart by his side again. "There is not much further to go. You might want to go get the others."

Mila cast her eyes ahead. In the distance, she could make out a bridge. "Very well," she replied, disappearing once more.

"You do not have anything to prepare?" Talikha asked.

Mike gestured to the rucksack on his back. "What can I tell you? I'm a light traveller." He looked over his shoulder to make sure Mila was out of earshot. "Look, if something does happen, if none of us make it back, you'll look after Emma and Sammy, won't you?"

"You don't need to ask that question any more than we would. We are the same, my friend. We always have been."

"Thank you."

"It is we who need to thank you. You are the ones taking the risks."

"We're all taking risks being down here. Be careful heading back. We've got no idea if there's some other psycho out there who has the same idea as Troy."

"I think we have seen the last pirates we are likely to see," Raj replied.

"I hope you're right."

"The river widens up ahead. This is the ideal place for us to stop." He turned to look at his friend and extended his hand. "You will never need to worry about Emma and Sammy while we still have a breath in our bodies." The pair shook hands and then embraced tightly.

"Thank you." Mike broke away and hugged Talikha too. "Thank you both." He crouched down and kissed Humphrey on the head. "You look after them, boy." Humphrey tilted his head a little then unleashed his immense tongue, slopping it up Mike's face like a wet paintbrush.

They all laughed. "He will miss you too," Raj said.

Mike stood up, wiping his face on his jacket. "Well, at least I'll have the smell of freshly licked dog bollocks to keep me company while I'm walking through the streets of Glasgow. Thanks, boy," he said, looking down at the Labrador Retriever, whose tongue now lolled out of the side of his mouth.

"So, we're ready to rock and roll?" Mya asked as she and Muppet joined them.

"In a few minutes," Raj replied.

"Good. Okay then." She cast her eyes up ahead, then to Mike. "You ready to do this?"

"Whether I am or I'm not, I don't suppose it really makes a difference, does it?"

Mya smiled. "Come on then."

*

Mike and Wren rowed while the others all looked back towards the yacht as it retraced its path up the Clyde. Even without the giveaway masts announcing their arrival in the city, some infected chased them along the banks.

"I really don't feel safe in this thing," Robyn said. "I mean what if they're in the water? Any second, a load of arms could reach over the side of the boat and drag us in."

"Very doubtful," Mike began. "If a load of arms reached over the side, we're probably more likely to capsize than get dragged in."

Wren and the others laughed. "Oh, thanks. That's a brilliant image to put in my head. Bastard."

"I wouldn't worry about it," Mya said. "I've seen those things in the water. They can get carried along by currents. They can trudge along the bottom, but we're pretty deep here. If there was anything in the river, the chances of them getting near us would be very low."

"Thank you, Mya," Robyn said, looking down into the river. "That's how you reassure someone." She glared at Mike.

"I'm much more worried about infected dropping off one of the bridges. That'd be a real nightmare."

The others laughed again. "I really wish I was on a different boat."

"Is it this bridge coming up where we need to moor?" Wren asked.

"No," Mya replied, looking at the small assembly of infected that grouped along the barrier, watching them approach, reaching out towards the orange dinghy as if somehow that would bring them into their grasp. "The George the Fifth is the next one. There's a narrow stone pier to the side where they used to run sightseeing boat tours."

"If there are any on the bridge when we get there, won't they be able to get to us?"

"If they figure out that there's a flight of steps at the end, there is every possibility that might happen."

"So, you're saying that we're going to hit the ground running?"

"That's a safe bet."

"I know a spot where we can access Hope Street. Easy peasy," Mike said, doing his best to imitate Mya's voice.

"I never said easy peasy."

"You never said that the infected would have an open invitation down to the pier to meet us either."

"You never asked," she replied, smiling.

"Somehow, I thought it would be my fault."

"I'm glad you are finding this amusing," Mila said. "What if there are twenty? Thirty? Fifty?"

"Listen. Wherever we land in the city, we'd run this risk. The good thing about the George the Fifth is that the steps down to the pier were built shortly after the bridge itself in the early part of the last century. "They're narrow, very narrow, and if an attack comes, they're going to be single file, two abreast at the most. With some good marksmanship," she said, looking towards Robyn and Wren, "we'll be able to cause all sorts of havoc. Some might even fall over the side into the river. The six of us are here because we are the most experienced and the absolute best at what we do."

"You don't have confidence issues, do you?" Mike said.

"It's the truth. I've never seen anyone handle swords like Mila. Robyn's and Wren's aims are second to none. Darren is one of the best shots I've seen in a long time, and I've had a lot of experience with this kind of thing."

"I couldn't help noticing you missed me off that list."

"Yeah, well. You're kind of a lucky mascot. Remember on *University Challenge* or *Blockbusters* when the contestants would have a stuffed toy duck or something like that by their glass of water? That's you." She flashed her teeth in a warm smile as the others all laughed.

"Gee. I'm lost for words."

"There's a first," Wren said, and they all laughed again.

She and Mike shared a smile. It was good that they were laughing. They knew it was false bravado. They were all scared, even Mya. This was a crazy situation. They were going to be in peril the second they stepped onto that pier. In fact, no. They would be in peril before then. The infected would be able to get the drop on them. They could even be waiting on the pier before they secured the dinghy.

"Shit! Shit! Shit!" Robyn said, kneeling up and nocking an arrow.

The Kingston Bridge was looming ever closer, and even more infected were lining it now, reaching over the thick safety railing. One in particular, though, was well over six feet five. It seemed to pivot on its belt line as its fingers danced and grabbed. For so long, all they had been able to hear was the noise of the oars and the slosh of the water, but now the growls of the creatures watching them from the bridge travelled to greet them.

"Don't fire unless you absolutely need to," Mya said. "We're not in Kansas anymore. We can't just resupply with arrows from your grandad's workshop. You lose one out here and it's gone for good."

"Let's head over to the other bank," Mike said. "Maybe if we can force them to move further along, there's less danger of them overreaching and dropping out of the sky on us."

"Good idea," Wren replied, lifting her oar out of the water momentarily and letting Mike adjust the course. He stroked powerfully, changing their direction before Wren put her oar back in the water and began to row again.

"It's working. It's working," Robyn cried, all the time maintaining her aim on the tallest figure, the biggest threat.

"Don't get too close to the other bank," Darren said as two creatures rolled down an incline behind a warehouse. They all watched as they dropped onto the muddy plateau below. When they rose, they were caked in filth, but neither beast cared as they waded into the water.

Both Wolf and Muppet, who had been observing with a low growl emanating from the backs of their throats, suddenly began to bark frantically.

"Shiiit," Robyn said, adjusting her aim and pointing at the creatures heading towards them instead.

"Don't," Mya warned. "If they get this far, we'll take care of them." She pulled a hunting knife from her belt, and Mila withdrew one of her swords, kneeling up at the same time.

"I really, really don't like this." Robyn turned her attention back to the infected on the bridge. "There must be like fifty of them up there or something."

"As long as they stay up there, that's all I'm bothered about," Mike said as he and Wren stroked even harder.

Mya looked down into the water and then back at the two creatures trudging towards them. "We might be too shallow across here," she said as Wolf and Muppet continued to bark, adding to the tension.

"I thought you could take care of them."

"Yeah. It's not them I'm worried about. If there do happen to be any on the riverbed and all of a sudden we're in water shallow enough for them to reach up, then we've got a serious problem on our—HAAA—FUCK!"

The dinghy rocked dangerously as something hit it from below. "What the hell was that?" Robyn screamed.

"What do you think it was?"

Wolf and Muppet started to bark louder, but now their attention wasn't directed towards the beasts advancing from the bank but whatever was making the boat rock.

The dinghy juddered again and again as fingertips and hands appeared out of the water. "Jesus Christ!" Darren hissed, withdrawing his Glock.

"Don't! We can't risk attracting more," Mya said as more hands crashed against the bottom of the vessel.

"We need to get back into the middle," Wren cried.

Mike immediately lifted his oar. "Go, go, go."

Wren turned them this time as more fingers broke through the surface.

"This is a bloody nightmare," Robyn cried.

"Okay. We're heading back to the centre. We're going deeper," Wren said, just as scared as her sister … as all of them. "Wolf. Stop!" The German Shepherd quieted immediately, and a second later, so did Muppet. But both dogs continued to survey the water around the dinghy.

"Never mind getting to the trucks; we're not going to make it out of the bloody river at this rate," Darren said. His eyes scoured the water, too, searching for more reaching digits.

Mya was transfixed by the two creatures that had waded in from the bank. Deeper and deeper they slogged until, finally, they each disappeared like shark fins beneath the surface. "Fuuuck!" she whispered to herself.

"Always reassuring when the most unrattleable person on the face of the earth is suddenly rattled," Mike said before letting out another grunt as he pulled back on the oar.

"I hate to be the bearer of crap news," began Robyn, "but we're back to square one with the infected on the bridge."

"It's too much of a risk to go back into the shallows. Just keep your eyes on them, Robyn. Hopefully, we'll get underneath and through before—"

"Oh, SHIT!" Robyn's scream was followed by a loud splash. Mike and Wren turned their heads to see the feet of one of the creatures disappearing into the water. They glimpsed up to see the line of infected on the bridge. The nearer they got the more the creatures leaned and looked like they were going to fall in too.

"Oh, SHIIIT!" Wren echoed.

Another splash and another exploded. "If one of them lands in the dinghy, we're all dead," cried Mike, angling his head back just as another creature caused a watery eruption as it vanished into the Clyde. Wolf and Muppet began to growl again, both showing their teeth as they stared up towards the bridge.

"Another few seconds and we're going to be bang underneath," Darren said.

"Scheisse!" Mila shrieked as two more monsters splashed down at the same time. She withdrew her swords and stood up in the centre of the dinghy.

"What the hell are you doing?" Robyn shrieked.

"It is no good. I cannot swing kneeling down."

"If one of those things lands in the boat, swinging will be the last of your worries."

"Oh Christ!" cried Mya. "The big one's going."

Everyone immediately knew what she meant. Even when Mike and Wren had briefly glimpsed over their shoulders, they had seen it. Its frame blocked out more of the sky than any of the other beasts, and as it hit the water, the noise sent a shudder of fear through all of them, followed by an actual shudder as a wave bigger than any they had experienced thus far hit the boat.

Mila splayed out her arms for balance as the dinghy rocked once more. "Keep your fingers crossed, 'cause we're going under," Darren said.

Other than the dogs, every other occupant of the boat held their breath as three, four, five, six loud splashes echoed around them. "Shit, shit, shit, shit, shit," Robyn cried out, still poised with a nocked arrow but shaking at the same time. The dinghy rocked haphazardly as disturbances in the water made it feel like they were at sea in a storm rather than on a relatively calm river.

They all breathed out a tentative breath as they crossed the threshold of the safety railing above. But the relief didn't last long as Wren let out a chilling scream causing both dogs to start barking feverishly.

The dinghy began to skew and dip, causing Robyn to let out a panicked screech too. Mila lost her balance, and now it was her turn to let out a terrified cry as she fell towards the water.

"MILA!"

17

Even though the dinghy was seemingly spinning and the force against Mike's oar was more powerful than it had been at any point in the journey, he reached out with his left hand, grabbing Mila's jacket. Mya seized her from the other side, and together they yanked her back. She still fell forwards, but now she somehow managed to stay in the boat as it continued its swirling journey beneath the bridge.

"Something's got hold of my oar!" Wren cried and everything became clear.

"Let it go. LET IT GO!" Mike shouted, his booming order echoing in the underpass as further creatures continued to fall from above.

Wren did as he said and watched the oar disappear through the rowlock. The oars they were using were not the ones that had originally come with the boat. Subsequently, the rowlock was still able to act as a fulcrum but in no way secure the oar, as they all now understood only too well as they watched it vanish.

"We're starting to drift, Mike," Mya cried as she realised the current, although not particularly strong, was causing them to float back out the way they had come, putting them in even more danger as the beasts continued to rain from above.

Mike crawled across to the bow as the oar that had sunk beneath the surface seconds before re-emerged and smashed against the starboard. "Jesus. It's still not let go," Wren shouted.

Robyn's face was drained of all colour as she aimed her bow into the murky Clyde. "This is like that scene out of *Friday the bloody 13th*. Any second, the ghost of Jason Vorhees is going to pop his head up and drag us all down to Hell."

"As long as we're staying positive; that's the main thing," Mike growled as he continued to row, each time switching sides with the oar, trying to get them away from the danger zone as quickly as possible.

Gradually they began to regain steadiness and balance. The creatures continued to drop from the bridge, but the harder Mike stroked the greater sense of relief they all felt. "I think we're out of danger," Mya said.

"Yeah. I feel totally safe now," Robyn replied. "I'm never going to sleep again."

"I wouldn't worry about that. The way this trip's going, we're not going to last more than half an hour," Darren replied.

"Oh, thanks. Thanks very much."

"It's alright, boy. It's alright," Wren said, calming Wolf and finally stopping his barking. Taking his cue from the other dog, Muppet stopped too.

"Do you want me to take over, Mike?" Darren asked as the other man continued to row hard.

"It's okay," Mike replied, clearly out of breath as he continued further under the bridge and towards the centre of the river. "Get ready because, in a few seconds, we're going to be coming out the other side."

They all looked back to see the raining bodies had finally stopped, but it did little to reassure them. Robyn looked up. "I really hope they're not all heading across the road."

"I doubt it," Mya replied. "They don't really have any reasoning capability."

"Yeah," Wren replied. "I'd have said that until one of them grabbed my oar and started to batter us with it."

"I wouldn't read too much into that. It was probably just a reflex or something."

"It's the 'or something' that I'm bothered about."

The only sounds were the slosh of the water and their breathing as they exited the underpass. Robyn aimed her bow skywards, expecting a replay of what had happened at the other side of the bridge, but as they re-emerged into full daylight, her fears were unfounded.

"So that's our bridge?" Mike asked, nodding towards the structure about three hundred metres ahead of them.

"That's it," Mya replied. "Are you sure you don't want someone to take over the rowing? We're going to have to stay as close to the centre as we can until the last minute. It's going to be hard work."

"I'm fine," Mike grunted stubbornly. They carried on for another couple of minutes, all the time getting closer and closer to their destination. As had happened at the Kingston Bridge, a swarm of creatures amassed on the overpass looking down at the boat as it travelled up river.

"Scheisse!" Mila hissed. "There must be sixty. More even."

"Yeah. When we get to the pier, it's all going to kick off fast. Robyn, Wren, I want you off the boat first. We can't be sure how it's going to play out, but try to get a couple of them at the top of the staircase before they've even begun their descent if you can. Hopefully, that will cause a lot more of them to fall. Fingers crossed, the rest of us will be able to finish the fallen ones off before they can rally themselves. Just keep doing that. Keep getting them as near to the top as you can. Like I said, it's a narrow staircase, which is one thing that's in our favour."

"Okay." Both sisters nodded and looked at each other, shaking their heads a little. They had been in a lot of bad situations before, but they both understood that nothing had been as dangerous as what they now faced.

Mike continued to row, pausing only for a second to whip his rucksack and jacket off. A line of sweat had formed down the back of his T-shirt. "This is definitely the bridge up ahead?" he asked. "This one?"

"Yeah. Why?" Mya asked.

"We're going to need to dock somewhere else."

"What are you talking about? There is nowhere else, Mike."

"There has to be."

"There isn't."

"Mya, that pier is about six feet above the water level. We're going to have seconds to get out of the dinghy. How the hell are Wolf and Muppet getting up there?"

"He's right," Wren said. "You can forget it if you think I'm going anywhere without Wolf."

"We're not leaving anyone behind," Mya snapped. "Give me a minute to think."

"I thought you knew this place," Mike replied.

"Yeah. I do, Mike. I knew there was a pier, but I'd never actually been down to it."

"Never mind the dogs. How are we going to get up there?" Robyn asked.

"I think I can see a metal ladder rising out of the water," Mike replied.

"I bet that's safe."

"Look," Mya said, clenching her eyes shut tight. "Wren, Robyn. You get onto the pier first, just like we said. Darren, you get up next. Mike and I will pass Wolf and Muppet up while Mila holds us in place and keeps her eyes peeled for anything in the water."

"That's it?"

236

"Feel free to speak up if you've got a better idea, Robyn."

"How deep do you think it is by the pier?" Mila asked.

"I don't know. I mean they used to moor paddle steamers there, so you'd think it would be deepish."

"Yeah," Mike said. "The further to the left we go the harder it is to row, so I'm guessing we're in deeper water."

"Let us hope, yes?"

They carried on for several minutes. Sometimes, when Mike stroked, it was hard to notice whether they moved at all. What they did notice was the army of creatures lining the George the Fifth Bridge. "That's an awful lot of infected for six people to take on," Darren said.

"Yeah," Mya replied. "It is. But unless you want half a million more making a beeline towards us, this is how it has to be."

"They're following us," Mike said as the horde drifted on the bridge with each stroke he made towards the pier.

"That's why we need to be quick. When we hit land, any wasted seconds could be the difference between life and death."

"I'd say about another minute and we're going to reach the pier."

They all looked up. The creatures still hadn't fathomed that the brightly coloured dinghy was going to stop at the pier. Like the ones on the Kingston Bridge, they just reached out towards it.

"Okay, this is it. Get ready," Mya said.

The dinghy tipped as Mila stood up and grabbed the rusted ladder. She took the hawser and weaved it around the frame, tying a simple knot while Robyn reached for the top rung and dragged herself up. The rusty construction screeched and shifted a little as she climbed. *Crap! Crap! Crap!* As soon as her feet were on firm ground, she spun around and extended her hand, which Wren took gratefully.

Wolf began to bark again, and as much as Wren wanted to turn around and comfort him, she knew to do so would be death for them all. The sisters drew their weapons. A handful of creatures were jostling for position at the top of the staircase, but at least ten were already making their descent. Both sisters fired at the same time.

*

Darren cast a sideways glance at Wren and Robyn as he reached firm footing on the pier but swiftly brought his attention back to the job at hand. Mike and Mya each had their right hand on Wolf's collar while linking hands beneath his hind quarters and lifting.

All the time, Mila kept a tight hold of the ladder with her left hand, surveying the water around them. On the off chance they were in depths shallow enough for the creatures to reach up, things would get very bad very quickly.

Wolf scrambled with his front paws, placing them on one rung and then the next as he rose. Finally, Darren grabbed his collar and yanked him to safety. The German Shepherd let out a short, sharp yelp, but a second later, he was by his mistress's side, baring his teeth and ready for battle.

*

Wren and Robyn had once been like chalk and cheese. It would have been hard to imagine two sisters more out of sync. But now it was as if a telepathic link existed between them. Wren had aimed for the first creature charging down the stairs. Robyn had angled her bow higher. Her arrow had taken down a beast about to descend the first step. Instead, it fell, causing a logjam at the top of the staircase as others collapsed in a heap.

Wren's bolt had cracked through the skull of her target and it had dropped like a sack of coal, causing those following it to tumble down the steep staircase. Heads smashed and limbs cracked as they bounced down the stone steps. Long before the first of them reached the bottom, though, Robyn had nocked another arrow, Wren had placed another bolt in the flight groove, and they had both fired again.

*

In all the time Mya had known Muppet, she had never seen him scared, but watching Wolf lifted onto the pier had sent a pang of fear through him, and he cowered in one corner. "Come on, baby," Mya said in her most soothing voice, which wasn't easy with the utter mayhem that was unfolding around them. "Come on, Muppet." She took a stride across and the dinghy tipped, causing Mila to clench the ladder tighter in an effort to steady them.

"We don't have time for this," Darren shouted down.

"Come on, baby," Mya said again, reaching out towards the mongrel, who recoiled from her. It was exactly the opposite of what she wanted to happen, but there was inevitability to it at the same time. Trying to scramble away further, her beloved mongrel slipped, suddenly disappearing over the side of the dinghy. "MUPPET!" she screamed, lost in horror. She could feel the heat of a furnace behind her eyes as tears welled. She heard Darren shouting. She heard the chorus of growls as the infected tried to reach them, but the only thing that mattered to her at that moment was her beloved dog. He had been the one constant in her life, the one faithful friend. *I've got to go in after him.*

She took another step, but then the dinghy rocked wildly as Mike dived into the river like a cormorant. By the time he resurfaced, Muppet was already paddling wildly against the current, his eyes wide with fear.

*

Fuck! Mike kept his eyes and mouth tightly closed as he disappeared beneath the surface. He tried not to think about what was below him. *I really hope this part of the river is as deep as we think it is.* The current worked with his powerful strokes and kicks and it was just seconds before his left hand clutched Muppet's collar and he forced a turn in the water, kicking even harder now with just his right arm free to swim with.

239

The rowing had been tiring, but it was as if he'd suddenly been given a giant shot of adrenaline as the cool water surrounded him. He looked across at Muppet, who was paddling frantically too. Mike turned his eyes to the dinghy, which tipped dangerously as Mya leaned over the side while Mila continued to hold on to the ladder with everything she had.

Behind them, he could see Wren and Robyn continuing to lay down fire while Darren remained frozen, watching the scene below. "Take him," Mike shouted, finally reaching the boat and pushing Muppet forward. Mya grabbed Muppet's collar and dragged him aboard before reaching out again for Mike. "Forget me. Get him up."

Mya nodded, guiding Muppet to the other side of the dinghy, thus creating a counterbalance for Mike to scramble in. As he did, he saw Mya and Mila lift the mongrel as Darren grabbed him from the pier. Muppet was clearly traumatised and the fear from before had been replaced with a new one. He was virtually still as his mistress and her friend helped him onto the dock.

"Okay," Darren said. "Chuck us the bags." The two heavy rucksacks containing the car batteries as well as spare ammunition and various other essentials were heaved out first as Mila now climbed out of the boat too.

*

Scheisse! The German samurai ran forward, passing between the two sisters and simultaneously withdrawing both replica katana blades. She had spent longer in the boat than their original plan had allowed and now everything was at risk. Wren and Robyn had done well to control the beasts but had clearly used far more bolts and arrows than anticipated.

Swipe! Slash! Kick! Two down, one in the river. Slash! Slash! Slash! Arrow. Bolt. Three more infected dead and about a dozen more rolling and crashing down the narrow stone staircase. Two more dropped over the side, splashing in the water. *Too deep. Don't think about them. They're gone.*

Flick! Stab! Stab! Kick! Wolf blurred on one side, flying at a creature rising from the writhing, wriggling mass that had formed at the bottom of the staircase. A dripping-wet Mike suddenly appeared on her other side and, despite the abject fear gripping her, a small level of reassurance returned as the plan was beginning to get back on track.

The pair stood as far apart as the narrow pier would allow, and as the next wave of creatures approached, they worked in sync, cutting them down with their blades like they were nothing more than overgrown vines.

*

Another swarm of bodies heaped, crashing on top of others, still trying to scramble up. Mya and Darren ran forward, she with her crowbar, shattering skulls with fearsome violence; he with a hunting knife, advancing, stabbing, slitting, and slicing before jumping back to gain perspective for the next threat.

"Shiiit!" Wren hissed as her target shifted at the last second and the bolt went over its head into the stomach of a creature further up the staircase. "Look out, Mya!"

Mya turned her head too late to see the beast almost on top of her. She let out a surprised cry as she fell back onto a carpet of already slaughtered creatures. Up until this moment, Muppet had been pacing with his tail between his legs. She had never seen him like this before, unsure and fearful, but seeing his mistress in such a dire situation it was like a switch had flicked inside him. He charged between Wren and Robyn, launching through the air and knocking the attacking monster backwards with hurricane force.

Muppet rolled once, twice, three times while Mya and the creature began to gather themselves, but the mongrel was up first, leaping at the beast again, knocking it face down this time and giving Mya enough time to bring her crowbar up and strike.

The crack seemed to echo across the Clyde as the beast fell still.

*

Mike and Mila rushed forward now, taking over from Darren and Mya as the next creatures began to scramble. The falls had left many of them with dislocated and broken bones, inhibiting some of the faster and more violent movements they were normally capable of, but the pair took no risks. They treated them all as if death was just one outstretched hand away.

Slash! Crack! Kick! Crack! Swipe!

One by one, the massacre continued. One by two by three by four, the monsters collapsed down the staircase until no more appeared.

*

Robyn and Wren maintained their focus and their aim for several more seconds until they were sure the coast was clear. Then they placed their bows down and ran forward, withdrawing their knives and joining the melee. Stab! Stab! Crack!

Many of the bodies were slow. Some were pinned down by multiple others, making it easy for the seasoned fighters to finish them off. It was only when they saw Wolf sit that they realised the danger was over for the moment.

*

Gradually, the others stood back too. Their eyes scanned the piles of corpses, looking for movement, and when they saw none, they retraced their steps along the short pier to grab their rucksacks.

"That went well," Robyn said.

"Sarcasm isn't really going to help us much right now, Bobbi."

"Too bad. That's all I've got left."

"That was some amazing shooting, girls. Well done," Mya said. "We'd better collect as many of the arrows and bolts as we can. I get the feeling we're going to need them."

"That's a happy thought," Robyn sniped again.

They began to search the bodies, but Mya pulled Mike to one side. "You're wringing wet," she said, rubbing her hand up and down his arm.

"Yeah. Water tends to do that."

Mya smiled. "Funny," she said before her face became more serious and she looked down at Muppet. "I've never seen him like that. I don't know what happened."

Mike pulled his T-shirt off and rang it out. "You told me once how you just looked up and found him there. He could have been wandering the streets before the outbreak for all you know. He might have escaped an abusive owner. You don't know what the poor little guy might have gone through." He pulled the T-shirt back over his head.

"Thank you anyway. Thank you for going in after him." She leaned in, giving him a peck on the cheek. "I'd be lost without my boy." With that, she turned and began to help the others in the search for bolts and arrows.

Mike looked down at his jeans and trainers. As he moved, it felt like he was still in the water. *This is going to take forever to dry out.* He looked at Muppet and now the mongrel stared back with what appeared to be a smile on his face while his tongue rested out of the side of his mouth. "I'm glad you find it funny." Mike reached for his jacket and bundled it into his rucksack before slipping it onto his back.

When they were sure no more arrows or bolts were salvageable, they began the task of ascending the staircase. It was littered with bodies, making it hard to find a steady footing. "Only hold on to the handrail where it looks safe," Darren said. It was sage advice. In some places, it had crumbled away as creatures had fallen and disappeared into the depths of the Clyde. In others, the rusted metal had become paper thin; all it would need would be one good push and the whole thing would collapse.

Mike went first, clearing some of the bodies where climbing over them would have been too hazardous. When he finally reached the top of the staircase, his heart sank as he looked up and down the street to see infected in both directions. For the time being, they hadn't seen him, but their presence was a reminder of just how dangerous this mission was.

"Shit!" he growled more to himself than anybody else when the first group began to move towards them as he helped Mila over the last of the bodies at the top of the stairs.

She took a deep breath. "I think you and I are going to be busy this morning, yes?" she said, withdrawing her blades. The two of them walked out into the middle of the road, gaining the attention of all the creatures and making sure the others had time to navigate the staircase before having to do battle once more.

Mike looked over his shoulder. The second pack had seen them, too, now. "Crap."

Mila turned. "Which side do you want to take?"

"Whichever." He shrugged and they stood back to back as Mila swivelled, taking the west approach while Mike took the east.

Robyn was next to appear from the staircase and she immediately nocked an arrow. "Come on, Sister dearest. We've got more work to do."

Wolf and Muppet stepped onto the street next, followed by Wren. Robyn had already fired by the time Wren had placed her first bolt in the flight groove of her bow. There were fifteen creatures heading towards them from the east and slightly fewer than that from the west, but as the excited growls got louder with each step the beasts took, they all knew that more could be roused at any moment.

Robyn fired again, bringing another RAM down before nocking a third arrow. The reassuring twang of the string rang out again and brought down another monster making several more stumble.

Wren stood by Mila's side. The creatures were still seventy or so metres away. Click. The first bolt whistled loudly before cracking straight through the head of one of the forerunners. She fired again. Another down.

Mya withdrew her crowbar, gently placed her rucksack on the ground, and went to stand with Robyn and

Mike while Darren joined the other pair. Mike and Mila suddenly broke away, running forward, knowing that they had to give time and distance to Wren and Robyn for them to be effective.

It worked. All the remaining creatures zeroed in on them. For a moment, Mya and Darren were a little bewildered by the seemingly rash action, but then they understood and ran forward too.

"Communication would be nice," Mya said under her breath as she withdrew her knife.

The first four beasts were on them at the same time. Both Mike and Mya kicked out, sending their targets flying backwards into more creatures, before striking their remaining attackers with juggernaut force. A saucer-shaped section of head spun just a couple of feet in front of Mya's face as Mike sliced with one of his machetes.

Before it had even landed, he'd leapt forward as an arrow took care of yet another attacker making several more behind it fall.

*

Darren felt redundant as he watched Mila work. She was like something out of a video game. Slash, swipe, stab, swipe. She did not relent. He stood there with his knife in hand, ready to take on any monsters that approached, but Mila had requested space when they had run forward, and that is what he had given her.

Wren took another attacker down, then another. But the battle to the west was over. She swivelled around just as her sister fired again. Mike and Mya continued to blur for a moment as they finished off the remainder of the pack. Then they all fell still.

Ever since they had ascended the staircase, something had nagged at all of them beyond the two groups of advancing creatures, and now that they had a moment's pause they all realised what it was. A drone rose from somewhere in the city. The Glasgow streets were labyrinthine and it was hard to tell where, exactly, but they knew that one wrong turn could lead them to meet up with thousands, if not tens of thousands, of infected.

"Jesus," Darren gasped. "There's no way we're going to make it out of here."

Wren looked down at Wolf. He had remained by her side rather than running forward with Mila to fend off the attack. It was uncharacteristic of him. It was almost as if he sensed a far greater danger in the air and so remained glued to his mistress to protect her.

Mya had ordered Muppet to stay with Robyn. She knew the fight would be brutal and fast. She didn't want to have to think about him getting caught in the crossfire, and now, as she looked back, the mongrel sauntered over towards her.

Mya was someone who would never accept defeat, but the reality of the situation was catching up with her quickly. They had barely got off the boat and already been run ragged. Without a doubt, as they travelled through the city, worse would be waiting for them.

"Come on," Mike said. "Let's get these arrows collected and then we can carry on."

"Didn't you hear what I said?" Darren asked, walking up to the younger man. "This is a suicide mission."

Mike shrugged. "I heard you. What do you want me to say? We're in it now. We have to carry on."

Darren picked up the heavy rucksack from where he had laid it down. "We need to come up with another plan because this isn't going to work."

"What other plan?"

"Maybe we head back out of the city. Maybe we can find resources on the outskirts. I mean this is a big industrial centre. There might be food warehouses, wholesalers, all sorts just waiting for us to stumble across them."

"There might be. There might not too. And we've got no idea whether the infected are centralised or spread out through the whole region. We could be wandering aimlessly for a magical food supply that isn't even there.

And while we're doing it, we could run into a massive swarm of those things."

Darren pointed in the vague direction of the drone. "I think it's pretty safe to say they are centralised, Mike. I'm listening to them right now."

"Stop this," Mya said, weighing in. "Mike's right. We're in this now and we don't have an alternative but to see it through. We can't just go off script searching for something we might never find."

"I don't like this. I don't like any of this. I don't have a problem putting my life on the line for our people, but I do have a problem throwing it away. Let's face it. We're their only hope. We've got kids back at home. We've got older people who can't look after themselves. If we don't go back, they're all finished. I say we need another plan. Look," he said, gesturing around. "There are offices and businesses all around here. Let's get into one of these buildings, find a Yellow Pages and a map and come up with something, the six of us."

"We—"

"We've only just arrived and we've nearly had our guts handed to us twice. We've been lucky, but this is a big city and I don't have high hopes that our luck's going to hold out, Mya. I want to go back with enough supplies to make sure we've got a chance to start again. I wouldn't have come down here in the first place if I didn't. But this is crazy."

"Crazy is looking for something that isn't there."

Darren shook his head. "This station we need to find, what's it called again?"

"Saint Enoch."

"Okay. Saint Enoch. Where is it exactly?"

Mya's left eye twitched a little as she pointed diagonally through an old building towards the heart of the city.

Darren put a hand up to his ear. "Exactly. You hear that? 'Cause I'm sure as hell I do."

"The time for thinking about a different plan would have been before we set foot on that pier, yes?" Mila said. "None of us wants to be here, but we are here now. Yes, it is dangerous. Yes, it is—"

"Dangerous?" Darren cried. "Dangerous is walking on a tightrope over an alligator enclosure. This is like doing it drunk while juggling knives and performing a fucking pirouette in the middle."

"Darren, mate," Mike said, walking up to him and placing a hand on his shoulder. "Wherever we go, we could face the same dangers. In a place the size of Glasgow, there could be a horde around every corner. And hell, this is fucking Glasgow we're talking about. The bastards'll probably nut you before they eat you." Darren let out a small laugh. "I've got two sisters at home and there is nothing I want more than to hold them again. If I thought for a second there was a better alternative, I'd take it. But there isn't."

Darren let out a long breath and closed his eyes. "This is a bad idea. It's a really bad idea."

"Yeah. But in the absence of any others, it's the only one we've got."

18

At sunup, Emma had been among the first to step foot outside of the centre. She had headed one of the groups, Vicky another, Andy a third, and Jules a fourth. They had separated the grounds into quarters and carried out a search for any stray infected that may have wandered in when the gate was down.

Kat and Ephraim stood on guard at the doors of the centre with Meg and Jenny. Jenny was under no illusions that her presence was merely needed to placate her beloved dog, who acted like an early warning system. Inside, Beck, Mel, Trish, Liz and Doug all did their best to keep spirits up while coordinating breakfast. Beck had a natural ability to put people at ease in even the direst situations, and while a full sweep of the grounds was carried out, the mood indoors remained buoyant as a result.

When the four patrol groups had finished, they did another sweep, and when Emma was as certain as she could be that the grounds were clear, she commissioned Andy and Rob to select a team who would man the gates and perform regular checks of the fences.

"All things considered, darling, I think the overall mood is a lot better than it could be," Jenny said as she and her friends all sat around one of the dining room tables, eating the meagre pickings that constituted breakfast. Dry crackers and jam washed down with hot tea were on the menu, and as simple as it was, they relished every bite.

Emma shrugged. "As long as people aren't screaming, crying and praying for death, I'll take it."

"That's the spirit."

"You know," Sammy began, "there are lots of oak trees in the woods. Soon, we'll be able to collect acorns."

"A few months? Sammy, I can't think past the next few days at the moment," Emma replied.

"Why do you want to collect acorns?" Ruby asked. It was the first time she had been out of her room for more than fifteen minutes since they had arrived.

"You can make flour out of acorns. If we collected enough, we could have bread through the winter months."

"Is that true?" Ruby asked, turning to Emma.

"Don't ask me. Sammy's the one who knows all about that stuff."

"Yes, she's right," Richard said. "There's so much fruit in the forest just there waiting to be gathered."

"Yeah, well, there wasn't that much fruit when we went out again yesterday," Emma said.

Ruth reached across and took the younger woman's hand. "They'll be back. They'll be back and things will start getting better. Things are already getting better."

"How do you figure?"

"We could easily have lost people last night. Thanks to your leadership, we didn't. You can feel the mood this morning."

Emma took a drink of tea and shrugged again. "How's Tommy?" she asked, turning to Ruby and changing the subject.

"Rocking back and forth on a chair in front of the window while reading a telephone directory."

"What, literally?"

"Yeah. But it's an improvement. At least he's reading again now." Ruby let out a sigh. "And on the subject of Tommy, I should probably head up there and take him some breakfast."

"Look, I'll get people to have a look around and see if there are any books or manuals or anything squirrelled away around here."

"Thanks, Emma," she said, smiling weakly as she headed towards the door.

"When are we heading out?" Sammy asked.

"After last night, I really don't think we should be going out there," Emma replied.

"I'm not scared."

"I know you're not, Sammy. But the fact is we got attacked last night, and I don't know if those things can smell the smoke from the fires we've been burning or what, but there's a chance that more might be heading this way, and I don't like the idea of us going out there right now. There are trees in the grounds; maybe we can have a forage around here."

"There are hardly any compared to outside. We're not going to find much, if anything at all."

"I tell you what," Richard said, "how about we take some of the children into the grounds today and Sammy can deliver a lesson on foraging?"

"I think that's a splendid idea," Ruth said.

"You don't need to patronise me," Sammy said.

Emma smiled as she witnessed the expressions of shock sweep over Ruth's and Richard's faces. "Sorry. That's her new thing. People patronising her."

Sammy turned to look at her older sister. "Don't make fun of me."

"I'm sorry, Sammy. Richard and Ruth weren't patronising you though. I think it's a great idea for a lesson, and at the same time, you can take a proper look at what we've got on the grounds. I'm pretty certain when I was on patrol this morning, I saw blackberry bushes, and there were croppings of dandelions all over the place. Y'know, the tea we've got isn't going to last forever. Making some dandelion coffee would be a good way to plan ahead."

Sammy looked at her for several seconds and then looked back to Richard and Ruth. "I'm sorry."

"It's alright, Sammy," Richard said. "I get it. But we really do need to plan ahead if we're going to survive down here and I think the sooner we show people what to look for the better, don't you?"

Sammy nodded. "I've got drawings."

"What do you mean?"

"Nana Fletcher had a big book with pictures of food that could be picked from the wild. I sketched a lot of the plants that Wren and I found so I'd be able to remember them better."

"And you brought these sketches with you?"

"They're in the back of my journal."

Emma suddenly turned to her younger sister. "You keep a journal?"

"Yes."

"You never told me."

"There's a lot about you in there. It's probably best that you don't see it."

The table erupted with laughter. "Fair enough."

"But I'll tear the sketches out and maybe we can use them. I'll go get ready."

They all watched her go. "How old is that sister of yours?" Ruth asked as the young girl disappeared out of the dining room.

"Fifty, sixty…. I lose track."

"She's a fuckin' force of nature. I know that much," Jules said.

"Tell me about it."

"So, what's on the agenda today?"

"After last night, I'm thinking we might need to bolster our defences a little."

"You've already got guards on the gates, which are locked I might add. Plus, there are roving patrols."

"Yeah. I'm thinking we might need something around the actual property too. Y'know, like a safety barricade of some kind."

"Isn't that overkill? And isn't it a bit premature, considering what's hanging over us? I mean if Mike—"

"Mike and the others will be back."

Jules shook her head. "There's no doubt in my mind about that. But what if they come back empty-handed? What if someone else knew about Hope Street? What if they beat them to it? Hell … what if the whole place went up in flames? We really can't be sure."

"Look. There is only one option for us at the moment and that's to treat this place as our home for the foreseeable future at least. With that in mind, I need to do everything I can to make sure that the people are safe." She finished her tea and stood up. "I'm going to see George."

The remainder of the diners watched as she headed through the door her sister had gone through moments before. Jules exhaled deeply. "I hope to Jesus you find what you're looking for down there, Mike," she said, looking out of the window.

"If anyone can, he can, darling," Jenny said.

Jules turned to her. "But what if he can't?"

"Then I suppose things are going to take a bit of a turn, aren't they?"

"Thanks, Jen. That's so fucking reassuring."

*

Shaw brought the bike to a stop. He had visited this house before looking for food, but that didn't matter. Now he was looking for something very different. He opened cupboards and wardrobes and even rifled through an old magazine rack that sat by the side of a threadbare old armchair.

The place had obviously belonged to an elderly person. The cathode-ray tube television in the corner had a layer of dust on it that suggested it had probably not been used since long before the outbreak. There were thousands of properties like this throughout the Highlands and islands and Shaw had visited plenty back when they were scavenging in and around Safe Haven.

He shook his head angrily as what he was searching for didn't magically materialise and he marched back out into the kitchen. He was about to exit the property when he stopped. He had noticed a pile of old newspapers on the top shelf of the pantry when he had searched the place before. It wasn't unusual. Knotted newspapers made good kindling to help get a fire started and most properties out in the sticks still had a real fire.

He headed across, pulling open the pantry door and reaching up, dragging the pile from the top shelf. He threw them onto the kitchen table and they splayed out. Finally, a smile broke on his face. Underneath the newspapers, he found a 2015 telephone directory and Yellow Pages. He had been lost, no, worse than lost. He had felt forsaken, but he realised now that much of that feeling had been self-realised.

The thought of heading back to his people, his family, had given him purpose and more than a little hope. Losing Barnes was life-changing, but losing Lucy, Hughes, and all those before and in between had been too. He was going to go back to the only ones who could help him though. He hadn't wanted to die. He hadn't wanted to give up. He hadn't wanted to walk out on the people he loved, but he had felt they deserved better. They deserved more than he could offer. What had become clear to him from the confrontation with Olsen's people was that he still had a purpose. There was a score to settle, and if it was the last thing he did, he was going to settle it.

Shaw flicked through the Yellow Pages, eventually finding the Skye Outward Bounds Centre. The telephone number in large bold lettering was of little use to him, but beneath it was the address. The display advert read, *A fun day of activity for the whole family. Just past Cirvhig on the A855.*

He had a vague idea of where he needed to go, but it would be a long trek. He reached into his rucksack and grabbed his water bottle, taking several thirsty gulps before tearing the page out and walking back outside. It was going to be another warm day and he didn't relish the prospect of travelling so far in mild temperatures, but there was something more important than his comfort at stake.

He climbed back onto the bike and began to pedal once more. He looked up at the blue sky and smiled. By the time night came, he would be back where he belonged; back where he was needed and back where he needed to be.

*

"Your feet are squelching," Wren said as she and Mike walked side by side with Wolf at her heel.

"Yeah. These bloody trainers were meant to be waterproof, too."

Wren giggled. "It was a good thing you did."

Mike shrugged. "It was a dog. I can't say I'd have done the same if it was a person who fell in."

Wren giggled again. "Thanks."

"I might have made an exception for you."

"Don't get me emotional."

Mike smiled now, but it was only fleeting. Wren could immediately sense something was wrong as she looked towards him. She reached for a bolt. "What? What is it?"

His eyes were cast towards the upper floor of one of the dirty brick commercial buildings further along the road to their left. "Err … I'm not sure."

"Okay. I don't think we're alone," Mya said as she and Muppet joined them.

"I saw a reflection like a mirror or something," Darren said.

"A mirror?" Wren asked.

"Yeah, like a signal mirror."

"Are you sure?"

"Pretty sure."

"Yeah. I saw it too," Mya said, coming to a halt. The others all stopped as well and looked around nervously.

"It's not enough that we've got half a million zombies to deal with. We've got to worry about some creepy bastards watching us as well now," Robyn said.

"I'm not worried about them watching us. I'm worried about what their intentions are."

"So, what do we do?"

"We'll take the next right. There's a road that runs parallel to this. We were going to have to get onto it at some stage. I just wanted to stay on the outskirts as long as we could."

"Are you sure you want to take that risk?" Mike asked. "I mean we could head across there and find out they're still watching us and, in addition, we're closer to the infected too."

The mirror in the distance glinted again. "What is that, Morse code or something?" Robyn asked.

"It's no code I've ever seen before."

"Nah," Darren added. "That's not Morse code. I don't know what the hell it is, but I don't like it."

"Come on," Mya said as they all began to walk again. "The sooner we get off this road the sooner—"

About thirty figures suddenly rushed out of the side street to their left and spread out across the road, blocking their way. They turned to look behind them to see a similar amount to their rear. They all held weapons of some description. A lot carried air rifles and air pistols. Some held baseball bats and machetes while others stood menacingly with homemade spears raised at an angle, ready for action.

"Crap!"

19

Beyond the line of figures in front of them another small army could be seen marching down the street. "We're not here to get into a fight with anyone," Mya called out.

Some were young, probably even younger than Wren. Most were older. She scanned their faces trying to figure out who looked like they were going to reply, but no one did. The army beyond continued towards them.

"What should we do?" Robyn asked under her breath as her hand hovered just a few centimetres from her quiver.

"We don't want to engage if that's what you're asking," Mya whispered.

"What if they want to?"

"I don't think there would be all these theatrics if that was what they wanted. They could have just started picking us off."

"What, with air rifles?"

"Trust me; a few dozen people with air rifles can do plenty of damage, and I don't know if you've noticed the ones with slingshots too."

"Mya's right," Wren whispered. "I spotted one with a pistol crossbow."

The drone of the infected continued in the distance as Mike, Mya, Darren, Wren, Robyn, and Mila just continued to survey the strangers. "If you're not going to let us through, and nobody's going to talk to us, this is going to be a very long morning," Mya said.

There was no verbal response and the line in front finally parted to make way for the other small army that had appeared in the distance a couple of minutes before.

Now someone did speak. "Well, what the fuck have we got here?" It was a man with a thick Glaswegian accent and wild, staring blue eyes. His head was shaved at the sides and his thick beard had been braided. He wore a T-shirt with the sleeves ripped off and carried a hand sickle. He broke from the others and continued towards the small group. "I said what the fuck have we got here?"

Mya was about to speak, but Mike took over. In his time in the young offender's institute he had met a hundred people like this. "Look, mate. We don't—"

"I'm not your mate."

"Okay. What should I call you? I've got a few ideas, but it's probably best that you choose."

"Oh God," Mya muttered under her breath.

Mya and Wren took hold of Wolf's and Muppet's collars as the man stepped closer. He was a good six inches taller than Mike and a lot broader. "So, you're a fucking comedian, are you?" The man turned to look at his people before his gaze set on Mike once more. "Come on then, funny man. Tell me a joke. Make us all fucking laugh."

"You hear the one about the dickhead who wanted to act like a big man in the middle of a city overrun with about half a million infected?"

"Please," Wren said. "He has a brain tumour. He doesn't know what he's saying half the time."

The man glanced towards Wren for a moment then looked back at Mike. His stare burnt into him as he tried to get a read on the younger man. Then he suddenly burst out laughing. It was a deep, raucous laugh, and he turned towards his own people again as some of them laughed too.

"I was right. You are a fucking comedian. It'll pain me to kill you because we do need humour in these dark times."

"Look, mate, pal, honey bunch, whatever the fuck you want me to call you. We've got no beef with you. Let us be on our—"

"Ohhh, you might not have a beef with me, smart man. But I've got a beef with you. You think you can just stroll into my city like you own the place? Do you have any idea what we've had to do to survive here? And you just come waltzing in. Others have tried. Usually, they're bright enough to come in groups bigger than yours, but they've tried and either left or died, and that's the choice you've got now." Finally, he broke eye contact with Mike and looked at the others. "What's in this city stays in this city. All the supplies, everything belongs to us. You've got this one chance to turn back and get the fuck out of here."

"That's it?" Robyn asked. "You'll let us walk out?"

The man nodded. "Aye. You just turn around, weapons, doggies and all, and you carry on as if you've never even fucking heard of Glasgow."

Mike felt a hand on his shoulder. "Come on, Mike. It's a good offer," Mya said, desperate to diffuse the situation.

A broad smile crept onto Mike's face. "That's not going to work for me."

"Oh shit," she muttered under her breath.

It was the Mohican's turn to smile now, and a booming laugh erupted from his depths once more. "Oh, man! I told you that you were fucking funny. I don't know if you've noticed, but there are six of you and like a hundred and twenty of us. By all means, try to get past and see what happens." He stepped out of the way so Mike was face-to-face with the solid wall of bodies.

"Mike, we'll figure something else out," Mya said.

Mike turned to look at her pleading eyes then looked back to the other man. He slipped off his jacket and his rucksack revealing the soaking T-shirt that was still glued to his skin. The Mohican looked confused as he noticed for the first time that the other man was actually wringing wet. Mike plucked the knife from his belt and dropped that on the ground too. "Fuck you. We're not going anywhere."

The Mohican looked more baffled than ever. "What the fuck are you doin', boy? Have you got a fucking death wish?"

"Nope. I've got a family back home that I'll do anything to see again."

"Then I'll ask you again. What are you doin'?" His brow furrowed as he stared at Mike. "Was the wee lassie right? Have you got a fucking tumour or something?"

"No. But I've come up against plenty of stone-cold killers. And they don't let people walk away carrying guns and weapons. If they have an advantage over someone, they take it. You could have taken us out, but you chose not to. I'm looking around at the rest of your people and they're not killers either. They're doing what they have to do to stay alive, just like we are."

"Exactly. And what we have to do to stay alive is protect what's ours."

"Michael?"

The faint, accented voice came from behind the Mohican and both he and Mike turned to the diminutive young woman who had spoken. For a moment, nothing registered with Mike. *This is surreal. How the hell does someone know my name?* Then a vague hint of recollection sparked within him. "Zophia?"

"Wait a minute," the Mohican said. "You know this walloper?"

Zophia stepped forward with a disbelieving smile on her face. "Michael," she said again.

"You know her?" Mya asked.

Mike was still more than a little bewildered as the young woman continued towards him. She took one of his hands in both of hers. "You said your family got out?"

He nodded. "Not all of us made it, but yeah."

"Um. Hello. Anybody care to tell me what the fuck is going on here?" asked the Mohican.

Zofia looked at him and frowned. "Hush."

The man put his hands up. "Fuckin' excuse me."

"And stop swearing."

The Mohican shook his head and stood back. "Of course, Your Majesty. Don't you mind me."

"Griz, I've lost it." It was a young Asian boy who had spoken. He was looking at a small screen that was attached to a remote control.

"Oh shit," hissed the Mohican. "This is obviously not going to be a short conversation. Let's get back to the hotel and we can figure out exactly what the hell's going on there."

Zofia looked at Mike and the others. "Come, we must hurry. The infected could be on the move."

Mike turned to his friends who shared Griz's confusion. "Who is this, Mike? What's going on?" Wren asked.

"I can tell you who she is, but I really don't have a clue what's going on. This is the nurse who came to visit us when Alex got bitten."

"But—"

"Trust me. I get it. I don't understand either. But I think we'd better follow them, don't you?" Mike picked his belongings up and followed the others.

The one called Griz was plainly the leader. He made sure all his people were on the move back up the street before he set off himself. He looked across at the young Asian boy. "Saffy! Talk to me."

"They were in front of Waterstones when I lost sight of them."

"What's going on?" Mike asked.

"When we're out, we always have eyes in the air to make sure we know where the horde is. A few of them we can handle, but if the horde ever found us, that would be it. Occasionally we lose one of the drones. It's too much of a risk to stay out here when we can't see what's going on." Griz looked back to make sure there were no stragglers as his people and the newcomers alike sprinted along.

"Where's this hotel?" Mike asked.

"It is where we live," Zofia replied. "One of the places anyway."

Within a minute, they had reached a modern-looking building that had clearly been adapted. Where glass doors had once hung, now two large metal doors stood. The windows had a collage of steel panels welded over them, and as Mike and and the others rushed inside, torch after torch flicked on to illuminate the dark interior of the foyer.

Griz hovered in the entrance while the doors were bolted behind them. When he was happy that they were secure, a second set of internal entrance doors, once again metal rather than glass, were bolted too.

Many of his people had already begun to ascend the staircase, but Mike and the others remained. "I'm sorry, Griz," said Saffy, who had stayed in the foyer with Zofia.

Griz reached out and ruffled the teenager's hair. "You did what you needed to do. As soon as you lost sight, you told us, and that's why we're all safe now. We've got more drones, but we can't replace someone's life, can we?"

"I suppose not."

"Now, go on. We'll be up shortly." Griz turned to Zofia, Mike and the strangers. "Now, would someone tell me what the ever-loving fuck is going on? You know this dafty again, how?"

"Let us go upstairs where we don't have to speak in torchlight," Zofia said, and she turned, leading them all towards the staircase.

Griz paused a moment and grabbed Mike's shoulder. "Listen to me. This is my home. These people are my family.

I try to be a reasonable man, but if you disrespect anyone, threaten anyone, or generally just piss me off, we're going to have a proper falling out, you and me. D'you ken?"

Mike nodded. "I get it."

They climbed floor after floor until they reached a large open-plan area that had once been the hotel's bar and restaurant. It was a generic, characterless place that could have been any one of a million similar hotels.

Hundreds of eyes glanced towards the newcomers as they paraded through. People of all ages, colours and creeds sat around tables as they finished their breakfasts, ready to start the day. All of them nodded towards Griz and Zofia respectfully but eyed Mike and the others with suspicion.

"How many people live here?" Wren asked.

"In this building, there are about two hundred," Zofia replied.

"This building?"

"Yes. We have—"

"We have a lot of talking to do before we tell you the ins and outs of everything that's going on here," said Griz, interrupting her.

They finally reached a partitioned lounge, which acted as a small private function area in days gone by. Griz gestured towards the chairs and he sat down too.

"How did you end up here, Zofia? I don't get it," Mike said as his friends, still baffled, just watched and listened.

"The field hospital fell and we realised by the reports that were coming in that the same was happening all over the city. There was nothing we could do but flee. We escaped into the country with—"

"We?"

Zofia nodded. "My sister Amelia and two more nurse friends. We escaped north. We spent the first few weeks in Cumbria then headed over the border."

"Yeah, but why the hell would you come to the most populous city in Scotland?"

"We were captured."

"Captured?"

"There was a man called Tuck. A bad man, Mike. He and his people captured us and hundreds more like us. They made us work. They used us as fodder for the infected while they raided towns and villages. They did unspeakable things." Her eyes hung heavy as she spoke and no more explanation was needed as to what those unspeakable things were.

"One day, we came into the city and that is when Griz saved us."

"Saved you?"

"He freed us. That was the beginning of the war with Tuck. We lost a lot of people, Mike." She looked down at the floor and shook her head. "A lot of people," she repeated with her soft Polish lilt. "But eventually, we won. Tuck and his army fled, and the people he enslaved are safe, and now we all live here."

"You all live in this hotel?"

"And others."

Mike frowned. It was the second time she had alluded to other hotels being occupied too. "I don't understand. How—"

"Let's not get ahead of ourselves, shall we?" Griz said. "Now, this is all lovely, you two having a good old catch-up, but what I want to know is—"

"And you," Zofia said, interrupting. "How did you get up here?"

Griz raised his eyebrows, lifted his hands up and flopped them down on his thighs. "Don't fucking mind me, will you?"

"Hush," Zofia said. "There are children out there."

"They can't hear a word."

"You will not swear around the children."

Griz's shoulders sagged and he shook his head. "Is there any point in me being here? Shall I just let you all have a nice blether?"

Zofia gave him a long stare until she turned back to Mike. "Go on."

"It's a long story, Zofia. We escaped Leeds with a couple of people you might have known. There was a doctor called Lucy and a nurse called Samantha."

A childlike smile lit Zofia's face. "Samantha and Lucy are alive?" she asked excitedly.

There was a long pause before Mike answered. "No. Not anymore. Samantha died on the journey up here and Lucy was killed a few months back."

Zofia's expression immediately changed. "Was killed? By infected?"

"No," Mike said, shaking his head. He looked towards Griz. "We're in a war of our own at the moment, Zofia. We had a settlement on the northwest coast where we lived until a couple of days ago. We were attacked and we had to flee; otherwise, we'd have been wiped out."

"I am sorry. You are the only survivors?"

"No. We've got just less than seventy more. We've taken refuge at a place on the Isle of Skye, but we've got virtually no supplies and that's why we're down here."

"So you thought you'd come here and take what's ours?" Griz said, turning to Zofia. "I told you."

Suddenly, Zofia looked a little uncomfortable. Yes, it was nice to see a familiar face from the past, and yes, their story was heartbreaking, but at the same time, her community was the one that mattered the most. "Mike, we have worked hard to build what we have here. It is—"

Mike put his hand up to stop her. "Look. This is where it gets complicated. We're not here to steal."

"Oh, so you're here on holiday then?" Griz asked. "My fucking mistake." He gestured towards the city. "Please have at it. Have a fucking ball."

"Listen. Prime Minister Beck's with us."

"Sure he fucking is. We've got Elton John out back. Would you like him to sing you 'Candle in the fucking Wind'?"

"I'm serious."

Zofia looked at Mike long and hard then turned to the other faces. "Why is he with you?" she asked.

"It's a long story, but this was his bodyguard," Mike said, gesturing to Darren. "And she is"—he pointed towards Mya—"well, in all honesty, I don't have a clue what she is, but she came up with Beck."

"So, what does this have to do with the price of bread?" Griz asked.

"There's a warehouse under the city."

Griz stared at the younger man. "Sure there is," he said, letting out a small laugh. "It's probably right next to the underground Tesco and the underground Vue cinema."

"Griz, Allie wants to know if you can spare five minutes?" said a woman as she appeared around the corner. The murmur from the expansive restaurant area was little more than white noise as they all spoke.

"I'm a wee bit tied up now. I'll pop down directly."

"Okay. Cheers," she said, smiling before glancing towards the strangers and disappearing once more.

"Go on, Mike," Zofia said.

"They built an underground station that never became part of the line. It was adapted as a bomb shelter, but when everything went south, they started using it as a supply depot. They were constructing a purpose-built survival complex in the sticks somewhere, but it wasn't finished in time, and a lot of the supplies that were going to stock it and help build a future after the fall are still sitting there."

A booming laugh left Griz's mouth and all the conversations in the restaurant beyond fell quiet for a moment before beginning once more. "Oh, man! That is priceless. We've got a guy here called Mad Matt. He lived on the streets until the fall and you could say he's not quite the full shilling. He talks about how there's a secret bunker underground with an endless array of food and supplies too. Of course, he also says that he taught Bob Marley how to water ski, Churchill and Hitler were the same person, and Elvis was actually an arc welder from Bolton." Griz sat back, smiling. "I knew you reminded me of someone."

"You are serious, Michael?" Zofia asked.

"He's dead serious," Mya replied.

"You're not buying into this?" Griz asked, sitting forward again and looking at Zofia.

"It is a long way to come from the Isle of Skye, is it not?" she replied, casting a glance towards Griz.

"On the subject of which," Griz continued, "I'm guessing that yacht was something to do with you."

Mike and the others all looked at each other. "How do you know about the yacht?"

"One of our drones spotted it. That's how we found you. Did you think we were all just out for a morning stroll?"

"Yeah. It took us a day and a half to get down here, and you can think what you want about us, but this is real. Beck is with us. We've been through hell and we're trying our hardest to get our people out of the other side. We're not here to raid your supermarkets or whatever else it is that you think we're here to do."

"Say I believe you. Say I trust that you're not here to rip us off and I let you head out there. What's your plan?"

Mike looked towards Mya. "Hell, we've told them this much; we may as well tell them the rest."

"We need to get to Saint Enoch Station. Access to this place is in the tunnel," Mya said.

The smile disappeared from Griz's face and he leaned forward further. "You don't go into the tunnels. You go into the tunnels and you don't come out again. If this place is so big, there's got to be another way in."

"This is the only way in. It's not the only way out, but it's the only way in."

"Then take my advice. Go back to Skye now. Hell, we'll even give you a packed lunch. If you go into those tunnels, that's it. You're dead."

"If we don't go into those tunnels, our people are dead."

A long silence hung in the air until Zofia broke it. "You could bring your people here."

Griz's eyebrows arched upwards again. "Can I have a word with you, Zofia?" he said, almost jumping up from his chair, grabbing the Polish nurse by the arm and guiding her out.

"This is just wasting time," Darren said. "It's nice that you're getting to catch up with someone from your past, Mike. But we need to get out of here."

"It's not exactly like we had a lot of choice coming here in the first place, is it?" Robyn said.

"Maybe we could come and live here," Mila said. "Why not?"

"I have no idea how these people have managed to survive as long as they have, but I'm not moving my sisters into the most populous city in Scotland," Mike replied.

"I don't know. No one seems to be going hungry here. They're not exactly wearing rags. I suppose they've pretty much got their pick of the clothes shops when they want something new," Robyn said.

"And there it is," Wren replied. "My sister's single best reason for moving to a city with six hundred thousand infected mulling around. She'd be able to change her wardrobe on a whim."

Mike suddenly looked down. "Actually, all things considered, I wouldn't mind a change of wardrobe right now."

Wolf and Muppet had been lying on the floor next to Wren and Mya up until this point, but now they sat bolt upright and looked to where Zofia and Griz had disappeared moments before.

Saffy and a girl who, in all likelihood, was his sister, came around the corner carrying two dog bowls. "Are we okay to give them some food?" he asked, smiling at the two dogs.

"I'm pretty certain neither of them will object," Mya replied. The two teenagers placed the bowls on the ground and the hungry dogs immediately dived in.

"Thank you," Wren said.

"We're getting some food together for you, too," said the girl.

Zofia entered a moment later with a couple of pairs of boots and a small bundle of clothes for Mike. "I wasn't sure of your size. You can get changed behind there," she said, nodding to a partition.

"What's happening? Is Griz letting us go?" Mya asked.

"He will be back soon. I am to give you the grand tour and he will catch up with us."

"We really don't have time for this," Darren said.

More people entered the room behind her carrying trays. "After you have eaten, I will show you around," she said again then exited.

Darren let out a long sigh and shook his head. "Look," Mya said. "Let's have something to eat, be good guests, and then we'll be on our way. We should be grateful this didn't go in a different direction."

"Amen to that, sister," Robyn said, shovelling a big spoonful of cornflakes into her mouth.

20

Most of the diners had disappeared from the restaurant and bar by the time Mike and the others began their tour. "Why here? Why this place?" Mike asked.

"Griz was the assistant manager here."

"Him?"

Zofia laughed. "He is a lovely man when you get to know him."

"I'm sure."

She stopped and turned to Mike. "He saved a lot of people. The council estates, residential blocks and old people's homes in the area; those who had no hope, no food, no way to get out of the city, he brought many of them here and to the other hotels. People do not go hungry or thirsty and they are as safe as they can be."

"But why here? Why in the centre of a city when the outlying areas would surely be safer?"

"There are too many old and infirm people to move. My sister and I run the hospital on the next floor up."

"Hospital?"

She nodded. "We do the best we can. We have lots of helpers." Zofia handed Mike a torch then turned and carried on to the staircase. She flicked her own lamp on and led them up. They did not stop on the hospital floor or the one after that. They continued until they reached the top. Zofia pushed the panic bar on the fire door and they all emerged onto the roof.

"Holy cow!" Mike gasped as they stepped out.

"Oh my God!" Wren said with equal surprise in her voice. It was not like the roof of any other building they had set foot on. Raised vegetable beds covered a large area of it. Walkways webbed in between allowing convenient access, and at the far end of the roof, dozens of panels fed into solar-powered generators common in the more affluent camping and caravanning communities, but something that had remained elusive to Mike and his people on their various scavenging trips.

"Those things are like gold dust. How did you get so many?" he asked, heading towards them.

"Griz is very resourceful. He also knows this city like the back of his hand."

"This is impressive," Darren admitted. "Very impressive."

"This is nothing. Come see," Zofia said, taking them past the line of solar panels to the west side of the roof.

"You built a bridge?" Mila asked, as incredulous as the others at the engineering and enterprise that had been employed.

The roof of the other building was about ten feet lower and fifteen feet beyond where they were standing, but a walkway had been constructed. People were busily working on the opposite roof and one of them waved at Zofia. "Morning, Asif. You okay?"

"Be happier if we got some rain," he shouted, lifting a handful of dry soil from the raised bed he was working on and letting it flow through his fingers.

Zofia nodded. "We have not experienced a time like this. Running out of water is not something you think could ever happen in Scotland."

Beyond the opposite roof was another and another and another. Each one had raised beds laid over their surfaces and a mass of bodies were already at work despite the early hour. "People live in those buildings?" Mike asked.

"Yes. And more on the other side."

"How many people do you have here exactly?"

"Over a thousand."

"Jesus."

"What the hell's that?" Robyn asked, pointing to one of the taller buildings on the other side.

"This is our water supply," Zofia replied.

"Eh?"

She gestured to a host of bathtubs, which were lined up next to the raised beds. "Each rooftop has its own smaller supply, but Griz and Diamond built—"

"Hang on, Diamond?" Mike asked.

Zofia smiled. "You will meet her. She is an engineer. Very, very clever woman. Anyway, they constructed these giant pools to be used as water towers collecting fresh rainwater." She pointed across to three taller buildings, and as they looked now, they could see pipes travelling across and down.

"And people live in those buildings too?"

"No. Not over there. They are just used for our water supply, but we are having to ration."

"What did they build them out of?" Mya asked.

"There was a big above-ground swimming pool supplier at the Atlantic Quay development. We got all the materials from there and Diamond, Griz and their team erected a network of linked pools, but now the water levels are dangerously low."

"This is incredible," Mya said, folding her arms. "The work and planning that's gone into this place is just amazing."

"Griz is responsible for many ideas, but Diamond is the one who makes it happen." Zofia shrugged. "Of course, we have lots of plumbers, builders and other skilled workers who help."

"Fuck me! I've been looking for you all over. When you said you were going to give them a tour, I thought you meant around the fucking bar," Griz said, emerging on the roof from the fire escape.

"I've told you. Do not swear around the children."

"Fuck's sake," he muttered under his breath before turning to Mike and the others. "Well, since my esteemed colleague so generously invited you and your people to join us earlier and has since shown you around the place, I suppose we'd better talk about ground rules."

"No need," Mike said. "We're not stopping."

"I told you, boy. Even if that booty's there, if you've got to go through the tunnels, it may as well be in Dracula's fucking castle. Nobody who goes down there comes out alive. It's as simple as that."

"We don't have a choice."

"You do have a choice. We're giving you a choice right now."

"You don't understand."

"I don't understand? Jesus, man! You don't understand!" he almost shouted, gaining the attention of many of those around who were busily sowing seeds in the raised beds. "It'll be the end of you if you go down there." He looked towards the others. "All of you."

"This isn't just about survival," Mike said.

"That's all it's about. That's all it's been about since this whole thing started."

"No. The people who murdered our families, murdered our friends. They've got to pay for what they've done."

"Revenge? You're saying revenge is worth dying for? Look, I've been where you are, boy. I know what it's like to lose people, and losing more still is no remedy."

274

"Really? You really know what it's like? D'you know what it's like to hold your wife's hand and feel it gradually turn cold? Do you know what it's like to see your little brother's brains splattered all over the kitchen floor? Do you really know what that's like?" Mya placed a hand on Mike's arm. Without realising it, he'd taken a step towards the other man. He exhaled a long, deep breath. "Olsen's got to pay for what she's done."

"Olsen?" Griz asked.

"Bernadette Olsen. The TrueBrit party."

"What she's done? I don't understand what you mean."

"It was her army that uprooted us. It was her army that killed my wife and brother."

Griz frowned. "No," he said, looking at the others. One by one, they nodded. "Fuck me. I always said she was dangerous. I always said someone needed to stop her or if she had her way, we'd be living under a fucking swastika rather than the Union Jack. Jesus. I thought one of the wee bonuses of living through the end of the world was never seeing her face and never hearing her name again. Fucking bitch."

"Griz!" Zophia said.

"No," said a woman with an accent a little stronger than Griz's, who was working by the side of her son. She stood up straight, massaging her back a little. "I'll allow him that one. Fucking bitch. The day that baby died." She snapped her fingers, trying to recall the name. "Jalila. That was her. The boat they were coming over in capsized. The father died too, but the mother lived. She lived long enough to identify her daughter. Her dead daughter. And that bitch was down in Dover talking about the migrant crisis at the time, playing up to the cameras, making out that these desperate people were somehow to blame for so many children in this country living in poverty and it wasn't the fault of the bankers or the CEOs of the energy companies or the corrupt politicians.

"And when the cameras were turned off, and she thought no one was recording, a mic picked up her conversation. 'Just one less terrorist for the state to feed and clothe,' she said, and her entire entourage laughed. A fucking baby. It was a fucking six-month-old baby. If she'd had the chance, she could have been a doctor, a teacher or anything. But that bitch didn't just revel in the fact that she was dead. She reduced her to a punchline."

The woman's face was red with anger. "So, yes," she said, looking at Zofia. "I will absolutely allow him that one. The fucking bitch." She looked at the others. "I'm sorry for what's happened to you and your people," she added before returning to her digging.

"I get it. I get why you want revenge," Griz said. "Honestly, I do. But heading down there will put an end to that. It will put an end to everything. Bring your people here. Bring them here to join us and at least your family won't have died in vain."

"That's the thing. They did die in vain. They died in vain and the people who did it are going to pay. I'm going to make sure of it."

"Look," Mya said, taking over. "We're going down into that tunnel. I fully intend for this to be the only trip we make to this city, so what's left in there is all yours."

"What do you mean when you say what's left in there is ours?"

"We're driving away with three trucks. From everything I've been told, there's enough down there to sustain a community for years, so I'm guessing there's a lot more than just three trucks' worth. The exit is in an abandoned underground parking garage near the river."

"Aye. I know the place. There's scaffolding and danger signs all over the place. It was like that for years before the outbreak."

"There's a reason they didn't want people sniffing around."

"We could help them," Zofia said.

Griz's eyebrows arched upwards again. "Tell me, is there any point in us having committee meetings at all or should we just let you make all the decisions for us?"

"Ah, shush," she said, smiling. "We could send a drone up so we could at least see if the coast is clear."

Griz turned to look at Mya. "You say there's definitely no other way into this place? I mean what about the car park? Is there no way in through there?"

Mya shook her head. "This is it. It's the tunnel or nothing."

"Fuck me!"

"Griz!" Zofia snapped.

He put his hands up. "I know. I know." He walked to the edge of the roof and stared out across the city, finally turning back to Mya. "I'll get Saffy to sort out a decoy for us. That's another drone we're not going to see again."

"A decoy?" Mya asked.

"We'll attach an MP3 player and a couple of speakers to a drone and fly it low around Saint Enoch Square then lure any infected away. It should give us access to the underground entrance, but it's not going to take care of anything that we find inside. You realise that, don't you?"

"*We* find inside?"

"You don't think my conscience will let a set of wallopers like you head there alone, do you?"

"I did not mean for this," Zofia said. "I meant we could help, not for you to go out there. What will Clara say?"

"What do you think she'll say? I'll be in the fucking doghouse again, but that's just my life now. I've come to accept it."

"Seriously. You should stay here with your people," Mike said. "This is our risk, nobody else's."

"When we built this place, it was with a view to helping everyone … everyone who deserved it, that is. For everybody up until today, all that's involved is putting a roof over their heads, feeding them and keeping them safe. Well, it's my own fucking fault for stepping out this morning to see what the fuck yous lot wanted, isn't it? You need help and someone who knows the city might be the difference between living and dying out there."

"Mya knows the city."

A smile cracked on Griz's face. "There's knowing the city and knowing the city. Me and my crew are proper fucking Weegies, boy. I could walk you around this place blindfolded and backward. Nah! I'm fucking going with yous, and if Clara wants a fucking square-go when I get back, then she can have one."

"I should say this to her?" Zofia asked.

"Oh yeah, please. I'm begging you."

"You need to tell her what you are doing. You cannot just go."

"I'll tell her I'm taking these gommies back to their boat."

"That is a lie."

"Jesus. It's easy to tell you've never been in a committed relationship." He turned back to Mike, Mya and the others. "Meet me on the ground floor in five minutes, and for your sakes"—he turned towards Wren, Robyn and Mila—"I hope you know how to use those things." He nodded at their weapons before turning and heading back inside.

"He doesn't need to come," Mike said.

"I know Griz. Once he has made up his mind about something, he cannot be talked out of it. I hope what you find is worth it."

*

It had been surreal meeting up with Zofia again after all that time. In some ways, they were practically strangers, but she had been there during one of the most turbulent and emotional times in Mike's life, and somehow that made him feel close to her. The fact that she was friends with Samantha and Lucy only cemented that bond further, but now, as they hit the streets, the small modicum of comfort he had felt at seeing her was gone.

The sound of 1990s dance music, with its loud bass and heavy drum beats, gradually drifted away from them as the decoy drone was launched. "He's a good boy is that Saffy," Griz said as they jogged along.

"Wait a minute," Mike called out.

"What?"

He pointed up to a sign. "This is Hope Street? We're only a few metres away from the hotel."

"That's why I've been asking you if there was another way down."

Part of Central Station's wall had collapsed and a giant section of pavement had disappeared beneath it. Rubble littered the street, and on the other side, a fire had torn through one of the shop units causing the roof and upper floors to spill out onto the road too. "I'm guessing they were being ironic when they called it Hope Street."

"Yeah. Of course. It was exactly like this, collapsed walls and all, when they named it that. Y'fucking walloper."

"I'll tell Zofia that you've been swearing again."

A smile crept onto Griz's face. "Like you could make my life any fucking worse. Come on," he said, turning to the others. "Let's get this over with."

They continued to jog down the street, carefully checking the side streets as they passed them. Wolf and Muppet kept pace on the flanks and both started growling simultaneously. Two creatures suddenly appeared from the doorway of an abandoned building up ahead and began to charge towards them. "Taking the one on the left," Robyn called, still moving. She raised her bow and fired, knocking her target back off its feet. Mila sprinted forward and sliced through the air, finishing off the other.

Robyn only paused for a second to pluck the arrow from her victim and wipe it clean before they were on their way again. "Jesus! Remind me not to pick a fight with you two," Griz said.

"Why are we heading down here?" Mya asked. "Wouldn't it have been quicker to just go under the bridge?"

"Aye," Griz replied. "But we'd also have been in sight of the infected. We need to give Saffy a bit of time to clear them. This way, we'll be able to get a good view of the square before we head out, so we'll know exactly what we're facing."

Five more creatures charged out of an alley ahead of them, lured by the loud beat of the music, which could still be heard over the drone of the horde in the distance, but now their attention had been won by fresh prey.

This time, Mike and Mila sprinted forward, coming to a halt side by side. A bolt whistled past Mila's right shoulder, cracking through the forehead of one of the beasts while the remaining four continued.

Mike took a side step and the beasts split into two pairs. He took another sideways stride to separate them further then he and Mila leapt forward, arcing their blades at the same time. The whirling stainless steel glinted in the morning light before disappearing into their would-be attackers' heads. The pair wiped their weapons clean before waiting for the others to catch up and continuing their journey.

"Got it," Robyn called again as yet another creature stormed in their direction. Another arrow flew true from her bow.

"This place is swimming with these things," Darren said.

"Yeah," replied Griz. "Welcome to Glasgow." They turned left and the growls began in the backs of the dogs' throats once more. A pack of fourteen beasts was almost across to the other side of the broad street when they caught sight of the small band of humans and began to charge. "Oh, man. Talk about shit timing."

Muppet and Wolf tore towards the creatures. Wren and Robyn came to an immediate stop and raised their bows while Mike, Mila, Mya, Darren and Griz all ran forward a few metres then spread out in a line.

Arrow. One down.

Bolt. Two down.

Wolf launched, knocking one of the creatures off its feet and sending them both tumbling. Muppet clamped on to another beast's leg, viciously tearing at the flesh. The creature fell forward, its nose cracking on the hard tarmac.

Another arrow flew, followed by another bolt. And the two sisters lowered their weapons, realising friendly fire was a real danger in such close combat.

Mila and Mike stepped forward, slashing and swiping. Mya parried her attacker's arms, bringing the crowbar around and down. A loud hollow crack echoed as her victim dropped to the ground.

Darren ducked the grabbing arms of his assailant, kicking out at its knee and causing it to topple. It crashed onto its side, and in a flash, Darren was on top of it, thrusting his knife through its eye, rendering it still.

Griz swept his sickle around with lightning speed. The blade sliced through the beast's neck as if it was no thicker than a handful of wheat. The gory head spun through the air, landing on the pavement with a thud.

Swipe, slash, stab. Mike and Mila hacked down three more while Mya sprinted forward, finishing off the two creatures Muppet and Wolf continued to tear at. The area fell silent but for their breathing for a moment as they all surveyed their handiwork. The sound of the music was even more distant now.

"I'll ask you again," Griz said. "Are you sure you want to go through with this? Because up here is nothing compared to what we're going to face down there."

Mya wiped off her weapon and returned it to her rucksack as she walked back to join the rest of the group. Wolf and Muppet trotted at her side. "You've done enough for us, more than enough. You should go back to your people. They need you."

Griz shook his head. "If you're going, I'm going."

Mya shrugged and shook her head. "Well … I guess we're all going then."

They set off once more. Even though Wolf and Muppet remained quiet, it did nothing to alleviate the tension or sense of foreboding. Their eyes searched out every alley, every doorway, every obstacle that horror might lurk behind. It only took them a minute or so to reach the end of the road, but it felt like an age.

At Griz's direction, they moved to the left, almost hugging the wall of the building they were using for cover as they went. "Okay," he said. "This is Saint Enoch Square. Let's hope to Christ that Saffy's managed to lure those gruesome fuckers out of the way." He took a breath and leaned forward.

How many times had he walked through this square? How many mornings had he got a coffee or a hot sandwich from one of the cafes on his way to work? *This place was once so full of life. It beat like a heart. It was something beautiful.* Now it was empty, a shell of the thing it once was. For a man who loved his city as much as Griz, it was like a knife in the heart to see it like this.

Even though not a single creature remained, the stench of death lay heavy in the air. Churned-up litter carpeted the streets as months of winter had robbed skips and bins of their contents.

A sad smile flashed on his face for a moment as he remembered Gordy, a craggy-faced street cleaner whom Griz often saw on his morning trek to work. They'd exchange the briefest of nods, occasionally a good morning if Gordy was feeling particularly sociable. *He was a funny old git alright.* He heard shuffling behind him and suddenly he was dragged back into the moment.

"It's all clear," he whispered, turning around. "It's not too late, y'know. My offer still stands."

"And we appreciate it," Mike replied before he and his friends filed past him into the square. Robyn and Wren, both with their weapons loaded and raised, moved out first, taking the flanks while the others jogged towards the subway entrance.

When they reached it, they all broke their surveillance of the surrounding area for a moment to stare down into the darkness beyond the escalators. Mike took a few steps in and withdrew one of his machetes, tapping loudly on the stainless steel siding.

"What the fuck are you doing?" Griz cried.

"If there are any down there, I'd prefer to get them up here where we're not just relying on torchlight."

They all waited with bated breath, listening carefully for the sound of pounding feet or chilling growls. They heard nothing and somehow that felt worse than hearing something. "In all likelihood, if there were any down there that could hear that, they were probably drawn out by the drone. It's the ones in the tunnels I'm worried about."

Mike reached into his rucksack and pulled out his torch and, one by one, his companions did the same. He flicked it on and shone the beam down into the blackness. He felt a presence by his side and turned to see Mya. "You okay?" he whispered.

"Having the time of my life. You?"

Mike smiled. "We're going to be alright, Mya. Yeah, it's dark down there, but we've got Muppet and Wolf. They'll let us know about any danger long before we'll see it."

"Somehow, that doesn't reassure me much."

"We'll be fine," he said again before beginning his descent. Goosebumps rippled up and down Mike's arms as he followed the beam of his torch. The warmth of the morning air was now forgotten as the cool breeze from the underground engulfed him. He could hear feet beginning to follow and the pitter-patter of the dogs' paws as they carefully negotiated the ridged metal steps.

Whispers from Wren, Robyn and Mila raced to catch up with him as a noticeable shift in the atmosphere seized all of them. He glanced over his shoulder towards the disappearing square of daylight. Suddenly, he understood what Griz had been talking about. Theoretically, the dark was the dark, and battling these creatures in a tunnel should be no different to fighting them at night, but there was something different about this.

He continued, finally reaching the bottom step and turning towards the platform. Billboard posters lined the short corridor as a sad reminder of the world that had gone before. A quiet reverence settled over the rest of the group as they followed. Memories of accompanying TV adverts for movies, cars and toothpaste flooded back to them all as the advertising panels caught in the beams of light.

Mike reached the platform and halted. Despite the long tunnels to either side of him, it suddenly felt very claustrophobic. "I told you," Griz whispered, joining him on the platform. "It's different down here."

The hair stood up on the back of Mike's neck as the ominous warning heralded an indistinguishable sound to their right. They panned their torches towards the tunnel, but the light diffused to nothing long before it reached the first bend.

"We need to head this way," Mya said, pushing her fears and doubts down deep inside and pointing to the left. "Beck said it was only four hundred metres, so let's hope he's right."

Griz laughed. "Only four hundred metres. You're not far short of half a kilometre with that figure. Half a kilometre in the pitch black with those things wandering around is plenty for us all to be killed several times over."

"Nice," Robyn said. "Thanks. I'm so glad you decided to come along now. I feel so much better. What do you do as an encore, hum a frikkin' funeral march?"

"I'm just saying. This is a really bad idea, and in my defence, I've been saying that from the start."

Mike jumped down onto the tracks and angled his torch into the tunnel. "We've already had the debate about this. We're going." He started walking and listened carefully, hoping to hear the others climbing down onto the track too. *I'm doing this for Sammy and Em. I'm doing this for Sammy and*

Em. He would never admit it, but there wasn't a cell in his body that didn't feel fear at that moment. *Griz is bang on the money. This is fucking mental.*

He relaxed a little as more illuminating rays joined his own, searching out the darkness. He felt something brush against his arm and turned to see Wren in the periphery of the artificial light cast by the torch she'd secured to the underside of the crossbow's barrel. "I'll have to get Grandad to attach this more permanently when we get back," she whispered.

"I like your confidence. When rather than if. That's the spirit."

"Don't you start." They continued, rounding the first bend, and now the temperature dipped even further. Wolf nudged Wren's leg. "It's okay, boy. It's okay."

"Remember," Mya whispered as loudly as she could without risking her voice carrying down the tunnel. "We're looking for a door on the left." They carried on slowly. There was a part of all of them that wanted to charge, just run as fast as they could and hope they could reach this magical door before they found anything, or, more importantly, anything found them.

After a hundred metres or so, Mike looked over his shoulder. Mya was directly behind him with Muppet at her side. Next came Robyn, Mila and Griz with Darren bringing up the rear.

Robyn stifled a small scream as she angled her torch beam to the right and saw several rats scuttling in the other direction. "It is alright," Mila said, taking hold of her friend's arm. "They are only rats going about their business."

"Yeah," Robyn said. "Me and rats don't have a great history. That's all."

They carried on and the metres ticked by. Even whispers seemed to echo down here, but the deeper they travelled the less any of them were inclined to speak. It was as if there was an inevitability to them running into the monsters that Griz had warned of.

A sudden growl began in the back of Wolf's throat and they all stopped suddenly. Mike withdrew one of his machetes, keeping the torch in his left hand to search the blackness ahead. The sound of running feet travelled through the tunnel towards them.

"I've got a problem," Robyn said. "I can't hold a torch and fire at the same time."

Muppet began to growl too.

"I was saving this in case we got into trouble, but it sounds as if we're there already," Griz said, reaching into his bag and striking a flare. He flung it over the top of Mike's head, and it cartwheeled, finally coming to rest on the tracks ten metres in front of them. They all put their torches away, drawing their weapons instead. The volume of the dogs' growls rose and the air became electrified.

Mya joined Mike on his other side and he heard a shivering breath leave her lips. He heard footsteps to his right and turned to see that Mila had replaced Wren as she now knelt down, taking aim with her crossbow ready to fire at anything that emerged into the red glow of the flare.

*

This is Hell. This is what Hell looks like, Mya thought. All the things she'd done in her life, all the people she'd killed for queen and country wrapped around her like a heavy shroud of human skin weighing her down. She closed her eyes for a second in the hope that the images of pain and torture she had inflicted would disappear, but it was too late. *This is it. This is my day of reckoning.* A small whimper left her mouth as the first demonic-looking creatures emerged into the arc of the red glow.

*

Darren had been to war. He'd seen horrors that he'd pushed down deep inside, but the worst of those were nothing compared to what he was witnessing. He'd known fear. He'd faced death a hundred times before, but this was a different type of fear. This was the fear of Hell and damnation. He'd never been a particularly religious man, but as the charging demons appeared through the smoke and darkness, he couldn't help himself. "Dear God."

*

Robyn fired, but her arrow disappeared through the red glow, through the smoke and into the seemingly infinite darkness beyond. "Uh oh." Terror gripped her as she nocked another arrow and fired again with the same result. "Oh fuck!" *This is it. We're dead.*

21

The first of the creatures was still several metres away when Wren fired. Her bolt disappeared into the neck of the front-runner, barely giving it pause as it emerged into the red light like some grotesque horror movie extra. It dived and Wren's heart skipped a beat as it zeroed in on Mya. In life, the creature had been a Goth. It wore a full-length black leather coat that flapped wildly as it flew through the air. Its pallid face juxtaposed with its dyed, jet-black hair made it look like a vampire rather than a zombie in the crimson glow. "Oh shit!"

*

Mya was frozen with fear as the monster shot towards her. She'd come up against hundreds of these creatures, but as the outstretched fingers of this one closed in, she knew this would be her last day on this planet. She wanted to raise her crowbar more than anything in the world. She wanted to fight and get the job done and emerge a heroine like she had done so many times before, but as soon as she had set foot in this tunnel, a grim certainty had gripped her.

*

She's going to go any second. She's going to go any second. She's going to go any second. Terror had shivered down Mike's spine, too, as he had first seen the arrows miss their targets then the vampiric monster launch towards Mya. *She's going to go any second.* He glimpsed Mya's face and knew at that instant she was dead.

No.

He dived to his left, parrying the creature's reaching arms. Mike was airborne too now but only briefly as the pair crashed into the wall. Mike stifled a grunt of pain as he landed heavily on the ground and watched his machetes somersault onto the track. The chink of steel against steel told him that Mila had entered the battle.

The lithe, black-clad figure he had tackled was on its feet again before Mike had even climbed to his knees. It lunged, and Mike jumped up, battering its arms out of the way with his right hand and seizing the ghoulish figure by the lapel of its coat. In one brutal movement, he hammered the beast's forehead into the wall rendering it dazed for a moment as it staggered back.

Not missing a beat, Mike lurched forward, grabbing the back of its head and smashing its face into the wall again and again and again and again. He heard the bone crack; he saw the splatter against the dark brickwork, but he continued nonetheless. When the creature could no longer stand, he still carried on, using his upper body strength to hold it up. As the sound of more charging monsters reminded him that there was a bigger battle to be had, he let the limp body drop to the ground like a discarded piece of rubbish. He bent over and picked up his machetes. The brutality of his first kill had empowered him and all the fear he had felt moments before had been turned to anger, fury … hate.

He ran across to Mila, who was waiting for the next wave of creatures to arrive out of the darkness. He turned to look at Mya, who was still staring down at the bloody mess he had left behind. He glanced behind to see Robyn and Wren with their bows raised. Griz had his sickle in hand but had still not entered the fray. Darren stood by his side, both men still not able to unglue themselves from the spots on which they were standing.

*

Two more charging creatures appeared. Arrow. Bolt. Both dropped to the ground. Robyn breathed a sigh of relief. The light and smoke did strange things to the eyes. This had affected her aim at first, but now she was getting used to it and she was feeling more comfortable, albeit still terrified.

*

Wren closed her eyes for just a second. *Thank God.* After her first bolt, she feared that she might not be able to hit a single target down there in the depths of the city. Seeing the two creatures go down lifted her confidence.

*

Four more RAMs reached the periphery of the smoky red glow and Wolf let out an angry growl, starting his charge. It was almost as if he was communicating telepathically with his canine friend as Muppet ran forward too.

They pounced at the same time bringing two more beasts down. Mila took a step away from Mike and the pair unleashed killer blows, each arcing down in perfect synchronicity, slicing through the heads of the attacking creatures.

*

Another line approached and, hearing Muppet's vicious protective growl as he continued to maul the monster on the ground, Mya finally forced herself to fight. *It's just a tunnel. The red light is just from the flare. There's nothing*

291

demonic about these things. They're just flesh and blood. She repeated it over and over in her head like a mantra as she kicked out, sending one of the beasts flailing through the thick smoke while she swung her crowbar at head height towards another. The heavy metal connected with the creature's jaw, snapping it like a brittle twig.

Even though it had no hope of being able to bite her tantalising flesh, it gathered itself and lurched again. This time, she brought the crowbar down with jackhammer force, stoving in the monster's skull with a single blow. Before it fell, she jumped forward, doing the same to the creature that had recovered from her kick. She took a breath.

It's just a tunnel. The red light is just from the flare. There's nothing demonic about these things. They're just flesh and blood.

*

Griz was a little in awe of how well the two sisters, Mike and Mila worked as a team, but finally he ran forward too, standing a few feet apart from the German swordswoman as seven more monsters broke through the hellish red haze. Arrow. Bolt. Five left.

Mya leapt towards another, Mike another. Three left.

Mila waited as two honed in on her. Griz's eyes widened as the final creature darted towards him.

At last, he swung, cleaving up and across. The curved blade of his sickle sliced through at an angle. The top of its head resembled a hairy skull cap as it flipped through the air. The monster collapsed and Griz jumped back instinctively, but there was no more danger; the creature was dead.

Another line of beasts shot out of the dark, and this time he was ready, gripping the handle of his weapon tightly as one of the monsters headed straight towards him. Another arrow and another bolt stopped two dead in their tracks and Griz relaxed a little more. *We can do this. We can do this.*

He whipped the sickle around the other way this time, burying the sharp point in the attacking beast's head. He jerked it back out again and he was about to edge forward, ready for the next attack, when a deafening crack made the tunnel quake.

*

Despite the threat of more creatures emerging through the red haze at any second, they all turned to see Darren with his torch raised in the opposite direction. He had fired with amazing accuracy considering the poor light and speed of the moving creatures, but now, as more shots boomed, a feeling of dread consumed all of them. They could see at least ten dancing shadows approaching.

Wren and Robyn raised their weapons again, and despite the dimness of the light, they fired in unison. Robyn's arrow lodged in the chest of one of the charging beasts making it miss a step and causing two more behind to stagger as they ran into it.

Wren's bolt lodged in the forehead of another, sending it crashing to the ground and those behind it to do the same.

*

There was only one possible way out of this now. Mya placed the crowbar in her rucksack, retrieved her torch, and drew her Glock. "RUN!"

This is crazy! This is totally crazy! She looked at Darren as he began to sprint towards her, still firing behind. Wren and Robyn broke into a run, too, each of their weapons still raised. More pounding feet could still be heard from the tracks up ahead, but for the time being, nothing could be seen beyond the red smoke-filled fog.

*

Mike ran forward, too, scooping up the flare and throwing it as far down the tunnel as he could. It somersaulted in the air over the heads of more charging RAMs.

293

"Oh fuck!"

He watched Mila blur in front of him, running first to where Wolf pinned down one of the infected. Slash! Then across to where Muppet did the same. Stab!

He turned to see the dancing beam of Darren's torch as he ran. He panned it back for just a moment to witness the scrambling creatures on the tracks start to gather themselves and give chase.

"Come on!" It was Mya who urged him forward, grabbing his arm tightly. The flare continued to burn brightly up ahead, but between them and it multiple silhouettes could be seen charging.

"It's no good," Wren screamed as they all ran forward. "We can't get clear shots this side of the light."

*

Mila was already fifteen metres ahead of them when she came to a skidding stop on the track. The chances of them making it out of this tunnel alive were diminishing by the second.

The frenzied growls of the creatures seemed to rebound off the walls and come at her from every angle. Another two shots rang out behind, but firing in the dark while running seemed futile. One of the dogs barked and she heard Robyn let out a frustrated cry as another arrow whistled by Mila's side and disappeared into the blackness.

"It's no good. I can't get an aim."

Mila exhaled a long, deep breath and extended both swords to forty-five-degree angles. Suddenly, the shots, the screams, the growls, the barks, the pounding feet all fell silent. The only thing she could hear was the sound of her own breathing. The only thing she could focus on was the wildly animated, monstrous silhouettes emerging from the eerie red glow ahead of her.

She whipped one of her replica katana blades up and around, slicing straight through the neck of the first lunging creature. Without missing a beat, she stepped forward, bringing the other blade around and down, chopping into the head of the next. She booted a third away while she tugged out the deeply buried blade from the second then advanced.

Her sword whistled until it sliced straight through the forehead of a fourth. She twirled, whipping her other blade around and carving through the neck of the beast she had kicked just as a fifth monster leapt towards her, which she dispatched with a single, lightning-fast hack.

Suddenly, the terrifying shadowy creatures were not all honing in on her and she looked to her side to see the unmistakable shape of Mike standing there with her. Another four were on them all at once and they both lunged forward together, chopping them down in unison.

"Come on," he shouted as Wren, Robyn, Mya, Griz, and the dogs all ran past them. Mila was still somewhere else as the words left Mike's mouth. "Come on, Mila!" he yelled again and now she was back. She was back hearing everything, absorbing all the terror just like the rest of them.

Mya was firing up ahead, Darren behind. The dogs were barking, Wren was calling out to Robyn, the demonic sounds of the creatures chilled the air, and their pounding feet gave the whole blood-curdling symphony a beat. From hearing nothing a moment before, now she heard everything, and Mike didn't need to tell her again. They both set off together as still more beasts appeared on the periphery of the red light up ahead.

*

Mike placed his machetes back in his rucksack while they ran, instead drawing his shotgun. He sprinted to catch up with the others, drawing level as they faltered a little with the advance of still more beasts, and then he took over.

BOOM! Two went down at once. *Might be dead. Might not.* It didn't matter. He stopped the advance of several more as he pumped the fore-end of his weapon and fired again. BOOM!

It was like a cannon going off in close quarters.

Crack! Crack! Crack! Mya continued to fire her Glock too. They were on the same page. Yes, they'd like to kill every last one of these things, but that wasn't the mission. They needed to clear a path. If they could make it to that room, then they would be safe.

BOOM!

*

"Oh, God!" Robyn cried as a reaching hand from one of the downed figures brushed against her leg.

BOOM!

Crack! Crack!

Wren looked to her side to see the familiar shape of Wolf matching her pace for pace. She wanted nothing more at that moment than to hold him and cuddle him, but as they continued to run for their lives from an advancing pack and seemingly into another, she wondered if she'd ever have the chance again.

*

"I see it. I see the door," Mila shouted, sprinting ahead, extending her blades and taking two more down. The red light was behind her now and its glow was fading more with each pace she advanced down the tunnel, but for the time being at least, she could still make out the hell-cast shadows as they closed in.

*

Mike chastised himself as he dropped a shell while reloading, but stopping to find it could mean death. He glanced behind to see the beam of Darren's torch bouncing up and down as the former bodyguard sprinted as fast as he could. The chasing creatures could be clearly seen in the arc of light cast by the flare now.

"Fuck!" They were about twenty metres behind, but there were at least thirty, maybe more. Mike slowed to a stop until Darren was nearly level with him; then he fired, pumped the fore-end of the shotgun and fired again.

Several of the front-runners collapsed to the ground, causing a pile-up. It wouldn't hold them long, but it would give them a few seconds, and every single one counted.

He turned and began to run once more.

*

Memories of the Paris tunnel where she had spent the night with Seb, up until that point the closest thing she had ever had to a best friend, came flooding back to Mya. She pulled the door open and shone her torch inside. The small room bore an uncanny resemblance to the one from that night too. Empty shelving units lined the walls, but it was the one on the far wall that she was interested in.

She could hear the chink of metal as Mila dispatched more infected, and as much as she wanted to help her and the others, she could only focus on one thing now.

Another booming echo made the tunnel quake behind her as she ran further into the small storeroom. The feet of the shelving unit screeched as she dragged it out of the way, and for the first time since she had entered the subway, a small flame of hope lit inside her. There was the door, and, just as Beck had said, a small keypad waited for the magic number to be entered.

This was time-proof, it was not something that depended on electricity or a battery backup, and as she began to enter the eight-digit code, she felt the strength of the spring mechanism below the sturdy metal keys push against her thumb.

Mya heard footsteps behind her and she could only hope it was her people. If it was the creatures, then everything was over anyway and it didn't matter if she entered the combination or not.

She keyed in the final number and a loud mechanical clunk rang out behind the door.

BOOM!

Mya closed her eyes. *Please, please, please.* She pressed down on the handle and pulled the door open. They were still a long way from safety, but a smile lit up her face. "Okay, everybody inside," she yelled, grabbing her Glock from the back of her jeans and shining her torch towards the door.

Wren, Robyn, Wolf and Griz filed through the outer door first. Glock fire, followed by another shotgun blast, raced to catch up with them.

"Mila. Get in there." It was Mike's voice.

Seconds later, Mila ran through the entrance with Muppet beside her. Without pause, they both disappeared through the inner door. Darren lingered outside for a moment, emptying his Glock. He ejected the magazine and reloaded as he ran into the small room and through what was hopefully their gateway to salvation.

"MIKE. WHERE THE HELL ARE YOU?" Mya cried, keeping both her torch and weapon raised towards the doorway as the dim glow of red and the diabolical song of the undead drifted into the small room, filling it with more foreboding with each second that passed. "MIKE?"

A final explosion from the tunnel erupted before Mike appeared at the entrance. He slammed the door shut behind him and bodies immediately began to hammer and smash against the thick metal. He toppled one of the heavy shelving units over then another as he continued backing away, his eyes still fixed on the torchlit entrance.

He felt a hand on his arm and he turned to see Mya. His eyes were wild, still in battle mode. "Is everybody safe?" He shook his head. "I just shut the door. I didn't check outside." He started towards the entrance again.

"Everybody's safe. We're all here."

The pounding continued. "We're all here?" He blinked, gradually coming to his senses.

She let go of his arm and grabbed his hand, squeezing it a little. "Everybody's okay, Mike."

The infected continued to batter against the door, but it didn't matter now. Still with the shotgun in his hand, Mike threw his arms around Mya and the pair embraced tightly. "You're sure everyone's okay?" he asked again, pulling away, still not able to believe they were in one piece.

"We're all safe. All of us."

22

Mike and Mya walked through the internal door into the rays of multiple torches that shone towards them. Mya turned and pulled it closed with a loud clockwork clunk as the locks re-engaged.

Robyn let out a small relieved laugh, then her sister followed suit. Darren was next; then all of them were laughing. There was nothing humorous about the situation they were in or the one they had just escaped, but a state of euphoria consumed them all. They shook hands and they hugged. They held each other tightly to make sure the others were real and the whole thing wasn't just some wonderful dream.

Even Griz joined in. "You really are a bunch of fucking mental cases, aren't you? I've never been so sure in my life that I was going to die. What in the name of Beelzebub's gonads was I thinking coming down here with you, you mad bastards?"

They laughed again. "If it makes you feel any better, I was pretty sure we were going to die too," Darren said.

"No. No, actually. In no way, shape or form does that give me even the tiniest modicum of comfort. And I'm telling you all now if any of you ever meet my Clara and mention one word of this, I'll butcher you all in your sleep."

They all laughed again. Even the dogs were wagging their tails. The danger was over for the time being and the relief in the air was palpable. They all bathed in the calm for a few minutes, getting their breath back, coming to terms with how close they had come to meeting a violent end, but, eventually, Mya took charge once more. "Okay," she said, shining her torch down the narrow tunnel. "Our job isn't even half done yet."

The others all panned their beams towards the path ahead and, one by one, they moved off. Good-humoured conversation continued as they all still revelled in the high that escape had given them. Mike was about to follow when Mya snagged him by the arm. "What is it?" he asked, concerned, wondering if there was some danger he hadn't picked up on.

"You saved my life back there," Mya said.

Mike shrugged. "You've saved mine before now. It just seemed polite that I should return the favour."

Mya shook her head and he could see sadness on her face in the glow of the torch beams. "I've never frozen like that before. I don't know what it was, but fear just consumed me. I couldn't move. I couldn't help myself."

"Yeah, well. We're out of there now, and, hopefully, we're never going to get stuck in another tunnel with a bunch of hungry, flesh-eating monsters again, so just forget about it."

She kissed him on the cheek. "I just want you to know that I'll never forget what you did."

"Look. I knew there was a good chance you were going to freak out given the circumstances and after you telling me about your fear of tunnels, so I just kept a closer eye on you than I normally would."

"I appreciate it. And if we're ever out swimming and I see a shark fin, I'll be sure to do the same for you."

Mike laughed. "I'll hold you to that."

"Come on. Let's catch up with the others."

By the time they reached them, none of the merriment had left their companions. They continued like a group of friends returning home after a good night out. They were still in a state of disbelief that they had emerged from the tunnel unscathed.

"Aye, aye," Robyn said. "What were you two up to back there?"

"Just deciding which one of you to shoot in the leg if we end up in another situation where we've got to run for our lives," Mike replied.

"Thanks. Love you too. Who did you go for in the end?"

"We figured Griz. Chances are even his own people wouldn't miss him." They all laughed, even Griz.

"Fuck you, y'wee southern shite."

"Watch who you're calling a southerner, old man."

"Old man? I'm thirty-six, you little bastard."

"Jesus. What happened?"

"Oh, man!" He turned to Mya. "It's a good job you're taking him out of the city, 'cause I swear I'd end up tanking the wee fucker before long."

They all laughed again. "Do you think they'll have Pop-Tarts?" Robyn asked.

"Who'll have Pop-Tarts?" Darren replied.

"She's wondering if the government vehicles where every single cubic centimetre of space has been accounted for to make sure mankind not only survives but flourishes following the end of civilisation will have Pop-Tarts. No, Bobbi," Wren stated confidently, "they will not have Pop-Tarts."

Robyn's shoulders sagged. "You can't know that for sure, though, can you?"

"Yes, I bloody can."

"How?"

"Bobbi, as much as you believe that Pop-Tarts are the key to survival on this planet, I'm guessing the nutritionists and other experts who advised the government on what was needed to maintain a healthy population had other ideas."

"It's possible though."

"Ugh. Give me strength."

The others chuckled again. It felt good even to laugh at the silliest things. For everyone other than Griz a long journey still lay ahead, and the day and probably night as well would be fraught with challenges and danger, but there was also a sense that if they made it through what they just had, they could make it through anything.

After a few more minutes, another door came into view. This had an identical keypad on the wall next to it and Mya entered the combination. The by now familiar loud mechanical clunk reverberated through the tunnel as the locks disengaged and the reinforced steel barrier opened inwards as she pushed the handle.

The light immediately diffused as they entered what looked like a giant loading bay. Twelve articulated lorries were parked side by side and again excitement rose within all of them as they moved the beams of their torches up and down. "Jesus!" Griz said. "Just one of these would keep my people going for a year."

"Somehow, I doubt that," Mike replied. "But we're here for three of them. The rest are yours."

"Yeah, right."

"I'm serious. Three of these will keep our people fed for a long, long time and I've got no intention of coming back to Glasgow in a hurry."

"Amen to that," Robyn said.

"You're serious? You're not joking me? Do you realise what a difference this will make? The risks we've had to take heading further and further for supplies and this is practically on our doorstep. It'll change everything. Sure, we're growing some of our food now, but it's not enough. Not yet." He shook his head. "This is something else." He let out a puff and gulped, doing his best not to get too emotional.

"You're a good man, Griz. There aren't enough good men left."

"You're alright, too, boy," he said, reaching out and putting his arm around the younger man. "You might be a fucking mad bastard, but you're my kind of mad bastard."

"Do you two need a moment?" Mya asked.

"Aye," Griz replied, giving the younger man a big kiss on the cheek and causing the others to burst out laughing once more.

"Okay. We need to check these trailers. Some of them might be full of farming supplies and shit, and as useful as they might be one day, right now we need food, ammo, medical supplies and so on, so split up and get to work."

They all walked around to the back of the trucks. Mike was the first to cut through one of the numbered zip ties and lever up the bolt securing the double doors in place. He opened the truck with all the excitement of a child on Christmas morning and shone his torch inside. There was a broad smile for the briefest moment until his eyes focused on the emptiness within. He panned the beam to the front of the trailer to see there was nothing but a pile of assorted cargo straps. "It's empty," he said, more to himself than anyone else.

Mya was the only one who heard him as she cut through the zip tie and unbolted the doors of the next truck. Muppet nudged her, still responding to the buoyant mood of the last few minutes. Mya moved the beam of her torch around the interior. "This is too," she called out, turning to Mike.

He walked across to her and they both moved on to the next lorry as Griz opened the doors. "Nuthin'," he said, immediately turning to Darren as the next truck was opened up.

They pointed their torches towards him. No words came out of his mouth as he shook his head. "This must be some kind of mistake," Mya said. "Come on; let's check the others."

Wren, Robyn and Mila found exactly what the others found. They moved on to the next three while Mike, Mya, Griz and Darren checked the next four. With each trailer they opened the mood in the air became a little more desperate until, finally, the last truck was unbolted, and seven torches all shone inside at the same time.

Robyn began to laugh, only it wasn't the good-humoured laughter she had shared with the others earlier. "Brilliant," she said. "Fucking brilliant. We've risked our lives for absolutely nothing. Twelve trucks of nothing, in fact." She carried on laughing as she walked away and sat down with her back against what was now a loading bay dock but at one stage would have been a train platform.

"This can't be right. We must be missing something," Wren said.

"Yeah. Twelve lorry loads of supplies. That's what we're missing," Darren replied.

"We need to check out the rest of the place," Mya said.

"What the hell for?"

She moved the torch beam to the dock and the doors beyond. "At one time, this was a functioning bomb shelter. It's possible there could be something here that we could use."

"I hate to break it to you, Mya, but sixty-year-old tins of food aren't going to be fit for rats, never mind humans."

"Look. I get what you're saying, but maybe we'll find a clue as to where all these supplies went or—"

"Will you give it up, Mya! Wherever the PM got his information from it was either bad or out of date or something. This mission is officially over and hunting around for scraps or clues is nothing but a complete waste of time." He walked over to where Robyn was sitting and shrugged off his heavy rucksack. It clunked on the ground before he flopped down next to it.

Mike began to punch the door of the final truck over and over. "FUUUCK!" he screamed.

Griz placed a hand on his shoulder. "Calm, lad. Breaking your fingers won't do anybody any good."

"You don't understand. This was it. Everything depended on this. We're finished. Our people are finished."

"No. No, you're not." Griz let out a deep sigh. "You're going to head back to Skye and you're going to bring all your people down here like I said you should do in the first place."

"We can't."

"That's shite. You can and you will. You said it yourself. You've got family. This is how you look after them. You bring them down here. You join us."

"About two minutes ago, you were saying that you're not growing anything like enough to feed the people you've got. How the hell are you going to feed more?"

"Yeah, we're not growing enough right now, but we've got supplies. In the early days, while we could, we raided supermarkets on the outskirts. We were well organised. We've got food and we go out regularly to get more. This is the biggest city in Scotland. It's the third biggest in the UK and it fell in a heartbeat. There are restaurants, pubs, cafes, grocers, convenience stores and a thousand places in between and beyond that we've not even set foot in. We lost a lot of good people along the way and seeing yous in action today, I know that our community will do nothing but thrive with you as a part of it. I'm asking you to join us, not just for you but for us too. You saw the people who surrounded you when we first met. A lot of them are little more than bairns."

"Yeah, well, we've got our fair share of kids and old folks too."

"So what? Kids give us a future and the oldies give us knowledge that fucked off into the ether the second Google went down. It's like Siri, what can I use as an alternative to toothpaste? Fucked if I know, you walloper, ask someone whose parents were alive during the war."

Mike and Mya laughed. "I'm telling you, it wouldn't work. We came from a rural community. Hell, my family has a goat, for fuck's sake. She stopped giving milk years ago, but she was my gran's and she's a part of our family. I already laid out someone for jokingly suggesting that they make her into stew. How the hell would I keep her safe? How would I feed her? We can't live in a city."

"I'm offering you safety for your people and your biggest stumbling block is a fucking goat?" Griz shook his head. "Trust me, boy; you are going to fit right fucking in. You'll get on like a house on fire with the Glasvegans."

"The what?"

"They were setting up a vegan café when everything went tits up. They were going to call their place the Glasvegan and they've got a fucking zoo in one of the hotels. There are hens that don't lay, a goose with a broken wing, and every time we go out, they seem to bring back a fucking injured pigeon or a kitten that's just been farted into existence or something. Seeing your goat would make their fucking year."

"You're serious?"

"Look. We've got Hindus living with Muslims living with Jews living with Christians living with a fucking all-girl black metal band who still walk around with pentagrams on their jackets, for Christ's sake. We've got straight, gay, trans, every colour, every creed, and they all have one thing in common. Fucking respect for each other. That's the only way this works. It's the only way we make it through. I vow on my daughter's life, if you come down here and anyone so much as looks at your goat in the wrong way, I'll give them a Glasgow kiss that they'll never forget, and trust me, the next day, they'll be serving your goat dinner in a silver bucket."

Mike still looked doubtful, but even in the torchlight it was easy to see the earnestness on Griz's face. "You mean it?" Mya asked. "You're serious about us joining you?"

"Have I just been talking to myself? Yeah. You need us and we need people like you."

"It's our only option, Mike."

"Moving into a city? It's crazy. You and I made each other a promise, Mya."

"Yeah, we did. And I still have every intention of seeing it through, but now isn't the time. Now's the time to get our people to safety and to consolidate. If we stay in Skye, we're going to starve to death. Maybe not you and me and the others here, but many of the rest will, and then Olsen will have won."

"She's right, Mike," Wren said, coming up on the other side of him. She angled her torch so she could see his face. "There's nothing about this that isn't crappy, but we're being given a lifeline here. Let's take it."

"We can't decide for everybody," he replied.

"No, we can't," said Mya. "But we can go back and tell them. And when they see we're empty-handed, and they realise that the last of our food will be finished before we reach next weekend, I think that will convince most people that this is our only option."

"Listen to them, Mike," Griz said. "Come and join us, lad. We'll throw you a welcome party. One thing we're never short of is booze. You and your people are going through a tough time. We're having problems too, but nothing like yours. I'm telling you now, though, I know together we'll be much stronger and things will be better for all of us."

Mike stared towards Griz for several seconds before finally nodding. "Okay."

Mya was happy to relinquish the twenty-five-pound dead weight of the car battery from her rucksack. She placed it at Darren's feet. "You know what you're doing with this stuff. Let's see if we can get one of these babies started, shall we?"

"So, that's it?" Robyn said. "We're coming to live down here?"

"I dare say it's going to be up to the council, and they'll probably want to put it to a wider vote, but in the absence of all other options, yeah."

"We're all just going to head back down here in the back of a lorry?"

"We'll have the yacht too, but I'd say we could easily get what's left of our people and our belongings in the back of one of these things," Mike replied.

"And what, we're just going to pull up outside one of the hotels and all climb out like we're on some package holiday?"

"Probably not. We'll have to work out the finer details, but I think Glasgow's going to have to be our home for a while."

"I'm going to check the rest of this place out," Mya said, hoisting Muppet up onto the loading dock.

"Yeah. Me too." Wren tapped the dock and Wolf leapt up by himself.

"Me three," Mila added.

"We'll iron out some of those finer details; then we'll be through," Mike said.

"I suppose that means you and me are jumping batteries and checking fuel tanks." Darren climbed back to his feet and helped Robyn up. He grabbed Mya's bag and his own and the pair walked towards the front of the first vehicle.

"So, how are we going to get seventy people into the heart of the city?" Mike asked.

"Fucking carefully."

"Useful. Thanks for the help." The pair heaved themselves up onto the dock and placed the torches down between them.

"I send drones up every morning. That's how I saw you in the first place. But I think the best option is if you find somewhere safe on the outskirts. A couple of you come in and tell us you're here and then we'll help. We'll lure any lingerers away and we'll check out the best routes. We'll get your people safe, and by that time, we might have got another one of these going," he said, gesturing towards the trucks. "The only thing that's stopped us hitting some of the big out-of-town places is lack of transport."

"Sounds like you're lining up work for us already."

Griz smiled. "After seeing how you handled yourselves today, there's going to be plenty of work. No such thing as a free lunch anymore."

"Thank you for this, Griz."

"I told you. You'll be paying your way."

"And we'll be happy to. But you didn't have to do any of this. We're strangers. You've got no reason to trust us."

"I did okay in school, Mike. I was no genius, but I did okay. I didn't go to college or uni. I let life educate me. There are lots of things I don't know and can't do. But there's one thing I'm better at than anyone else I've met, and that's sussing out my kind of people. And you and your pals are my kind of people." He gestured to the trucks. "This turned out to be a bust, but I know that, from today, things are going to get better for all of us."

Mike sniffed. "In fairness, they can't get much worse, can they?"

Griz let out a booming laugh. "You've made me smile more today than I have in the last six months. Like I said, we need people like you and your friends. Today hasn't gone to plan, not by a long shot. But I'm going to go to sleep with a big smile on my face tonight because all the things I wanted for my people that seemed just that little bit out of reach don't seem that way anymore."

"I think you're putting too much faith in us, mate."

"No, Mike. I'm putting exactly the right amount of faith in you. Now, come on, let's see if there's anything worth grabbing in the back before we get you on your way."

EPILOGUE

It had been another long day and it was nowhere near over for Emma. More work had been done digging what had once been a nice lawn at the rear of the property. George, Jack and James had begun building a crude but sturdy fence around the main building. Everyone had been fed. Regular patrols of the perimeter had been carried out, and before she could even think about resting, she needed to draw up a rota for guard duty.

"Are you alright, darling?" Jenny asked, popping her head around the corner of the office door.

"I'd be happier if I didn't have to wind this thing up every two minutes," she replied, gesturing to the dynamo lantern on her desk before throwing her pencil down and leaning back in her chair.

Jenny smiled and walked in with Meg by her side. "I'll ask around tomorrow and see if anyone would be prepared to make a trade with you. We can't have our leader working in the dark."

"Please don't call me that."

"What should I call you then?"

"Err … Emma?"

"Shaw was the chairman of our council, thus our leader. You're our new Shaw; thus, you're our leader."

"Stop saying thus. You sound like a lawyer."

Jenny smiled again. "Anything I can help you with?"

Emma shook her head. "Nah. Just working out a guard rota. How's everybody doing out there?"

"Pretty good actually. The PM and Doug are holding an audience in the dining room. They're dishing loads of goss about what went on at the last European leaders' summit."

"Sounds riveting."

"It is, actually. Get him to tell you which prime minister has a penchant for wearing leather thongs and fishnets. I'll give you a clue. It's not one of the girls."

Emma curled her nose up. "Eugh. Gross."

"Wait until you hear who it is."

Emma chuckled. "I'll make sure that's the first thing I do when I've finished here."

They both turned suddenly as they heard the main door burst open. Footsteps pounded towards the office and their eyes fixed on the doorway as Finlay appeared.

"Somebody's coming," he said between heavy breaths.

"What the hell do you mean somebody's coming?" Emma asked, climbing to her feet, opening her desk drawer and grabbing her Glock.

"Somebody on a bike. As soon as we saw them, Rob told me to come and get you."

"Jesus, what now?" Emma asked, rushing past him and towards the main door. Jenny and Meg followed her out as raucous laughter erupted from the dining room.

The sun was not yet completely down as Emma began to jog to the main gate, but it would not be long before darkness fell and another night of uncertainty settled over the Skye Outward Bounds Centre.

Fear gripped Emma as her jog turned into a run. She glanced behind to see Jenny was trying her hardest to keep her in sight while Meg cantered comfortably by her side. When the main gate finally came into view, it was already opening and a shiver ran through Emma. *Who the hell are they letting in without consulting anyone? Jesus! What's wrong with these people?*

She only needed to travel a few more metres to see. Tears of happiness flooded her eyes and streamed down her face. She flung her arms around Shaw and he reciprocated. They squeezed each other tightly. "I'm sorry," he whispered. "I'm so sorry."

She kissed him roughly on the cheek and stepped back. "What happened to you?"

"I don't know. It all became a bit too much for me to deal with."

Emma took hold of his hands. "I get it. I've been there. But we're family. You lean on us when you need to and we lean on you."

It was he who squeezed her hands now. "I'm sorry."

"Stop saying that. You're back now. Don't worry about anything. You're back and we're going to take care of each other."

His head dropped and he started crying. She pulled him into her and held him as he sobbed. He was a long way from being well or being the man he once was, but coming back to his family was a start.

A deep heaving sound made both of them turn. Jenny stood there, barely able to believe her tearful eyes. She put both hands up to her face and then reached out, beckoning her friend towards her. "I'm sorry," he said, letting go of Emma and rushing into Jenny's arms.

She held him close, kissing him on the side of his head as he wept on her shoulder. "It's alright, darling. It's alright. You're home now. You're home."

THE END.

A NOTE FROM THE AUTHOR

I really hope you enjoyed this book and would be very grateful if you took a minute to leave a review on Amazon and Goodreads.

If you would like to stay informed about what I'm doing, including current writing projects, and all the latest news and release information; these are the places to go:

Join the fan club on Facebook
https://www.facebook.com/groups/127693634504226

Like the Christopher Artinian author page
https://www.facebook.com/safehaventrilogy/

Buy exclusive and signed books and merchandise, subscribe to the newsletter and follow the blog:

https://www.christopherartinian.com/

Follow me on Twitter
https://twitter.com/Christo71635959

Follow me on Youtube:
https://www.youtube.com/channel/UCfJymx31Vvztt B_Q-x5otYg

Follow me on Amazon
https://amzn.to/2I1llU6

Follow me on Goodreads
https://bit.ly/2P7iDzX

Other books by Christopher Artinian:

Safe Haven: Rise of the RAMs
Safe Haven: Realm of the Raiders
Safe Haven: Reap of the Righteous
Safe Haven: Ice
Safe Haven: Vengeance
Safe Haven: Is This the End of Everything?
Safe Haven: Neverland (Part 1)
Safe Haven: Neverland (Part 2)
Safe Haven: Doomsday
Before Safe Haven: Lucy
Before Safe Haven: Alex
Before Safe Haven: Mike
Before Safe Haven: Jules

The End of Everything: Book 1
The End of Everything: Book 2
The End of Everything: Book 3
The End of Everything: Book 4
The End of Everything: Book 5
The End of Everything: Book 6
The End of Everything: Book 7
The End of Everything: Book 8
The End of Everything: Book 9
The End of Everything: Book 10
The End of Everything: Book 11
The End of Everything: Book 12
Relentless
Relentless 2
Relentless 3
The Burning Tree: Book 1 – Salvation
The Burning Tree: Book 2 – Rebirth
The Burning Tree: Book 3 – Infinity
The Burning Tree: Book 4 - Anarchy

CHRISTOPHER ARTINIAN

Christopher Artinian was born and raised in Leeds, West Yorkshire. Wanting to escape life in a big city and concentrate more on working to live than living to work, he and his family moved to the Outer Hebrides in the north-west of Scotland in 2004, where he now works as a full-time author.

Chris is a huge music fan, a cinephile, an avid reader and a supporter of Yorkshire county cricket club. When he's not sitting in front of his laptop living out his next post-apocalyptic/dystopian/horror adventure, he will be passionately immersed in one of his other interests.

Printed in Great Britain
by Amazon